V. K. Mina's work has b
Review, Manushi and *Wasafi*
She lives in New York City.

THE SPLINTERED DAY

V. K. Mina

First published 1999 by Serpent's Tail,
4 Blackstock Mews,
London N4 2BT

Website: www.serpentstail.com

Typeset by Avon Dataset Ltd, Bidford on Avon, B50 4JH

Printed in Great Britain by Mackays of Chatham plc

10 9 8 7 6 5 4 3 2 1

Contents

Acknowledgements

Parts of this novel first appeared in *Christopher Street*, *Turnstile*, *The Kenyon Review*, *13th Moon* and *Streetlights: Illuminating Tales of the Urban Black Experience* (Viking).

My thanks to all the editors concerned, particularly the late Dorisjean Austin. Most of all, my gratitude to Michelle Hill, for her arul and her acuity.

She waits with a ruined heart every night . . .
just for a glimpse.

—Mirabai,
trans. Andrew Schelling

Bit by bit the splintered day has ended,
The night is all in shreds . . .
What does defeat mean, or waiting,
When an endless trek is my allotted fate?
When my heart was gifted to me, as companion,
An unrest walked alongside.

—Meena Kumari,
trans. Syed Sirajuddin

Chapter 1

How I Made Love to a Negro

Since you walked out on me . . .
there's just your cruelty circling
my head like a bright, rotting halo.

—Nina Cassian, *Lady of Miracles*
trans. Laura Schiff

I read a few chapters of Dany Laferrière. You might think I already knew how to make love to a Negro, but I was tired, so very tired, so obviously there was something I wasn't getting right. My stomach turned and turned.

The first time I read the book, I was sixteen. I found it at an alternative bookstore on Almond Street. I was still a virgin. My experience consisted of two white boys who'd kissed me and a Sikh who ate my pussy badly. I loved the book. What *profondeur,* what glamour it had, what wisdom about interracial sex. So long surrounded by whites, I saw my dark self easily in Laferrière. I forgot my other selves: my eleven-year-old self getting beaten up by white trash Angel and enormous, West Indian Jasmine; my pussy self of labyrinthine crimson and brown folds so easily crushed; my woman self who would one day feel so guilty because I had inveighed against Driss for having a white wife, and then he left her six-and-a-half months pregnant for a Brazilian from Bahia.

I loved the book because our hero satirizes the white women he sleeps with for their submissiveness, to him and to their illusions. Their desire for him is only a version of imperialist fantasy, and so our hero punishes them with ridicule, sniggering as they do his dishes. I understood how he felt: I was everyone's first Indian girl. One man in Florence while kissing me in a hotel stairwell paused to discuss his passion for Sanskrit philosophy, someone else pulled away from my mouth to ask me why Indian women wear dots on their foreheads. These things happened after I read the book, but they are the best examples of what always happened. Except with the Sikh, I guess, but that was too lousy to matter, and he liked me with too much hysteria.

By the time I read the book, I was almost wondering if I was subconsciously racist because there were few black men I was attracted to. There had been one Nigerian with fine bone structure who'd said, not two feet away from me, that as a rule he didn't like black girls. And even though there were plenty of Indian-black couples at school, the girls were either impossibly fair like Sukhinder or mixed beauties from the West Indies like Anne Mohan, and I knew that for the Nigerian, I was one of the black girls. So you see Laferrière's charm.

Claude, too, called me black. When I demurred, he accused me of wanting to be white, so I was left with nothing to say. He was the kind of black man whom white women fawned on, so I was puzzled by his interest in me. He was very "downtown" and hip, had spent half his life in clubs, and whatever I looked like, or however I had lived, I was still a gauche and pudgy middle-class girl awed by the chic I did not have. I was amazed he wanted me, so glamorous did he seem. OK, also dissolute, but I wasn't going to marry him.

Claude called me black because I wasn't white or yellow, but he differentiated me from the dark-dark-skinned girls. "If I am with a girl that dark," he said, "it's only fucking." I was uncomfortable; I wasn't used to being on the other side. "It's not prejudice," he said. "I like black women. I just don't need to lie down next to a jet-black girl who will scare me when I wake up in the morning." I nodded absently. But when I told him I didn't like flat noses, he turned his flat-nosed face away from me, and said I had been brainwashed by white people.

I first met Claude with Joyce at a Japanese bar in the Village. It turned out that this bar was a famous den of iniquity, and everyone we ever mentioned it to knew that it was a hangout for drug dealers. A friend of Joyce's had even moved out of a nearby apartment because of their preponderance. It was common knowledge, only we didn't know it yet. The place was empty except for us, and Claude. I had never seen anyone like him. I had seen dreads on Rastas (and sants) before but his were different: thick, neat locks that fell to his jaw. I don't think he had his beard then, and I wasn't sure how attractive I found him. He spent a long time talking in a low voice to Joyce, who was becoming increasingly tipsy from all the sake she was drinking. I sat making an airplane out of the napkin of Joyce's drink. On the stereo system, Barrington Levy sang, "Two months later, she said come and get your son, because I don't want your baby to tie me down, because you are old, and I am young, and while I'm young, I want to have some fun." Except it was thirteen months later, and I said what are we going to do, because you are an illiterate, unemployed drug dealer and I am young, and while I'm young, I want to be happy.

I was surprised when he wanted me to write my

3

number on the airplane, and Joyce slurringly told me he liked me. Neither of us thought he would ever call. Whenever I blame Joyce for taking me to the bar, she reminds me that she told me not to go out with him. He was too ornery and too horny, she said. But he was an adventure I was determined to embark upon.

Meeting him at the bar for our first date, I eyed another man and the hurt look in his round, brown eyes peeking through his dreads thoroughly seduced me. He is vulnerable, I thought, and blanched only slightly when his pale, feline friend talked openly about selling drugs as I sat between them in his friend's jeep. How exotic it was, not the dreads but the clubs and the drugs, like a story I had read in *Christopher Street*, like Henry Miller, like the girls I had despised and admired in high school who wore leopard coats and short-shorts to go dancing all night with strangers and with eyes half-closed like gay Paris with absinthe and debauchés. Within a certain circumference, I wanted to be debauched.

I was amazed to discover myself pregnant – I mean, hadn't we almost always protected ourselves? I hadn't been promiscuous. I didn't like babies. I'd always said my womb would reject the idea. But I soon discovered my womb had no such discernment.

I took to bed. I spent days staring at the peeling plaster on the ceiling, my stomach churning, anxious, sweaty, senses filed so sharp I could barely breathe. Fresh paint from the hallway, the broccoli in the garbage pail, my own juices skewered me. I felt sick and dizzy from the smell of toothpaste and orange soda and laundry detergent. I opened the window to air the apartment and the merengue played by the people in the building opposite clanged into my head. I sank into bed and fire engines screamed up my legs. In the distance, I heard what simply could not have been – a man crying, "Allahu Akbar," over and over again. Almost any food made my stomach turn, but I dreamt helplessly of garlic rasam and porichche kute, helplessly and hopelessly.

Before I was certain I was pregnant, I thought I was going insane. I was obsessed by the thought of dying, the snuffing out of my bright, beautiful consciousness. I picked out therapists from the phone book and begged them to tell me what was wrong with me. They took my money and asked me about my childhood. I went to a restaurant and sat immobilized over a plate of jerk chicken, imagining the annihilation of a chicken's mind. I prayed – not to God, since I had no faith – but prayed Claude would come and save me.

Finally, I took a taxi to the Japanese bar he still went to, though he'd long since stopped working there. I clutched the seat-belt sure that the car would veer off the road, sure that I would die, sure that the headlights of cars passing in the opposite direction were turning towards me and coming closer and closer. I wanted to tell the driver to slow down, but that was so out of character that I simply couldn't do it. I dug my nails into my palms until the orange paper lantern outside the bar grew bright and large. I paid the driver and lurched out into the rain.

5

I'd known Claude for a little over a year by then. He had told me he was leaving me in the spring, about a week before he was supposed to return the three hundred dollars he'd borrowed from me. And maybe a month and a half after he had hit me with my telephone until my lips and nose were bloody. To be honest, I'd hit him too, once. And a few days after he hit me, he was mugged and those thick lips of his were bloodier than he had made mine. I took him back when he called me at 6 am after the mugging mostly to see how badly off he was. "You don't care, do you?" he said, sinking into my bed. I sat on the futon, laughing. "I care about as much as you cared when you hit me," I said, which of course was far from the truth.

When he tried to come home in the fall, I found it easy to forgive him for hitting me because he'd never done it again, or for not returning my money because he promised to repay it. It was easy to think around anything I didn't like, wanting him to take me in his arms. I loved to sleep next to him, my face against his breast, his skin always so much warmer than mine. He had the right equipment for me to feel like a child — broad shoulders, strong arms, a hard flat chest, small nipples I sucked shamelessly, curled against his waist.

It wasn't just lying in his arms — I had memories which tempted me with their warmth. Claude bringing me ginger-ale and Fisherman's Friend cough drops when I was sick. The time I told him about someone else's lovely eyes, and he said in his butterscotch voice, "I have nice eyes." Once, I was drunk and bawling that I knew he would rather be with a white girl, I apologized through drunken sobs for not being white, and he said, drawing me to him, that the girl he wanted was a beautiful Indian. Claude said plainly what could have been lines in a song. "You make me feel hurt," he said once, "and you know I love you." And artlessly, he uttered clichés which were fresh in his mouth. When I asked him why he came to my house only to sink into slumber — or rather I screamed, "You don't come here for me at all. All you want is a bed to sleep in. Why are you in my house?" — he said, simply, "You do something to me." He cooked rice and vegetables for me, saying, "I'm your Daddy, and I'm going to take care of you." The time after we broke up when Irene and I ran into him at a coffee shop, he said hello and left, only to return to me sitting at the counter, only to leave, only to return again. Finally, he asked if he could come home with me.

Eventually, in the fall, the leaves fell to the ground, and he tried to come home again. He claimed he'd never left. I let him into my bed, but I would turn his lines onto him, this Laferrière hero, his skinny black dick his access to the world, who said to me when I asked him why I should wash his clothes or buy him presents or why he never took me out, "I fuck you, don't I?" So for weeks, I told him I couldn't afford his sex. At any kind gesture, caress, I moved away, explaining I had no money to buy it. He held me against his breast at night, rubbing my hip, and I told him about every handsome man I knew until he clasped his hand over my mouth. But finally, he said, "I'm lonely, I miss you" and kissed the top of my head and I said yes. He came hurtling in, telling me how tight I was and how he knew I had been faithful to him – which I had been – and he told me he wouldn't come inside me and he called out my name. Over and over again. And then he came.

It was the first time anyone had come inside me, and not being in love, I was revulsed by his semen, but I felt too languorous for a fight, and besides, I thought it was over. I didn't know it had just begun, not even when I found myself screaming and screaming until my throat was raw, naming his every misdeed. All I wanted was for him to pull me to that chest, sponge up my rage, but instead he put on his shirt and left, wordlessly.

For weeks I heard nothing from him. I was sure he would call, but he didn't. That accouterment of drug dealers, his beeper, was no longer in service even before that night. I didn't know how to reach him when the time came except to stand out in front of the bar, pregnant, in the pouring rain like in some hokey country song. He stood under the awning.

He waited impatiently for me to start and finish what I had to say. He didn't have the beard which made him look as old-fashioned and kindly as his name. "I think I'm pregnant," I said. He shook his head. It's not possible because he used a condom. It's not possible because he no longer wanted me and I was using it as a ruse to win him

7

back. He told me he wouldn't talk to me unless I paid the gas for his car. I gave him what money I had and he drove me home, on his way to another bar.

But still, I missed him, like when I watched a video with Bobby Brown entwined with a lovely girl on a beach. If it's not good enough, he would work harder, he sang. But it's not good enough, and he's not working at all. I watched the video enviously, yearning for that embrace, flesh against flesh, the warmth and womb-like comfort of Claude against me.

If it wasn't Claude on my mind, it was dying. I called everyone I knew, on the other coast, in other countries, to talk about dying. "It could strike so suddenly and then you're extinguished," I said. I was terrified to go to sleep. When my stomach churned, bowels loose, I didn't know whether it was fear or sickness. Fear became a sickness. "I don't want to die," I would say over and over again. I tried to calm the panic by telling myself that I wouldn't know, that it would be like fainting, or being knocked unconscious. Late at night, I was still alert, my sweat sticking me to Irene's yellow vinyl sofa, curled against the armrest, waiting for the blow to be struck.

One night, Claude called me to say he wanted me to have the baby, we could give it to his grandmother. That night in the rain, he'd snarled, "What should I say? Let's go buy a ring?" I had put my hand out to touch the glass wall of the bar. He had continued, more softly, "Are you going to have an abortion? You are a child to be having a child, and I'm not up to taking care of a woman and a child." But then he decided it was about time some woman had a child for him. He was calling me from a pay phone, and when he was about to get cut off, he said, "I'll call you back." He called the next night, while I was sleeping. I took the cord of the phone in my hand when I heard his voice, and pulled the line taut until it yanked out of the jack.

The abortion was more pain than I had ever experienced, the anesthetic alone made me feel like I was being stabbed in the stomach with a pair of scissors. The doctor hushed my screams, saying I'd frighten the other patients. I vomited and wept and went home. All night and the next morning, my skin boiled. I stumbled into the hospital, whimpering like a dog. The other women stroked my forehead, brought me cups of water through the hours I waited. I was scraped again, the doctor telling me that this time I should lie still to avoid any problems. Irene waited for me in the recovery lounge. I came out and sat in the recliner, and she sat beside me, her elbows on her knees. The radio was on, playing something syrupy by Ashford and Simpson, and I asked her, again, why he couldn't be with me.

"Forget him, for God's sake!" Irene cried out, worn out from the demands I was making on our friendship: taking care of me, my refusing to sleep, sitting with her because I thought I wouldn't accidentally die if I wasn't alone, telling her every boring detail of how I felt about Claude. I didn't explain why I talked because she knew why and she didn't explain why she was fatigued of listening, because I knew why.

I hadn't seen him since that night he drove me home and he hadn't slept next to me since the night we'd fought. I wanted him in that desperate, ashamed way that a starving person wants someone else's leftovers in a garbage can. I wanted him the way a baby wants to feel strong loving arms. Only thinking of him and the sadness it brought to the back of my throat stopped me from thinking about dying.

I thought of Dany Laferrière. Of course, I found Claude exotic. Because of him, I had read Jacques Roumain, and the lines had meant something: *vers vous je suis venu avec mon grand coeur rouge et nu, et mes bras lourds de brassées d'amour.* I bought him a mustard shirt and made countless pots of spaghetti and bought bottles of wine. I had sucked his cock, and well, too. I'd been impressed by certain of his pronouncements and I'd asked him if I was disturbing him when I clanked his dirty dishes as I washed them. I'd liked his dreads.

At the end of our first date, we sat in a diner, eating hot bagels with melting, salty butter, and I, for the first time, touched his hair. I put my fingers through the woolly locks and massaged his head. He was uncomfortable at first, because he was used to women – white women – liking his hair. And I knew from my own life exactly how he felt.

Sometimes he would say that I was using him for sex. "Sex we have, where you come and I don't?" I'd reply. But other times, he would say that he wouldn't go out with white women because they wouldn't respect him. But he treated me not much differently than Laferrière's hero treated his white girls. And reading the book again, I wonder which of the white women were listening attentively because they were impressed a black man could speak intelligently, and which were genuinely interested, which didn't want to disturb him because the sight of a black man reading was the goal of *la mission civilisatrice,* and which didn't want to disturb him because they were polite, which were using him for the sexual skill they presumed him to have, and which loved him. It's all very to well to tell us how to make love to a Negro, but even that's only half of the story. I took such a long time to come to this, but I am no longer sixteen, and I need to know: how could I have made him make love to me back.

Chapter 2
Jeannie

Some in this world insist
that a certain whatever-it-is
that has no taste of
joy or sorrow
no qualities
is Release
they are fools . . .
the undoing of the knot
of her sari
that
is Release.

– *Srngaratilaka*,
trans. Jeffrey Masson and W. S. Merwin

Neelam's worry was never about why she was what she was, or what she wanted, but that what she wanted would be unconsummated. Oh, there had been women who had liked her, liked the way she sucked their breasts, liked having her on their arm, liked dancing with her, but she wanted to be wanted. It wasn't so much that she wanted a "butch" as that she wanted a woman who would desire the corporeal reality of her, her breasts, her stomach, her cunt, and this didn't seem altogether likely. Why would a woman want her pussy? She had never been overcome by a desire to eat pussy. It didn't repulse her, she was willing to do it, but the idea didn't excite her particularly.

The night Neelam met Jeannie began with Neelam sitting in Sheridan Square after yet another failed date. The only other people left in the park were the homeless men. Neelam stretched her arms out on the back of the bench. Her blouse was short-sleeved, and the metal of the bench was cool against her skin. She sighed. It had been a long damn day.

First, she'd gotten out of work late. She had rushed downtown to make her blind date with a pudgy, androgynous Chinese-American dyke who was not what she had been expecting. After the movie, they'd walked down Seventh Avenue and Neelam had suggested they go to the Box for a drink. The Chinese-American dyke said she only went to Crazy Nanny's, the white bar, because she had heard that the women at Pandora's Box smoked crack in the bathroom. The date ended soon after.

Neelam stayed in the park after her date left. She didn't feel like going home. It seemed such a shame not to be out on such a ripe summer night. She took a sip of D & G's and watched the people going by.

Years ago, her mother used to pass the long, empty days sitting in the garden, doing the crossword puzzle in every magazine or newspaper she could get in the village they lived in. Neelam would sneak the Australian tabloids into the room in which she slept. There she sat hunched on the tile floor, pigtails dangling, poring over the pictures of bare-breasted Page Three girls, listening for the sound of footsteps, ready to shove the magazines under the mattress if anyone came to the door. "Why does that girl *sneak* magazines away?" her mother once asked her stepfather. He had shrugged.

A cop came into the park to get the homeless men out and Neelam rose along with them. She tossed the empty bottle into the garbage bin and turned the corner.

The Box wasn't very busy. There were some women at the bar but the only person dancing was a vogueing transsexual. Neelam set her bag down on a chair on the edge of the dance floor. Jeannie was standing against the speaker with her arms crossed.

Jeannie was pretty in a thick, Junoesque way, at least if Juno was wearing jeans shorts and a football jersey, but Neelam walked by her and into a corner of her own. She wasn't in the mood for rejection, and Jeannie was too femme for Neelam to think that she would have any success with her. Although Neelam hadn't aligned herself yet, people presumed she was a femme because of the low-cut, high-hemmed way she usually dressed. She went along with it because she thought she was too small and unathletic to do otherwise.

Neelam stood with her hand on her waist, listening to the music, then turned to face the mirrored wall. She slowly started dancing with her reflection. Behind her, and therefore before her, diamonds of colored light slid across the walls and the floorboards. On the other side of the room, Jeannie was talking to a slim, dark girl in an orange Lycra bodysuit. Neelam watched them for a few minutes to see if they were together, but the girl in the bodysuit noticed her and Neelam had to turn away. Neelam went up to the DJ booth to make some requests and then down to the bar.

The bartender, Jamie, was a *puertorriqueña* who looked like Nargis. "Mimosas are on special," Jamie said in her throaty voice.

"I'll have a screwdriver."

Jamie shrugged and smiled, revealing the gap between her two front teeth.

"Are you having a good time?" Jamie asked, bringing her her drink. Neelam didn't answer. Out of the corner of her eye, she could see Jeannie dancing with the orange body-suited girl. Neelam sipped her drink. She repeated to herself the fundamental tenet of Hindu philosophy: root out desire, root out the "I."

But she found herself drawn to tempting illusions. It's the drink, she thought, setting it down. Alcohol made her want everything more loudly, and they always say you will never meet someone when you're looking. She fiddled with her coaster. She caught herself in the mirror behind the bar, brooding over her drink like Amithab Bachchan, and laughed.

In her childhood of movie-going Sundays, Neelam had identified with Amithab completely. Amitabh, after all, was the angry young man. He was misunderstood, father-less, illegitimate, forced outside the law by injustice, forced to rely on only himself, a drinker, a club-goer, wrecker of revenge, an urbane, melancholy man who won in the end or died. Neelam was all these things. But to her confusion, she also identified with his heroines. She wanted to wear makeup and lots of heavy gold jewellery and zari-bordered silks and be beautiful and have designs in henna on her hands and brow and writhe and sing mujras like Rekha and Zeenat Aman and Parveen Babi. She was torn between being Amitabh and being the heroine, knowing that she was both. And if she was corrupted by being both, how would she have the only solace Amitabh ever had – the love of a beautiful, sympathetic woman?

Amitabh movies stirred her and consoled her and discomfited her. She watched Helen swivel her hips in the den of the dacoit Gabbar Singh and felt a strange wave of something between queasiness and joy. She watched the scene in *Muqaddar ka Sikandar* where the rich girl who will grow up to be Raakhee comes out of her house in the dead of night. The poor boy who will grow up to be Amitabh is sleeping on her front steps. He has nowhere to go and no one to help him. The girl leans forward, and without waking him, covers him with the blanket. Which one did she want to be? The girl or the boy? She thought about it until her head hurt. The blanket, she thought finally, but it was an inadequate answer.

Neelam took her half-finished drink to the dance floor. One of the songs she had requested had come on. She set the drink on a speaker, and danced with a slowly disintegrating edge of self-consciousness. The DJ played her anthems one by one: "Coming on Strong," "Ride the Rhythm," "Love Dancing," "Let No Man Put Asunder." She jumped and glided. "Hot Stuff." "I Will Survive." Songs she had heard through the years; she had only imagined she would find herself in places like the one she was in.

Robyn, her best friend in junior high, was the first person Neelam ever told. Robyn said that she too was open-minded enough to try it. Neelam couldn't articulate how what she meant was different. It was years before she told Robyn she had fabricated her crushes on boys they knew, simply to have stories to interest Robyn with, simply to be Robyn's friend.

But Neelam had always known she wasn't the only one. Neelam was from a post-Stonewall generation, and there were books to tell her lesbians were everywhere. She also learned that they were with each other out of feminism and they would be with men if men weren't such patriarchal pigs. Either that or they were lesbians because they were tomboys. She'd read *The Color Purple* and she'd loved Celie and Shug, but she could hardly identify. She'd examined her own pussy years before. Besides, she didn't quite relish the idea of sleeping with a bisexual woman. Shug eventually left Celie for a man. That's the way it was. And more importantly, Shug wasn't so much overwhelmed with desire for Celie as moved by her oppression. This was not quite Neelam's dream of love.

Neelam had stopped watching Jeannie, and barely noticed her when she brushed by. She danced with her eyes closed, the better to feel the beat. "You used to hold me, you used to touch me"; she moved her hands along her arms. She took advantage of the extra room, sauntering down the length of the floor. "You used to squeeze me, you used to please me."

Finally, the DJ played some lethargically slow Jodeci song and Neelam sat down. She gulped down the rest of her screwdriver. The no-name vodka hit her straight between her thighs. She pushed the table away from herself so she could stretch out her legs and wait out the slow set.

Other women had close friendships that turned into sexual love but Neelam couldn't imagine looking at her friends that way. It was not the way she wanted it, but she supposed that was the way it happened. At fourteen, she had gone on a date with her bank teller, but that was the only time a woman outside a bar had ever flirted with her. And in bars, she met women with lovers, with chemical dependencies, live-in boyfriends, bizarre fetishes – one woman from Texas had kept asking Neelam if Neelam would have the baby if she made Neelam pregnant. Neelam wished she didn't want it. She wished she could be content with her work and her interests and her apartment. She wished she could be a repressed Bible-thumper, like the bank teller. But she couldn't.

The transsexual who had been vogueing up a storm a little while back was sitting at the table across the aisle, next to Jeannie. Jeannie leaned over to whisper to the transsexual who turned around and looked at Neelam.

Neelam ignored it. The transsexual turned around again. What the hell was he . . . she . . . it looking at? What the fuck were they talking about? Neelam sucked her teeth.

16

It was bad enough that she had to accept that a woman like Jeannie wouldn't want her, but did she also have to accept that Jeannie would make fun of her with some transsexual? Just as she was crushing the empty plastic cup, the transsexual loomed over her. "My friend is too shy to come over, but she'd like to dance with you."

Neelam wondered if it was some kind of prank. She resigned herself to falling for it. Neelam nodded. "Okay."

Jeannie strode to the dance floor and Neelam followed, eyes lowered. They danced and Neelam felt too embarrassed to look up. She was suddenly hyperconscious of her body, and her movements were stiff and deliberate. A little liquor made Neelam feel dainty but a little more made her acutely aware of her heaviness. Jeannie asked her her name, where she lived, where she was from. "I'm Indian," Neelam said, stopping to catch her breath.

Jeannie pulled her closer as the siren of "Housecall" began to wail. She leaned down and whispered in the shell of Neelam's ear, "You know you have rhythm." Neelam blushed. Suddenly, everything was going right, and her anxiousness was eased. She rested her face lightly on Jeannie's chest, the soft cotton jersey against her cheek so she could smell Jeannie's musk. They were in a corner, near the speaker and through her half-closed eyes, Neelam could see the lights fading down until the dance floor was dark.

When they became tired, Jeannie bought her a drink and after Neelam downed it, Jeannie took her outside for a breath of fresh air.

The air outside was in fact heavy and moist, hot summer night air that was waiting to break. Jeannie stood against the brick wall of the bar. "Do you want to see some pictures?" she asked. Neelam nodded. There wasn't anything else to do.

Jeannie fished her wallet out of her backpack and showed Neelam some faded snapshots of women in jaunty

17

toques sitting around a table. "That's my grandmother when she was young." Jeannie flipped the page and showed her a heavily air-brushed studio picture of a woman with a big white bow in her hair and a radiant smile. "And that's my mother."

"Where's your girlfriend?" Neelam asked flirtatiously.

"I don't have a picture of her," Jeannie replied, putting her wallet back.

"You have a girlfriend?"

"Yes," Jeannie said. "Don't you?"

"No. What the fuck are you doing plying me with alcohol?"

"Being friendly." Jeannie pulled the strap of her backpack over her shoulder. "I wasn't making a move on you." Neelam pouted. "Come on, let's sit down." Jeannie led her across Seventh Avenue and through deserted side streets to a church with wide, white steps. They sat down on the top stair.

Neelam was silent. She has a girlfriend, Neelam thought. She has a girlfriend. There was always something wrong. Neelam sighed. Her butt hurt from the rough concrete stair. The air was like a layer on her skin. She watched the flies buzz around the streetlight in front of the church and screwed up her eyes until it was all a blur. She could hear crickets and cars and some people having a conversation around the corner. Why were there crickets in the city? "I told that boy he was out of his mind. He can take his fine self and jump in the river. I do not need to be taking this," a husky voice said. The other person laughed. Neelam was suddenly hungry. She realized she had barely eaten all day. She'd bought a bag of sour cream and onion bagel chips right after she got off work, but she'd had to stand and hold the bar on the train so she hadn't had a chance to eat them and then she forgot. Neelam took it out of her bag and ripped it open.

"Do you want one?" she asked, as chips tumbled from the packet. She held one out. Jeannie shook her head. Neelam put it in her mouth and held out her salty fingers.

Jeannie looked down Neelam's outstretched arm to her fingers tipped with a paste of onion flecks and salt, and then back at Neelam's face, and said, "You know how bad I want to suck them."

Neelam felt her pussy clench. She just barely leaned towards Jeannie and they kissed, Jeannie's tongue sliding into her mouth. Jeannie said, "Are you trying to make me unfaithful to my girlfriend?" and kissed her again. Just then, a man came out of the church and Jeannie pulled Neelam towards her to let him pass by. Neelam sat triumphantly ensconced between Jeannie's thighs, Jeannie's arms around her waist. The alcohol was beginning to wear off and everything seemed in sharper focus. Jeannie's arms felt heavier around her, Jeannie's bare legs warmer beneath her hands.

Soon a white straight couple came to sit at the bottom of the stairs and they rose. "Do you want to go to the pier?" Jeannie asked. Neelam nodded. It was, after all, what gay people did. Jeannie led her through the streets. Before they crossed the West Side Highway, Neelam said she needed to use the ladies' room, so they stopped in at Kellers.

When they entered, Neelam saw that they were the only women among the dozen people in the place. The rest were what Neelam thought of in decades-old slang as "rough trade." Jeannie checked the bathroom for toilet paper, and gave Neelam some cocktail napkins before standing guard over the lockless door. The toilet was filthy, but Neelam couldn't afford to discriminate after two drinks. She washed her hands.

When she came out, Jeannie was sitting at the bar. "Will you buy me a drink?" Neelam gently pushed her luck. Jeannie nodded. Neelam climbed onto a torn leather barstool and ordered a ginger-ale. It was something cheap at least. Jeannie didn't order anything for herself. They sat for a few minutes watching two skinny men in jogging suits play pool. Neelam sipped the cloyingly sweet ginger-ale. She felt giddy like a little girl, a spoilt little girl. It felt so good. She put her drink down, and they went across to the pier.

"How come you don't have a girlfriend? Are you really picky?" Jeannie asked, heaving herself onto the low wall. Jeannie had just been laid off of her job as a secretary in some city government office.

Neelam shrugged. She who had once said she would never sleep with someone who hadn't read Flaubert had gone out with a sorter at UPS who was thinking of getting her GED, a prison guard, a secretary, various fillers of the unemployment rolls. And Marita, who was not worth mentioning. "I don't know what it takes. Tell me about your girlfriend."

But Jeannie wouldn't say anything beyond the woman's name and that she was from Barbados. She wouldn't tell Neelam what she did. "She's not a prostitute, is she?" Neelam was suddenly afraid.

Jeannie sucked her teeth. "I wish she was. Then maybe she'd be making some real money." She looked down at Neelam, who was standing in front of her. "What do you do?"

"I work at a museum up in Harlem," she said. "I go to school, I teach kids math in an after school program." She said it with an edge of spite.

"I guess you're very productive."

"Freud said civilization was built on sexual frustration," Neelam replied, carelessly, looking at the lights on the river.

"Frustrated?" Jeannie asked, pushing her braids back with both hands. "What is it that you want?"

Neelam looked up and told her.

"You got a light?" A group of banjees from the other end came up behind Neelam. Jeannie produced a fake gold lighter from her bag. Each of the men lit their blunts in turn. One man offered them a hit. Jeannie and Neelam shook their heads, and the men left, a refrain of salsa trailing after them.

Neelam and Jeannie were the only ones left on the pier. The sky was gray and troubled, and the river was like a slick, black sheet smudged with Jersey lights. It looked as if the river and the sky had exchanged places. Neelam turned away. Even the highway was almost empty. Up the road, a neon pink sign for a triple x place of some kind blinked and flashed. A police car screeched past. Jeannie was looking down at her hands. "My nails are kind of long," she said. "Do you have a nail clipper at your house?"

Neelam pressed herself against Jeannie. "Yes," she said, winding her arms around Jeannie's waist. "Yes."

21

She drew back. Jeannie was beautiful. Her bright, sloe eyes, her red-red lipsticked lips. Jeannie held her by the shoulders and Neelam felt Jeannie's fingers pressing into her flesh and Jeannie's braids grazing her ears and neck as Jeannie kissed her. "Let's go," she said. "We can take a cab."

Jeannie hopped down from the wall. Neelam was walking to the island in the middle of the highway to catch an uptown taxi.

A car full of boys stopped at the light. One of them shouted, "Are you lesbians?"

"Yes," Neelam said over her shoulder. She was laughing.

"Baby, I could eat your pussy," he said, craning his head out of the window.

"Yeah, but you don't have a pussy for me to eat," Neelam shouted back.

Jeannie touched her hip. "Listen," she said. "You know I'm not working, right, so we have to split the cab." Neelam pouted. This was not exactly romantic. Nothing ever happened to her the way it should. "Alright?" Neelam shook her head with a toss. Jeannie began to walk away towards the mouth of Christopher Street.

"Jeannie!" Neelam called out. A taxi had stopped and Neelam was holding the door open. They got in and Neelam leaned her head on Jeannie's shoulder and watched the lights swim by and Jeannie slipped her hand between Neelam's thighs.

It had been a couple of months since a woman had touched Neelam. Since Marita. Neelam inwardly winced. Marita was in her late thirties and not quite pretty, with a voice corrupted by years of smoking. From the beginning, she had known Marita was living with someone but Marita had said they were breaking up. Weeks later and with no progress on that score, and since she found Marita's kisses slobbery and repulsive, and after the rather annoying discovery that Diane had courted Marita similarly when they first met, Neelam let go. She had liked the idea of being courtly with an older plain woman who had never been cherished before, but she was hardly going to follow in some squat, uneducated former lover's footsteps. It was somewhat humiliating to think that she couldn't draw Marita away from Diane. She had a whole lot more going for her than both of them put together. She had declined when Marita suggested they stay friends. She didn't find her interesting on that level. As she joked to Simon, "You date someone because you wouldn't want to know them as a friend."

Finally, they got to her apartment. "It's a little messy," Neelam said, opening the door. After a quick glance at the time, Neelam went into the bathroom to run the bath water. It was nearly one in the morning. How had it gotten so late?

Neelam felt soiled by her long day. Besides, she had

taken a leak at Kellers, and she didn't want Jeannie to touch her without washing herself. She put the plug into the drain of her clawfoot tub, and ran the water. Then, she searched for the cherry-scented bubble bath amidst the clutter on the sink.

Jeannie had locked the front door and was sitting on the edge of her bed, under a tacked-up drawing. "Can I use the phone?" she asked.

"Yes," Neelam said, over the sound of gushing water. "Who are you calling?"

"My girlfriend," Jeannie replied. "I told her I'd be there when she got home from work, so I have to call and make up something."

Neelam said nothing. Jeannie was not being particularly tactful, but after her own behavior right before they caught the cab, she had not much right to complain. Besides which, Neelam knew from Jeannie's gaucheries that she wasn't used to this kind of thing. But she couldn't help herself with me, Neelam thought happily.

She unbuttoned her blouse and took off her pants. She was wearing a lace white one-piece with satin cups. Nice underclothes gave her an extra bit of confidence on a date, but she didn't think of why she was wearing it. It suited the moment, that was all.

Jeannie came in and fingered its satin spaghetti straps. "I guess you were planning on bringing someone home with you," she said.

"I've never done this before," Neelam said truthfully, but the idea of herself as a deliberate, lingeried seductress was not displeasing. She reached over and turned the water off. She put a finger in the tub. The water was nice and hot. The mirror was covered with steam. Jeannie pulled off her jersey and hooked it on the doorknob.

Neelam undid her ponytail. "You are beautiful," said Jeannie.

23

"I know," Neelam replied.

"I know you know."

"But no one loves me."

Jeannie said, "You know if I didn't have a girlfriend, I would scoop you up." Then Jeannie scooped her up.

They sat in the bathtub with Neelam's back against Jeannie's chest. Neelam could feel Jeannie's nipples. She felt aroused and happy. She splashed the hot, soapy water over Jeannie's strong legs. There should have been music in the background, but Neelam knew it would spoil the mood to go turn some on. Without a great deal of gentleness, Jeannie tried to enter her. "Didn't you ask about the nail-clipper," Neelam said, wriggling away.

Jeannie rose, splashing water on the floor. "Where is it?" she asked, waving her hand over the sink counter, over the tubes of lipstick, bottles of perfume, a pink soap pig, a toothbrush in a jar full of cowrie shells. She upset the contents of the jar that held the nail clipper, and clipped her nails, letting the cuttings fall on the floor. "There is a wastepaper basket right over there," Neelam remarked, getting out of the tub.

"Now you'll have to clean before you invite the next person up."

Neelam wrapped herself in her blue towel. "There doesn't have to be a next person, you know," she said, tentatively, going into the other room.

But Jeannie had a girlfriend, she thought. She felt cold in the bed and got under the covers. She threw the towel on the floor. "Turn off the light," she said, and Jeannie did.

Jeannie crawled into her bed, shoving the blanket aside.

Neelam knew what the inside of her own pussy felt like.

She had felt it. And though it was fine, she couldn't imagine a woman wanting to be there. What for? It wasn't that she thought it was icky, just uninteresting, and yet she wanted a woman to want it. Her fantasies always abruptly veered into trying to imagine why exactly a woman would want it. She knew that she wasn't overcome by the desire to be inside another woman, so why would another woman want to be inside her? Women probably did it out of politeness. Trent said he sucked dick because he liked his dick sucked. This was simply not good enough for Neelam. But fags have anal sex, which they can both feel. What a ridiculous thing a lesbian was. Two polite women doing boring things. Didn't any woman want it? She was forced to admit that she never looked at a woman and wanted to suck her pussy or get inside her. The thought just never occurred to her. She never thought at all about the act of sleeping with a woman she knew. Neelam somehow felt that it was imping-ing on the woman because the woman might not want to sleep with her. Neelam rarely appeared in the fantasies she used to get off and the other kind rarely managed to overpower this kind of deliberation. When she did succeed in suspending her disbelief, she felt like she had cheated. The only way she believed a woman could want another woman was out of pathology, like the Texan. The Texan wanted to be a man. In fact, the Texan liked to pretend her lovers were men. The Texan wanted to be a fag. This was too much for Neelam. She never had much luck when she tried to explain her quandary to other people. They would describe scenarios where two women could come at the same time, but that wasn't the point. She wanted a woman to be stimulated by what was stimulating her, not by the idea of stimulating her. "You think too much," Trent said.

"What choice do I have? I never have any sex," Neelam replied.

As Jeannie got inside her, she wondered what was

going on in Jeannie's mind, but knew better than to ask. Why were women so ridiculous, she wondered. Why couldn't she just believe?

"Do you have any lubricant?" Jeannie asked.

"But I'm so wet," she said. She leaned forward to suck Jeannie's breasts. There wasn't much else she could do in the position they were in. Jeannie's pussy was beyond the reach of her hand. She wondered if Jeannie was having a good time. Neelam wondered if Jeannie was bored with probing her guck. Straight women had it so easy. All they had to do was lie there and a man would be satisfied.

Jeannie made her lie back. Jeannie went deeper inside and Neelam arched up to accommodate her. She didn't want to tell Jeannie to stop but it was beginning to hurt. Finally, it was too much to bear. "You're hurting my clitoris."

Jeannie said breathlessly, "Can't you move it?" Jeannie was staring at her as if she expected a response to her absurd question. She doesn't want to stop, Neelam thought with astonishment, she wants to be inside my guck. If she is unwilling to stop, then it means she wants to. Neelam felt both ecstatic and in pain, as if her lungs were frozen, and just beginning to thaw. She moved Jeannie's hand out and pulled Jeannie on top of her. "You didn't even come yet," Jeannie said, reproachfully.

"It doesn't matter," Neelam replied, ridiculously happy. She wants it, she thought. It's not just to make me happy.

Jeannie shifted to lie beside her. "I have to go soon," said Jeannie. "My girlfriend is expecting me." Neelam rose and put on her satin nightshirt.

Neelam turned on the light and looked at Jeannie, her naked body. Jeannie was about to draw the covers over her, but Neelam stopped her. She parted Jeannie's legs. "I've never really seen a pussy," she said. Jeannie laughed and unclenched her thighs. Right after Jeannie left, Neelam felt cold and sluttish and guilty, but not for long. She was full of Jeannie, and when a friend from high school whom she hadn't talked to in eons called her, she couldn't help telling Kinnie about what had happened.

Kinnie was initially discomfited, but then her curiosity overcame her other emotions. "So when did you know you were..."

"What's there to know?" Neelam replied. "Ask me when I knew a woman could feel that way about me."

Not that Neelam always believed, but thinking of Jeannie always made her feel better. Once, after eyeing a dark, hard dread all night, just as she was getting her coat from the coat check because it was obvious that this eye contact thing was not working and she was ready to go home, the dread touched her elbow. The woman made mildly flirtatious conversation and asked for her number, and just as Neelam was settling in to enjoy the moment, the woman said, "Let me ask you something. I see a lot of Indian girls with acne on their faces, is that a really common thing?"

Neelam reeled from the shock and rushed out the door. It had been almost a year since the time with Jeannie and that was the last time she had been with a woman. She felt ugly and empty, she felt like it would never happen. The drinks she had downed and the ache of celibacy made her feel weak and insecure. She would never find anyone, she thought, crying, but then she stopped, because she thought maybe she was overdoing it and besides she would find someone. At least the women were getting better and better, so one day, she would actually have a girlfriend.

She undressed and got into bed, remembering Jeannie's pussy. It had such pink petals. She had wanted to suck it, but it would be her first time, and she knew she would be depressed later if her first time was on a one-night stand. She had contented herself with a swipe of her finger to taste Jeannie, and Jeannie tasted slightly bitter, like apple seed or pink champagne. Jeannie's pussy was so pretty and rimmed with dark, tightly napped hair like a pink rose surrounded by baby's breath. She had leaned closer to the pink jewel at its heart, and she had seen, Neelam remembered with a smile, possibility.

Chapter 3
Cocksucking for Beginners:
A Recipient's Guide

> Miz Literature, in a trance, takes me in her mouth
> …An act so…I knew that as long as she hadn't   ²⁹
> done it, she wouldn't be completely mine. That's
> the key in sexual relations between black and
> white: as long as the woman hasn't done some-
> thing judged degrading you can never be sure.
>
> –Dany Laferrière, *How To Make Love to a Negro*

Lili has brought home a book about Edouard Manet from
the library. Carefully, she rips out "Brunette with bare
breasts," and tacks it up on her wall next to a semi-naked
picture of Billy Idol on the cover of *Rolling Stone*. Then she
puts the music on low. She is in a deep David Bowie phase
which is off-schedule with the rest of the world, but she
plays "Changes" anyway. She sits at her desk, cutting out
pictures. She wants to make a collage for the front of her
plastic three-ring binder.

Lili is thirteen, and pretty in a buxom, '50s way. She

wears the latest fashions, which at the moment is neon sweatshirts with slogans. Hers is neon pink with "Make it Big" written on it. Lili is at her social peak. She is making quite an effort to fit in and, for once, it seems to be working.

She props her shaven legs on the edge of her desk and cuts out a picture of Prince. She cuts out a picture from the newspaper of a Palestinian boy in a kaffiyeh holding up a flag. She trims a photocopy of a Nicole Hollander cartoon. It is past three in the morning. She is trying not to listen to her mother screech at her stepfather. Lili pouts. She isn't allowed to make noise after nine, but apparently it's OK for her mother to screech at all hours. Lili takes out her glue stick and starts rubbing the back of the picture of Ian Stanley sitting in the sun with his wrist glistening.

"You are damaged goods!" her mother screeches. "You aren't a man! I should've just bit off the useless thing when I was sucking it!"

30   Lili purses her lips. Do I really need to be listening to this, she asks herself. I mean, do I? Why didn't her mother bite it off? If he is as beneath her mother as her mother says, why is she sucking his dick at all? Lili glues the picture on. At least it's her stepfather who is the target of her mother's hostility now, which means she will be spared for the next few days. She begins to glue the next picture, then gets bored and sets everything aside. She gets into bed and starts reading *Fireweed*. Really, she thinks, I need to get away from these people.

She hears her mother's bedroom door slam. Her stepfather opens her door and shuts off the light, then walks on to the living room where he sleeps. "Asshole," she mutters. She thinks it's not a bad thing after all to know he is impotent. When her mother asked her if she should have an affair with Albert, the Japanese man who works with her, Lili voted yes. Lili turns the light back on and settles in to read.

*

Lili is now twenty and heavier, and no longer interested in the latest fashion. She hasn't seen her mother in six years, and doesn't think about it. She is engrossed in her man, Maxim. Maxim is tall and strong and macho. Lili has dated only wimpy, skinny types before, but now that she lies on a hard chest when she sleeps and follows a man with a sense of direction when they go out, she realizes what she has been missing. She likes it when Maxim leads her around. With everyone else, it is she who has to take charge.

Lili has just come off a relationship with a slender Berber alcoholic who claimed to adore her and when she realized this smacked a bit too much of her mother and her stepfather, she left the Berber to his fate and embarked upon a real man. The Berber mended Lili's ego and his mission accomplished, Lili threw him out of her life. She could not stand his drunkenness anymore, and she could not stand the cigarette burns he left everywhere. Lili discovered he was thirty-four, not twenty-eight. He was a virgin when they met. Lili had been desperate to lose her virginity and he was handsome. His friends had set them up together. They didn't warn her about what she was getting into.

31

She hates them, and him. He disgusts her. She cannot remember caring for him. He calls her fifty times a day to tell her she is a slut, a whore, a bitch. He comes by once to pick up a letter that has come for him and in a burst of cheerfulness she starts telling him about Maxim. The next time he calls, all he says on her machine is "Fucking nigger." That's the end of any feeling Lili has for the Berber. Every time she thinks of him, she can taste the half-cooked chicken he left in the oven the night he tried to stab her and she got her super to throw him out. The chicken was cooked on the outside, so she bit into it, and then tasted the raw meat and nearly vomited.

Maxim isn't a diligent lover and, for a little while, Lili misses the Berber's attentiveness, but she likes Maxim's self-assurance. She likes his masculinity. Maxim is new, he is fresh, and Lili thinks she can cleanse herself of the Berber with him.

Lili regards Maxim with a mixture of adoration and irritation. Maxim is standing in front of a pay phone. His leather-jacketed shoulders are slumped into the booth. They are somewhere near Shaheen, and Lili is wondering if she should go get some channa battura. Her mouth gets wet at the thought of hot, spicy garbanzo beans. But Maxim is scowling. "Gitmaman," he yells into the phone. "Look, I been on your ass for fucking three weeks now, three fucking weeks and you haven't done shit."

Lili puts her cold hands in her jacket pockets.

"Emmanuel. Emmanuel, I ain't playing with you. I need my money, man," Maxim says.

The more she thinks about it, the more hungry she is. They have already spent an hour waiting for Emmanuel in his apartment. His girlfriend let them in, and Lili and Maxim sat with her in silence, Lili in desperate boredom flipping through the girlfriend's old *Vogues*. Finally, they left to page Emmanuel. He doesn't have a phone at home.

"Where the fuck are you?" Maxim says. "Alright, I'm coming down. Alright. Alright." He bangs the phone down. "Fuck." He turns to Lili. "We're going to Brooklyn."

"I don't want to go to Brooklyn," she says.

"Look, you see I'm fucking having problems. I got to get my money over there. You don't want to come then you go home. See ya. Do what the fuck you want." He begins to walk toward the subway station on 28th and Lex. Lili runs after him. She can't stand it when he is mad at her when she's not mad at him. It's cold and her ears are red and her stomach is growling, but she wants to be with him. Doesn't this man ever need to eat? She doesn't want to say anything. Because she is heavy, she is always embarrassed to bring up the subject of food.

"Maxim, if he said he'll be at his house and he wasn't, what makes you think he'll be in Brooklyn when we get there?"

"I got to fucking find him," Maxim says. He puts his fists in his jeans pockets. He is walking fast and she is struggling to keep pace. She is wearing heels because he said he was going to take her out.

In the subway, she leans her head against his shoulder. He does not pull away. From his neck, there is a faint scent of Old Spice. Lili bought it for the Berber, but it remained on her bathroom counter when she threw him out and now Maxim uses it. The train stalls once they are in Brooklyn and the lights flicker out. The people on the train heave a collective sigh. An elderly woman takes out an orange from a cloth bag clutched between her legs. A girl with a green scarf on her head dog-ears a page of her romance novel and closes it. Maxim swears. Lili, whose hand has been resting on his thigh, strokes him lightly to soothe him. The feel of the denim irritates her fingertips, but touching him soothes her too. She passes her hand over the bulge of his crotch. "That's all you think about," Maxim says, lifting her hand by the wrist and setting it in her own lap. "I got fucking things on my mind and all you think about is dick." He purses his fat lips.

"Oh please," Lili says, raising her head off his shoulder. She hates it when he says that. She is used to thinking of sex as a way to be generous to a man. "What dick?"

"If your hole wasn't so big, you would know."

"If your dick wasn't the size of a toothpick, I would know." Lili's voice is raised over the rumble of the train starting up again. The lights come back on.

"You're fucking disappointed aren't you because you

33

thought every black man got a fucking tree in his fucking pants," Maxim says.

Lili sits up, her back straight to give her every inch of her height. "No, I'm disappointed because you are illiterate, uneducated, abusive, unemployed and a drug-dealer."

"Then why are you my girl?" Maxim looks at her through his dreads.

Lili is silent. "Bad taste, I guess," she says, reluctantly.

After a few minutes, Maxim says, "You just like to fight don't you? You're a fighting girl. Macho girl." He says it with affection in his dark, scraping voice.

Lili leans back against him. She likes to hear herself being described as macho. "Maxim, you know you do satisfy me in bed," she whispers into his chest. It's the only kind thing she can think of to say. She wants to make amends. She realizes it is also the wrong thing to say. He shrugs her off his shoulder. It is their stop.

Maxim leads her through empty streets lined with identical houses with porches and no gardens. The only people out are a few young men standing against cars, listening to low compas. Lili wants to be inside somewhere warm, eating channa battura. Maxim pauses to speak in Creole to two teenagers. They are dark and scrawny and are sitting on the hood of a brown and beige stationwagon. Lili looks away. All around her, the houses are quiet and no lights are on. The night is sharp and windy. Why am I here, she wonders. If they kill me now, no one will ever know.

"This is my girlfriend, Lili," Maxim says, pushing her forward. Lili smiles politely.

"Are you Indian?" one of the teenagers ask. She nods. "From Trinidad?"

She has been asked this a thousand times. "No," she says coldly, "From India."

The teenagers nod. "Be seeing you," Maxim says, and they walk on. They go to the apartment Emmanuel is supposed to be in. Of course, he is not there. A sleepy and wrinkled Haitian woman answers the door, and they retreat. Maxim curses. Lili is still flying high from the teenage boys and says nothing.

She is not used to being thought pretty. She is used to being told she is intelligent, but to be found attractive is new and exciting. When Maxim first met her, he told her she shouldn't be such a club kid, she should read some books. This is what she likes about Maxim. She is used to being seen as a fat nerdy book-reader. Who besides Maxim would think of her as a club kid, one of those hip, superficial, good-looking women she has always longed to be?

Maxim holds her hand as they cross the street and lets go as soon as they are on the other side. He leads her to yet another apartment building. They clamber up six flights of stairs because the elevator is broken, Lili trying to pant discreetly. "Fucking thing is like never working," Maxim says. He motions her to be quiet and opens the door to the apartment in which he lives with his sister and her family.

35

Maxim goes into the bedroom where his sister and brother-in-law are watching television. Lili has seen the brother-in-law on a previous visit when Maxim stopped by to change his clothes. The man is enormous and misshapen. The stepsister she knows only by her rudeness on the phone. Sometimes, even when Maxim is there, she will say he isn't home and Maxim will have to grab the phone away. Maxim says she does this with every girlfriend he has ever had.

The apartment is decorated in late-twentieth-century lower class. The living room is marked off from the dining room by brass gates to keep out Maxim's nephew. The living room carpet is fluffy and white and the sofa and cushioned chairs are plump and plastic-covered. Brass lamps with white shades sit on the end tables, which are glass with brass edges. There are huge black ceramic vases of orange nylon flowers. The walls are decorated with brass-framed slick posters of a black woman in a Nefertiti headdress and a sunset over a lake. Two tall glass and brass bookshelves are lined with Woolworth's ceramic curios of little white boys dozing under haystacks and curtsying blond girls, the kind of commemorative plates that are advertised on late-night TV, brass-framed pictures of an incredible array of family members at various stages in their lives. There is a picture in a round frame of a gawky, teenaged Maxim before he got dreads, muscles and sex-appeal. The lowest shelf has about twenty books. Maxim hasn't turned on the light in the living/dining room area and Lili has to strain to read their titles. A book on numerology, a mystery novel in French, Harlequin Romances, and an accounting textbook. She settles down in a chair and amuses herself by reading the steamy parts of a romance novel in a ridiculously breathy inner voice. When she hears footsteps, she assumes it is Maxim and doesn't raise her eyes.

36   "Hello," a woman's voice says. Lili jerks up. Maxim's sister is very fair, her hair is chestnut and disheveled, and Lili can see her huge brown nipples through her sheer nightgown.

"Hi," Lili replies. The woman looks her up and down with scorn and turns. Maxim comes out of the bedroom. Lili sets the book back and is about to return to her seat at the dining table. Maxim's sister touches him lightly on the arm. The light in the corridor bathes their faces and the stepsister's bare shoulders. Maxim's skin shines like burnished gold against his mustard turtleneck. His sister's skin is paler, her negligee glitters. Maxim takes her elbow and bends down to say something Lili can't hear. The sister presses by Maxim and goes into the kitchen. A tap is turned on.

"Alright, let's go," Maxim says. Lili frowns. "I'm sorry I made you wait. Let's go." Maxim doesn't say goodbye to his sister and Lili doesn't either. When they get back down to the chilly street, Maxim says, "They didn't have any money to lend me, but my brother-in-law says I can pick up the twenty dollars he lent to François."

Lili is already tired. It's nearly midnight, and they have been waiting and wandering for hours. She doesn't like to go out without a clear plan. This is another thing that she can't tell Maxim. She knows what he will say: you don't have anything important to do, why you acting like a white man?

Lili sulks. She had been thrilled when he said earlier that evening that he was going to take her out. She didn't expect it to be a walking tour of Flatbush. She says, "It's bad enough that you're a drug-dealer, but can't you even be a good one and have some money?"

"Why don't you go home?" he says. She's not even sure where exactly they are, so she says nothing. They walk through some more identical-looking, poorly lit streets. Lili crosses her arms over her breasts to keep warm. Her feet hurt. She thinks of all the work she should be doing to prepare for the next day. "I need to get a car," he says after a while. She is still silent. "So my girl doesn't have to freeze her butt off."

Lili looks up.

"Don't you always tell me that your butt gets frozen?" he says. "I don't want my baby to have a frostbite butt." Lili laughs and really looks at him; she notices once again his broad shoulders, small snack-like hips in hip-hugger jeans. He tosses his mane of dreads. Her heart is flooded with desire, as if she tries to dam it up at other times. She is suddenly proud of herself that he is hers.

"Remember François?" Maxim says when they arrive.

"We met at Sticky Mike's," François says, leering at her. Lili can't tell if the leer is intended or François' attempt at flattery.

Lili is seated in the cramped kitchen and she watches quietly as people walk by in the corridors. The apartment

37

apparently has four or five bedrooms and the living room contains bales of cloth and several sewing machines. Lili sips the cognac François has given her and stares at the discolorations on the wall near the stove. She thinks of how she would redecorate the kitchen. She leaves the drink unfinished. Her stomach is empty, and another drop would push her over the brink. For what seems like an hour, she is alone. Lili is bored and feels like everyone else has forgotten her. She wonders where Maxim is. Finally, a woman comes in to heat up a bottle of formula. Then, a man married to an Indian woman comes to meet her and says she looks just like his wife. "Yeah, we all look alike," Lili says.

"That's true," Maxim says, entering the kitchen. "All these Indian girls look fucking alike." Lili tries to tell if he is joking or if he's drunk, but Maxim seems to be his usual self.

Eventually, they leave and Lili says she is ready to go to bed. She is sleepy. She got up at seven in the morning to go to work while Maxim stayed in bed until she came home. She sits in angry silence all through the subway ride, waiting for Maxim to ask her what the matter is, but Maxim doesn't seem to notice. Once at home, she is too weary to be angry. "I would have taken you out tonight, except you were tired," Maxim says, as she undresses. She nods, and gets under the covers. She is still hungry but decides against eating since she is just about to sleep. "Where's that wedding music thing?"

"On top of the stereo," Lili says. She wonders again why Maxim thinks *Bolero* is wedding music. He gets into her bed.

Lili curls up with her back against his warm, hard chest, and she can feel his erection against the small of her back. Her whole body aches, but she raises her ass onto his dick. He pulls aside her underwear and enters her. It is painful, and she has to switch onto her back. They pull off their underwear and she hands Maxim a condom from inside the pillowcase.

He climbs onto her and Lili brings Maxim's cock to the rim of her vagina. Unlike the Berber, Maxim isn't always erect, and Lili feels like she must take advantage of the situation when it occurs. She sometimes worries that Maxim doesn't find her attractive. Maxim plunges into her. It's uncomfortable, but she never says anything unless it hurts. Maxim turns her over onto her knees. Maxim is the first man she has ever let do this because she has always thought the position bestial, but she wanted to give Maxim the first of something and so she is obedient. He pushes into her, and sweetness shoots up her body. She tries to put Maxim's hand on her breast. He yanks it away and says, "Do it yourself." She flinches, but says nothing. After he comes, Maxim switches the tape to the other side. He doesn't like the roughness of the later Billie's voice, so he sifts through the tapes until he finds some Verdi arias to play.

He used to listen to opera on Saturday mornings when he was a kid. Strange and serendipitous are their points of connection, Lili thinks as he goes into the bathroom to wash himself. She begins to masturbate. As usual, he comes back too soon and she has to stop before she comes. He doesn't like her to do it. She has to wait until he falls asleep before she continues.

After she comes, she turns toward him and curves her body behind his. This makes her limbs ache in the morning but she loves the warmth of his skin against hers. She puts her nose against his back to smell his musk.

She hugs his waist tightly. It disturbs her that Maxim hardly ever holds her like this, and sometimes she makes him but then the point is lost so she doesn't do it very often. Still, he lets her cling to him the entire night, and she does.

When she wakes up, it is late in the afternoon. She has missed her physics class. She doesn't care. She can always

39

retake the class, but Maxim won't always be lying next to her. She looks at him. He has shaved his beard, which accentuates the wide flatness of his face, and she doesn't find him all that attractive. She rises. She puts on a pair of dungarees and a spinach-colored sweater. She examines herself in the mirror. When they were first going out, Maxim said just looking at her turned him on, but lately he rarely wants to make love, and he never tells her he finds her attractive. She hopes things will change when her Victoria's Secret order arrives. She doesn't know what else to do.

Before she gave up the pussy, everything was better. She teased him mercilessly, sleeping naked next to him, rubbing against him, licking his earlobe, telling him he could get inside her and changing her mind at the last minute. Sprawling beside him and asking if he would rub violet lotion over her skin. Those were the good old days when she didn't think she would sleep with him, when she didn't even particularly like him, when he was only a novelty. Now, she feels trapped like an asteroid spinning around him, too fast to get up to him and too slow to get away. She quietly locks the apartment door and goes out into the sun-drenched street.

At the bagel store, she tells the clerk to make the coffee extra sweet for her man. She likes saying this. She buys a newspaper and a magazine and goes home. She has another class that evening, but she isn't sure if she will make it. It depends on when Maxim leaves. She isn't allowed to ask when he's leaving because then he'll say she's throwing him out. She finds this rather bizarre because when she wants to throw him out she bluntly tells him to get the fuck out. Not that he leaves because she says it. Sometimes, she is tired of his coming and going as he pleases, and she tries to take a stand, but no matter her rudeness or throwing things, he lies in bed and refuses to budge. She knows she simply shouldn't let him in when he comes to her building early in

40

the morning, but if she tries to ignore the buzzer, he presses on it harder until her longing for him overpowers her. It never takes long.

Once in the apartment, she undresses again and gets back in bed. He opens his eyes. "Hey Daddy, I bought you some coffee," she says.

"Thanks," he grunts, inching away. She tries to embrace him. "You are fucking cold from outside and I'm naked. Can't stand to see me sleeping." He withdraws further. She lies flat on her back and stares at the ceiling. He covers her with her flannel sheet and then puts his leg over her. She turns to him and smiles. "Your body is cold," he says. "You know you never wear enough clothes when you go outside."

She puts her arm around his waist over the blanket. She says, "I think you're losing weight."

"I'm not fucking eating," Maxim replies. "My sister's getting a big fucking mouth. I can't live there no more, man." He sucks his teeth. "And you're my fucking girl and your fucking fridge is like always empty. When it comes to fucking, you're always ready but you don't fucking put back all the vitamins you want to take out of me." He pauses. "Shit. I'm not happy. I am not fucking happy."

"I do love you." She raises her head to look at him.

"Please, I am talking about fucking money and you got nothing to say but I love you." She lies back on his chest. "Next week I am going to cut my dreads off so I can get a fucking job." They are silent for a while, she gently stroking his arm.

At the beginning of his first date with Lili, Maxim quit his job because he had a fight with a co-worker with whom he is still friends. At first, Lili tried to help him. She made lists of jobs she saw advertised and scoured the newspapers, but he didn't show much interest in what she found. Maxim's own search consisted of many phone calls tracking the girlfriend of a cousin's neighbor who knew about a position as a waiter. Lili gave up trying to help. It isn't her job to take care of him. As much as she wants to say something, she bites her lip and refuses to get involved.

Finally, he goes to the bathroom and she sits up and reads the newspaper. When he comes out, he turns the television on. She turns the volume off. He dresses and sits down on the futon with her phone. "Yo Chris," he says. She looks up. He sees her looking and lowers his voice.

"I don't know why you're whispering. I know you're a drug-dealer," she says.

"Shut the fuck up, alright. Women want to know fucking everything. Mind your business," he says. The rest of his phone calls are to other Haitians and he talks in Creole.

Since he is dressed, she knows he will leave soon. When he sets the phone down, she tentatively asks if he's going. "Yeah," he says, standing. He puts on his cowboy boots. "I need to buy another pair of jeans, so I'm going downtown. I don't have a girlfriend to buy me some jeans." He looks at her. "Black jeans. Size 28."

She is doing the crossword now. "Don't forget the coffee," she says, nibbling on the pen's cap. He stands next to the dining table and drinks the coffee. He eats half a bagel. He turns the television volume on. There is a news broadcast about the status of Haitian refugees. Respectful of patriotism, she doesn't complain about his turning on the volume after she has turned it off. "If Aristide was in power, man, my butt would be out of this stupid place and I would be back in Haiti," he says. He strides toward the door. "Close the door for me, please."

"Give me a hug before you go," she says. He gives her a quick squeeze and then pounds down the stairs. She shuts the door and sinks back in bed. She pulls the covers up, and with one arm across her head, thinks of him and masturbates. Thinking of him turns her on more than when he is there. She has a hot, explosive orgasm. She washes her hands and goes to school.

She thinks of him throughout her economics class. She sits in the back row and does a sketch of him. The professor is handing something out. She quickly closes her notebook. When he walks away, she continues her drawing. Maxim's dreads are hard to draw. She is using a pen, so she can't rectify her mistakes. She is still puzzling over the problem when the class ends. She gathers her things and goes back home.

She has two messages on her answering machine. One is from Morgan, whom she met at a club a few days ago. The other is from Cicely. She calls Cicely first. "You down to go out?" Cicely asks.

"Always," Lili replies. It will keep her from calling Morgan back. She spends the rest of the evening bathing and dressing with the stereo turned on really loud. The man who lives upstairs pounds on her door until it shakes, but she ignores him. She puts on a diaphanous mauve dress and indigo tights. She wears Vamp Red lipstick and kohl and electric purple eye shadow. She sprays herself with Diorissimo.

Cicely comes to her house at midnight and they take the subway. Lili finds Cicely boring, but she likes going out enough not to care. She's the kind whom Lili meets with to go to bars, rather than the kind Lili goes to bars with as an excuse to meet. Cicely's only subjects of conversation are who she wants to date and what diets she wants to try. She is the only person in the world around whom Lili is silent.

In the bar, Cicely is immediately lost in a sea of people she knows. Lili sits down and waits for a good song to come on. Cicely will spend the whole evening flirting and gossiping. In the months she has known Cicely, Lili has seen her dance only once. Lili scans the crowd for someone she finds attractive. In her first ten minutes, she habitually searches for the one person whom she decides will make or break her night. The person she selects is very tall and broad-shouldered with dreads the color of sand. Mr Sandman, Lili thinks to herself, and smiles. Mr Sandman, bring me yourself. The Sandman is in the center of the dance floor. A crowd gathers to watch the Sandman dance. The Sandman is enjoying every minute of it.

Lili dances with other people, but her eyes are locked on the dread. She knows she is making a fool of herself. The last person she danced with brings her a Long Island Iced Tea. She decides to ignore the Sandman but they make eye contact on the dance floor and Lili ditches her partner to give the Sandman an opportunity to ask her. "Will you dance with me?" the Sandman says with a slight Jamaican accent, and Lili is about to respond when she realizes that the question is actually directed toward the graceful, tea-colored girl next to her. The girl says no and the Sandman shrugs. Lili is astonished.

Of course, Lili also realizes that no one will ever ask to dance a girl who has just seen them shot down, and she will not meet the Sandman that night. She tries to find Cicely to tell her what happened. When she finally finds her, Cicely says, "Well, what's your sob story this time?" and Lili tells her she is going to get something to eat.

There is a pizza shop right outside, but Lili goes to a different one a few blocks away. She misses Maxim.

She buys a slice and casually saunters by the bar Maxim is usually at on Thursday nights. Nearly every man inside is a dread and at first she can't tell if he is there. Then she recognizes the turtleneck he was wearing when he left her house and she enters. He wheels around. "What are you doing here?" he says. The blonde he has been talking to recedes.

His friends watch her expectantly. "I missed you," she says simply. She offers him a bite of her pizza and he refuses.

He says, "Let's go outside." They turn the corner, to the front garden of an overhanging apartment building. He sits on the garden's raised concrete border. "So what's up?" he asks, peering at her with his round eyes.

"I was in the neighborhood with my friend and I just thought I'd see you." Maxim looks at her like he's sure that couldn't be the end of what she has to say. "I guess you were busy with that blonde."

"She's the girlfriend of the guy sitting next to her." Maxim pulls her towards him by the hem of the jacket she is wearing. "Listen, I am going to be honest." He pronounces it awe-nest. "I don't want you here. I'm doing business, and I don't like having you around when I am doing business." He slips his hands in the pockets of Lili's jacket. She pulls away. She has about fifty dollars in her pocket and she doesn't want him to know. "See, that's the easy way to make you leave."

"I'm leaving," she says.

"Lili…" His voice is growly. "Lili, is just that girls and business don't mix."

"What business?" she asks, her head tilted back. Her back is slightly arched, so the hem of her dress rises.

He smiles. It is almost a blush. "Look, come back in an hour and we'll go to Nell's."

"I'm not taking you," she says darkly.

"What the fuck. I didn't say nothing about that. Come back in an hour." He rises. Her audience is over. "And be good."

She shrugs and walks away, tossing the paper plate the slice was on in the garbage. She wipes her mouth with a napkin and balls it in her fist. She walks the twisting streets back to Cicely.

"Where were you?" Cicely asks.

"I got a slice," Lili replies. She hasn't told Cicely about Maxim and she isn't about to start now. Cicely begins to tell her that greasy food isn't good for her, but Lili walks away.

Lili decides not to go back in an hour. She doesn't want to always give in. In the next hour, though, no one speaks to her and the Jamaican she likes is dancing with a sleek Latina with high cheekbones, so Lili finds herself returning to Maxim.

The bar is almost empty. Some twangy Haitian music is playing and Maxim is sitting in the window seat. She sits in his lap. His hands reach to her breasts. She slaps his hands away but he tweeks them again. She rises. He wants to walk to Nell's. She is wearing heels and wants to take a cab. He agrees. She knows that means she will pay. If she protests, he will say it was her choice and that he isn't working. Her feet are hurting, so she decides to go along with it. At this point, she has already come to him, and she doesn't want to stage a scene.

She thinks of the pale Jamaican with the sand-colored hair. Something about the Sandman's cheekbones and soft lips has settled comfortably into Lili's imagination. Lili thinks of the Sandman's skin as being the color of Brie and she laughs. "What you laughing at?" Maxim asks. She shakes her head. "You met someone?" Lili looks out of the taxicab window. "You met someone with your friend over there. Maybe your friend is your boyfriend, I don't know. Is it that gay motherfucker?"

"Why would my boyfriend be a gay man?"

"I don't know. Do I know your business?"

"Do I know yours?" Lili says, paying the cabfare. "I mean besides being a drug-dealer and a K-Mart gigolo."

"Your mouth is always flapping, isn't it?" Maxim replies. He goes to the grocery store next to Nell's and buys a beer. As they stand outside Nell's, he gives Lili six dollars and tells her to pay for him.

"Why, you want to pretend like I pay for you?" Lili says as they go up to the crowd milling outside the velvet ropes. "Don't want your friends to think you have a girl and you aren't scamming her?"

"Fuck, I just don't want the beer to drop. You are just fucking sick." Maxim tucks the beer into his jacket. "When the fuck do I ask you for money?" Maxim is trying to signal the bouncer he knows to let him through. "You are just selfish, don't like to give nothing."

"What about that shirt I bought you? What about all the food you eat at my house?" Lili is incredulous. A pretty, bosomy girl standing next to Lili briefly turns. The girl's braids are coiled in a complicated chignon on top of her head and Lili stares at it in wonder.

Maxim continues, "You don't even fucking cook. I'm your man and you can't fucking cook for me except for spaghetti. And that shirt cost like what, ten dollars? Maybe you found it in the garbage can, I don't know."

"And what the fuck do you ever give me?" Her attention is back on Maxim.

"I fuck you, right?"

"No, you fuck me wrong," Lili says as the bouncer lifts the rope for Maxim. She hooks her finger in the loop at the hem of his jacket and follows him.

"So why are you always grabbing for it?"

Lili doesn't bother to respond because he is already sailing past the cashier towards a host of dreads he knows. What could she say in any case? I want you to like my body? The only things I have to offer are my pussy and my money and I don't want you to like me for my money? I don't know how else to please a man? Because when you are inside me, I feel like you are a part of me? She stands by silently as he chats with his friends. Maxim knows everyone,

47

though he often told her the people he called his friends aren't really his friends. "The only person I really have is the woman I sleep with, and that's only you," he told her. And the only person she has in the world is him. She feels so wifely, so normal, standing next to him as he talks to a group of less-attractive versions of himself. "And this is my girlfriend," he says, and she smiles demurely.

He leads her around the curving banister down the stairs to the basement. She pushes past the dark red velvet curtains at the bottom of the stairs. The dance floor is already full. When she feels cynical, Lili thinks of the crowd as the zozo posse and its clients: white and Japanese people who want to buy drugs, and white and Japanese girls with jungle fever.

Maxim takes her to the back of the room near the DJ booth. He sets his Heineken on a speaker and hangs his jacket on the ornate base of a wall lamp. Lili sways self-consciously to the music. Maxim has told her she can't dance. Maxim is not looking at her. He surveys the scene, his head tilted back to keep his dreads out of his face, one hand in his pocket, on hand holding the bottle of beer.

He spots Chris dancing with a skinny white girl in tight jeans and a dirty striped T-shirt. Her hair is long and stringy, and with one look, Lili knows the girl is not terribly bright and couldn't possibly have a good job. Chris could do better, she thinks. Chris is rocking from foot to foot like a bear in a circus. When Maxim and Lili are alone, Maxim often does imitations of the way he dances. Chris is thin, but he dresses in shapeless, baggy clothes, no doubt to better suit the bear image.

Chris sees Maxim and comes over, sending the white girl on her way. Chris has a delicate-featured face, and if he were just a little better looking, he would be effeminate. He wears a cloth cap to hide his budding dreads. "Hello," Chris says, and Lili shrugs her shoulder.

The first time she met Chris, Lili told Maxim that she liked Chris' eyes, and Maxim said, "Those fucking light-skinned boys, man, that's all it takes." Maxim, though more golden than Chris, is light-skinned himself, but Lili understands his insecurity. Ever afterwards, she snubs Chris so Maxim won't think women prefer Chris' kind.

"Ignore her," Maxim says. "The girl has no fucking manners." He turns his shoulder and they are engrossed in conversation.

A chubby Buppie asks Lili to dance. He is short and she is one of the few women available to him. For lack of anything better to do, Lili agrees. The Buppie moves with surprising fluidity to the music, which is a house remix of a disco song that was bad enough the first time around. At least it has lyrics. Lili finds it hard to dance well unless she can sing along to the song. In any case, she can't really dance with much freedom because her dress ends an inch below her crotch. The chubby Buppie casts glances at her thighs. Beads of sweat glisten on his skin and on his hair. She can tell that he uses Indian Hemp or something similar, because his hair is greasy and fragrant.

A circle of men cheer on an East Asian writhing on the floor. He is dressed like a b-boy and has dreads coagulated with wax. When the East Asian rises, the men pat him on the back with a mixture of pride and kindness. Lili recognizes them as the regular Monday night crew, men who do hard, attention getting moves, a lot of work on the floor, and then, with repressed, hetero-black-man nonchalance, pat each other on the back a good half hour afterwards. They hardly ever dance with girls, though one particular man seems to know every female in the place. He even knows Lili, and smiles when they make eye contact. What is his name, she wonders. It's something to do with candy. Kit Kat? Baby Ruth? Starburst? Skittles?

A slim girl in '70s-style maxi-pants and a crocheted

black top and braids to her butt comes up to him. She is beautiful, and Lili stares at her enviously. The girl is dark with flawless skin and the deer-like face that some East African women have. She has that lean, angular model-look, except with more kalai.

Once again, Lili is the fattest girl in the room. Nearly all the women there are beautiful in a done-up, elegant way that leaves Lili feeling sloppy and uncontained. The white girls are a different story, because many of them are insouciantly clad in expensive T-shirts and jeans. One really cheap, other borough, teased hair white girl wears a boustier several sizes too small and her blue-veined tits bulge out of it. All the lesser members of the zozo posse go to pay tribute to her mammaries.

Chris walks away and Maxim takes Lili's elbow. She thanks the chubby, sweating Buppie and excuses herself. "Do you want a drink?" Maxim says.

"Yeah," she says, grinning. "I'll have a madras."

"Good, give me the money," Maxim says. She is startled. "I'll buy you one." She does want one, and she doesn't want to fight through the crowds and back with it, so she acquiesces. She hands him the money and stands with her elbow on the speaker. It's time to get out of this, she thinks. She is tired of the constant struggle not to be suckered. She is tired of having to protect herself – you have to defend yourself against the whole damn world, and isn't the point of having a man to have someone with whom you can set your armor down? Her anger is the clots of milk skimming the surface of the coffee she keeps sweet, weak and hot for Maxim. But if not him, who? She looks over what the room has to offer.

There were zozos and suit-wearing Buppies, one or two b-boys, preening superdancer fags, Eurocool types with slicked-back hair, the occasional leering and pock-marked Indian, miscellaneous others too irrelevant to notice. Irene dislikes the place because everyone there is always vogueing on something. This is probably true, Lili thinks, but she likes it when she's vogueing on being slim, and hip, and artistic, and chic.

The atmosphere of clubs – the darkness, the pulsating music, the beautiful people, alcohol and possibility – makes Lili want to quit school and take an internship at *Interview* and support herself with some waitressing job. She wants endless Wild Nights, Wild Nights with the City. Then she realizes that she would be a lousy waitress and she would hardly make enough money to pay her apartment's rent, and she finds *Interview* pretentious and irritating. She wishes she could be Maxim, but she is too chicken to do anything illegal – not that the police care about small-time dealers like Maxim – and she is not the type to be a whore. If only she could stand taking money from men, but she can't. It nauseates her enough to take money from her family. She just doesn't like the idea of being bought. The alternative seems to be doing the buying.

Maxim comes up to her with the drink. "How much of it did you drink?" she says. Her voice is lazy and snide. She sees it is more or less untouched. He scowls. She feels guilty for trying to hurt him.

"Take your fucking drink," he says. So she cajoles him to have some. He refuses, and then he sees someone and he is gone. She gulps down the drink. It's a rum and Coke, and it is ghastly. It burns going down. She sets the glass on the speaker, half-listening to the zozo beside her. He is giving the white girl Chris was dancing with a long and convoluted explanation of the color symbolism of his wool cap.

The middle-aged, red-uniformed Bangladeshi busboy squeezes past Lili, pausing only to grab her glass. Then Lili hears "Jump," so she starts shaking her rump and ends up dancing with a Latino in front of her. She moves closer to get away from the white girl's cigarette fumes, and the

Latino tries to press his hips against her. She pulls away and says coyly, "My boyfriend will get jealous."

The Latino smiles and lets go. "I don't blame him," he says. "You're beautiful." Lili edges sideways, still pursued by the cigarette smoke. The rap music gets more and more down, the beat more insistent and the tune forgotten. It must be Public Enemy by the time Maxim comes back. He stands next to her still dancing with the Latino. As soon as she sees him, she turns and puts her arms around his slim waist. The Latino smoothly turns away.

"He said I was beautiful," Lili says into Maxim's chest.

"Are you?" He moves out of her arms. "Are you beautiful?"

"I don't know," she says. She looks at him. He is whistling along with "My Mind is Playing Tricks on Me." He coils and uncoils his small hips. She moves in front of him so he is between her and the wall. Her whole back is tensely conscious of him behind her, trying to gauge whether his body is moving with an awareness of hers.

The club is even darker because some pseudo-cool type has turned out all the wall lamps. The only light is from the doorway to the lounge and from over the bar. She wipes her brow. Her perspiration intensifies the smell of her perfume. The music's tempo slowly rises, and her tempo too. She thinks of the Latino calling her beautiful and gets warm over her cheekbones like when she has had a lot to drink. As she moves, her dress floats out around her. A passing man stops to ask her to dance, his hand reaching out to hers.

Out of nowhere, she sees Maxim's hand push the man's hand away. "That's okay, she's mine," Maxim says laughing. He puts his hand on her stomach, his arm encircling her waist. His cheek is pressed against the side of her head, and his stubble is tickling her. She glows; she is beloved. She is overcome by how handsome he is, how lucky she is that he is hers. She is aware of all those thin beauties, those white models, that he could be with, girls just inches away from her, but it's her he is embracing and he said she is his.

"Daddy," she purrs.

"I know if I wasn't here, you'd be all over him," Maxim says. "I go away for like three minutes and you let some guy rub up on you."

"Maxim, I don't let even *you* rub up against me." Lili puts her arms around his arm, clasping her to him. "You know you're my Daddy."

Maxim laughs and calls her Lili again. They aren't dancing anymore. She is luxuriating in the feel of his arm around her. Somewhere along the line, he has put his leather jacket back on, and the zipper towards the cuff is pressing against her waist. In a few minutes, Maxim says, "You fucking pissed me off so I didn't tell you before, but when the bartender gave me the drink, she put her hand on my dick."

53

Lili lunges forward to see who the bartender is, but Maxim still has his arm around her and she can't move away.

"Hey, she was just playing," Maxim says. "You're so jealous."

"I wish you were jealous." She is pouting now, but only in a half-hearted way because she is sure of being contradicted.

"I'm jealous," he says. She smiles like a spoiled child. "When that man tried to touch you, I didn't let him, did I?"

This is as close as they get to billing and cooing, and she likes it. She rubs the back of her head against him. Soon, they will be home and she will have a chance to run her tongue over him, suck on his tiny nipples, and maybe he will gently stroke her hip as he has once or twice. She turns around and presses herself against him. He squeezes her shoulder. He is sweet sometimes. Just sweet enough to keep her coming back for more. Just sweet enough for her not to want to really hurt him. He feels so good. She tells herself to savor his smell, the feel of his turtleneck, his hard, broad chest against her.

Lili has read too many novels by old people reminiscing about fleeting youth, so she is desperately aware of being in the prime of her life, and she enjoys herself with a relentless awareness that all good things must come to an end. Notice how good he feels, she tells herself, because you won't have him after a while. He'll leave you, so notice his soft skin and his fat, juicy lips and his snack-like hips and the way he puts his arm around you.

"Ready to go home?" he asks.

"Just let me go to the bathroom."

Lili enters the powder room, and goes past two girls standing in front of an enormous mirror. They are discussing Sinead O'Connor, one of them trying to peel one of the postcards papering the wall. A third girl is lying slumped and silent in a plush red chair. Lili takes a leak in the adjoining room.

"That bitch just wants to get a black man so fucking bad. I mean, she says Desiree Washington's a bitch and Mike Tyson is a hero, she's all into Rastafarianism, praying at the altar of Bob Marley, what does this shit spell?" a hoarse voice says.

"I'm telling you. That's what all them bitches want. They talk that feminist shit but they ain't going to stand up for a sister. They just want some black dick."

"Who doesn't?"

"I can do alright without the tired old fools here."

A third voice says, "Hey, I feel really weird."

"You want to go home, Sandra?"

"Nah. I don't think I could if I wanted to."

"Um, that guy musta sold you some nasty shit."

The hoarse voice says, "Please, I take it and I never felt fucked up on it."

The second voice says, "Yeah but you didn't take from the same bag Sandra took."

Lili is still standing in the stall, not wanting to flush because she might miss out on something.

The hoarse voice says, "That's 'cause I take just any old Negro home when I get on that shit and I already made one trip for that penicillin, you know what I'm saying."

Sandra says, "Yo, this shit is getting strange." The chair squeaks. Lili flushes quickly and walks out. Sandra is kneeling on the floor. The other two are trying to hoist her back onto the chair.

"Maybe we should make her barf it out."

"How you gonna do that?" the hoarse-voiced one says.

Lili is washing her hands. "Who did she buy it from?" Lili asks, wiping her hands with brown paper.

The hoarse-voiced girl, who is ebony dark and has what someone else would call cock-sucking lips, says, "One of them dreads."

"Maxim? Did you get his name?"

The two girls give Lili dirty looks for trying to engage them in this irrelevant conversation while Sandra is crazed out, but Sandra gets into it. She lifts her head. "Hey, I think so. Light-skinned?" Lili nods. "Big face?" Lili nods again. "I guess that's him. He had a big ole face." She spreads her hands to show Lili how big.

When Lili comes out, Maxim is sitting on one of the couches with another man and a Japanese woman. The woman is neat and kempt if not really pretty. Her coat is soft and camel color, and obviously expensive. She has that trim, composed look that Lili envies East Asian women for. Indian women radiate messiness. The man is ugly. His skin is thick and shiny and his face looks like it has been melted out of its natural definition. He leans into Maxim as Lili plops down beside her man. "Coolie?" he asks, indicating Lili with his chin. "Guyanese?"

"India," Maxim says, putting his arm around her shoulders. "She's Indian."

The ugly man says, turning to her, "So when are you going to give Maxim a bouncing baby boy?"

Lili ignores him, pulling Maxim closer to her by his shirtfront. She whispers to him, "Have you been selling tonight?"

"Did you see me?" Maxim shakes his head as if Lili is incorrigible. She tells him about the girls in the bathroom.

"You asked some girl in the bathroom? This is some stupid shit. Did you see me selling drugs?" He rises, sucking his teeth. "Michel, man, this girl is a trouble-maker." She knows that this is his line and he will not deviate from it. She will not know if it was him. She wishes he trusted her enough to tell her everything or was so discreet that she never found out about it. He doesn't trust her enough to level with her or respect her enough to make sure she knows nothing. He respects her enough not to admit it, but that's as deep as it runs.

They go up the stairs. The top floor is nearly empty. A lone couple sits on the stage kissing as they pass by. A fleet of yellow taxis waits outside the club. A homeless man hobbles over to ask the few stragglers for some change. A vendor is selling hot pretzels and shish kebab. Smoke rises from his stand.

Lili pulls her jacket closer to her. She knows she should have worn something heavier but she hates her winter coat. It's so heavy it makes her shoulders hurt. She wants to buy a new coat. Something flashy and cinematic. Maxim walks beside her, silent. Behind them, Michel and his girlfriend are bickering about going home. The girlfriend is tired but Michel has the key to their house and wants to have a cup of coffee with Maxim. Lili also wants to just go home. She wants to take a cab but that would mean paying for Maxim again, and she's not up to that.

"Michel, just give me the key, and I'll let you in when you come home," the Japanese woman says. She is milk white, and looks elegant and dainty in her subdued-colored coat. The man next to her is wearing jeans, a silk shirt and a tacky multi-colored vinyl jacket. He wears a gold signet ring on his pinkie and it flashes when he mock slaps the air.

"That's all I'm going to give you," he says.

Lili looks at him with all the scorn she can muster.

"You better be careful," the Japanese says.

"I'll be whatever the fuck I fucking want to." Michel walks quickly so he is almost beside Maxim.

Behind him, the Japanese woman says, "You shouldn't swear so much." Michel turns and mock slaps her again. Lili stares at her. Why is she with this ugly obnoxious man? 57 "It's just because he's uneducated," the Japanese woman says to Lili. "He doesn't know how else to express himself but swearing and hitting." Michel sucks his teeth. "And you better be more careful because you already sent me to the hospital for six stitches."

Michel pauses to look at his girlfriend. Her heels tapping furiously against the sidewalk, she catches up to him.

"Six stitches?" Lili ignores Maxim gently tugging at her sleeve. "You should have left him."

Maxim has stopped walking. "Leave their business, O.K.," he says softly. He leans against the green post marking the subway entrance.

"He put her in the hospital for six stitches," Lili says, resting against him. Maxim waits for her to finish. "This is normal to you?"

"Look, I am not the kind of man who hits ladies, but

you know it's between them. And they made up." He tilts his head toward the Japanese woman and Michel. They are arm-in-arm.

"Maxi, let's get coffee," Michel says.

"Let's go to the coffee shop," Maxim says to Lili. He has an eyelash on his cheek and she wants to brush it aside but her fingers are cold and he will yell if she touches him.

"I'm going home," she says and turns the corner. She is about to step down the stairs into the subway station when Maxim grabs her around the waist and starts to heave her toward the coffee shop. She kicks his legs, her heels jab into his yielding flesh, and he lets go. "I am sleepy and I'm going home." They are in the middle of the road. The lights change and one or two cars begin to approach them.

"A quick coffee, okay?" Maxim's voice has a hint of pleading. She thinks that he doesn't want to lose an argument to his girlfriend in front of his friend, so she acquiesces. As they walk up to the shop, Maxim says, "You just want to show off that you're a macho girl in front of them."

"I am not like her, Maxim, I want you to understand that." She opens the door of the shop. Michel and his girlfriend are sitting down on the stools at the counter.

Maxim orders a coffee. "Give me a dollar," he says.

She glares at him. He reaches over and puts his hands in her jacket pocket and she has to yank away. She walks out of the coffee shop, to the subway. Maxim reaches into his pocket and pulls out some change.

She buys a token and is going past the turnstile when Maxim comes running down. He slides behind her and they both go past on the same token. The attendant doesn't look up from the magazine she is reading. The train comes quickly for a change and they sit opposite each other near the door to the next compartment.

"Let me ask you something," Lili begins. "What does Michel do?" Maxim doesn't answer. "What is his job?"

"How the fuck should I know? I mind my business. I'm not nosy like you. I don't ask girls in the bathroom, oh you bought some drugs, who you bought them from, what he look like." Maxim does a singsong imitation of Lili's voice.

"Does he have a good job?"

"You know nobody going to give a Haitian man a good job. A dread man got no chance in this country."

"So how does he buy silk shirts and expensive shoes and a gold signet ring?"

"His girlfriend. Not all women are cheap, like you. I had a Japanese girlfriend, man, she was so nice. Not ugly like most Japanese women. You should see her, so beautiful. And when I woke up in the morning, she'd be like 'Oh Maxim, here's $200 for you' or whatever. She bought me a nice fucking VCR. I didn't appreciate it. Now when I need a good woman, what do I have?" Maxim looks away.

59

Lili is hurt and she wants to punch him in the face. He is very quick and he would no doubt grab her wrists before she got close to him. "Do you take me out? Do you buy me a VCR? Do you give me $200?" she says loudly. This is not supposed to be the ending of the evening. They were supposed to go home, make love, he was supposed to slide his fingers inside her and make her come, which he's the only one ever to have done, and they are supposed to tell each other stories about their childhood and fall asleep entwined.

"You're a user," Maxim says. "You just like using men, but I am not like that, okay? I'm twenty-seven years old and I don't have time for bullshit. You are not going to play this using thing with me." His voice isn't raised but his accent is more pronounced.

Lili, whom arguments always trap between rage and

sadness, says, her anger pushing up in her heart and displacing everything else like the Loch Ness monster surging up in the center of the lake, "How could I use you? What can you do? I can't use you for a night on the town because you don't take me out. You can't help me with my homework. I can't use you as a maid because you don't cook or clean or do the laundry. So what can I use you for? I can't use you for your money because even if you have any you don't buy me things. It's not like being with you is such a good time and I'm using you for my own amusement. You can't fix things. I certainly can't use you for sex, because sex is where you come and I don't. What is it that I can use you for? You better let me know, because I'm a user, right, so I want to use you except that I really don't know what use you are." When all the words have come out, she is silent and exhausted. The train stops at 59th Street, and Maxim bolts out onto the platform and he is gone from view before Lili has even fully assimilated what has just happened.

Her throat is sore, and she has managed to give herself a slight headache. The homeless man who was sleeping sits up in his seat. He looks at her and she stares intently at the grime on the floor. I guess he'll catch the train to Brooklyn and go to his sister's house, she thinks. Her chest cavity feels hollow. She feels guilty and sad. She didn't want to drive him out. Her whole body aches for him. There is a glaze of wanting over her arms and shoulders and down her thighs, just wanting to touch him and hold him. Her heart feels as soft and open as wet pussy and she misses him. She is afraid she has driven him away. She is afraid she will never see him again.

She wants to call him, and as soon as she gets home, even before she checks her answering machine, she pages him, her man, her Maxim. Whatever their problems, she knows she has a nasty mouth, and she shouldn't emasculate him in public. She plays her messages and unlaces her shoes. Maxim has called her. His message is so sweet and vulnerable. He says he loves her. She shouts with joy and she runs around the room in a happy jig and tosses her shoes so they knock down her coat stand and all her jackets fall in a pile. She pages him again. Maybe he'll come, she thinks. She peels off her pantyhose soggy at the crotch and throws it into the laundry hamper. She changes into her nightshirt and sits on the futon, reading Raj Thapar's autobiography with little concentration. Maybe he'll come, she thinks. Sometimes, unexpectedly, late at night, her buzzer rings and he has come to her and her heart soars. After a night at some club, so his clothes stink of cigarettes as she hugs him. She complains that he uses her apartment like a hotel room, but she can't turn him away at the door as the shrink on "Oprah" advised. It feels too good to be near him. When she wakes up in the morning after having slept next to him, she is radiant, she is all-powerful, she is blessed. She pages him for the tenth time.

61

He doesn't call her, and she decides to get into bed. Maybe it's all for the best. Maybe he won't come, and despite the vulnerability and love in his message, she will be able to resist him and this mess will end. All she really wants from him is for him to be open to her, to need her for her, to be pleased by her. Her, not her money. Then, she goes over their three months together, and she thinks, fuck what he wants. She knows she deserves better. All this hoping and scheming and simpering for a little loving is ridiculous. "He is an unemployed, uneducated drug-dealing 'ho," she says out loud.

She goes over to her stereo and presses "play." She doesn't remember which tape is inside. Soon enough, she hears Billie moan. She gets into bed and she is skimming over Thapar's life during the Emergency when Billie Holiday sings, "I cover the waterfront, I'm watching the sea, will the one I love be coming back to me?" She closes the book. What you are feeling is Billie, not Maxim, she tells herself, but she does not know. The buzzer finally rings. He comes in and she is so grateful, she calls out his name. He strides into the room and throws his jacket on the futon.

He undresses down to his blue and black tiger-striped underwear and gets into her bed. He lies beside her, his back to her, and she runs her tongue down his spine and in little curlicues all over his back. She is happy he has forgiven her rudeness, so happy he will still give himself to her despite her behavior, happy he cares, he gives her his love. He turns and she caresses his chest. She runs her hands down his stomach to the hair on his concave belly. His chest is hairless, but he has a layer of fur on his abdomen and she gently tugs at it. She slips her hand into his underwear and pulls out his stiff cock and moves down to gently lick the head of his cock poking past his foreskin. She takes his cock into her mouth, sucking on it so he can feel the warm walls of her mouth, curling her lips over her teeth so as not to hurt him. She holds him in her mouth and gently sucks, careful not to be too hard. He opens his thighs a little, so she knows he likes it, and she is so pleased she sucks with renewed vigor and urgency. He puts his hand on the back of her head and presses down gently, not hard enough to gag her, but just enough for her to know how well she's doing. She has a good rhythm now, and her mind begins to wander. She thinks they have to work things out, because she loves him, she needs him, and he loves her, he needs her. She flicks her tongue over his dick. Cocksucking is an incredibly boring activity – cocks have all the flavor and pungency and texture of a rubber hose – but she likes it because it's practically the only time their hearts are open to each other and he says yes, it's you, it's you with every shudder of his body. She lifts her head. He pulls a condom out of the pocket of his jeans which are lying at the edge of the bed.

As he fucks her, she lies contentedly thinking of how pleased he seemed when she sucked him off. She thinks remembering his excitement will turn her on immensely when she masturbates thinking about it. She thinks of the Sandman she saw at the bar earlier in the evening. How attractive the Sandman was. She wonders where the Sandman is right that minute. Maxim comes and goes into the bathroom to wash himself.

She turns on her side and goes to sleep as soon he is next to her.

The next day, after he is gone, she moves her tape recorder next to the answering machine to record the message Maxim left. He is hardly going to write her love letters, so this is the only memento she will get and she plans to save it.

The first few messages are the Berber spouting obscenities. Then, Cicely. "Bitch, you left without telling me. I spent half an hour looking for you. Call me." The last is Maxim's trembling, almost crying voice:

Why are you   always acting so stupid?
Now, you make   me feel hurt,   and you know I love you   andyouknowyou'rehurtingme
    whenyoukeepsayingshitwithyourmouth.   You make me feel me feel   so bad.   You know I'd love to see you cry.

63

Chapter 4

The Dress You Wear, Your Perfume

> A violet by a mossy stone,
> Half-hidden from the eye.
> Fair as a star when only one
> Is shining in the sky.

> – William Wordsworth,
> *She Dwelt Among Untrodden Ways*

Montego Bay was one of those trendy downtown stores which sold bright clothes, African and Caribbean music, beaded and cowrie shell jewellery, a few painted ceramic dishes. The store had just the right mix of exotica and expensiveness to make it popular, and the staff was chosen for maximum ethnic visual appeal.

Which is why I was there. I agreed to take over for Simon, who had gone to D.C. to visit his latest flame – pun most certainly intended – because I was vaguely attracted to Louise. She had a head long and oval like a Benin mask and a quarter inch of hair. The short hair and the shoulders-up way she carried herself made her look quite dykey, but I soon found out that she was merely an Afrocentric dancer.

By that time, it didn't matter, because it was all about Opal.

"Me?" said Opal.

"Yes, you," said Louise, handing her the phone. "It's your boyfriend."

"I don't have a boyfriend."

"You'd have him if you played harder to get," said Mona. She exacto-knifed a box open. It was full of books from Heinemann.

I picked one up and flipped through it. *Mayombe*.

Another customer came in, a white man with moussed hair and an expensive, avocado-colored suit. Even before he opened his mouth, I knew he'd have a foreign accent.

"I'll stack the books," I said, and Mona slid over to offer him her assistance. I dragged the box over to the plastic rack on the other side of the cash register. Opal was sitting behind the counter, the phone cradled on her shoulder. She giggled.

Her legs were slightly open, her pantyhose stretched taut over her thighs. As if she knew I was watching, she sat up and pulled her dress hem down. She shifted so I could no longer see her face. Her back was arched and her butt stuck out even more.

Opal always looked startled, caught in the act, her wide-open eyes, her arched back, that protruding butt. She had the slim frame, big butt, and small tits body of girls in rap videos, except she was wholesome. Opal was wholesome. She was corn-fed and church-going and she believed in God and unity and the black family. She didn't wear makeup so her inner Nubian beauty could shine. She usually didn't have her hair done, so she wore caps a lot, X caps or a red velvet Kangol. Opal was plain-faced, but she had beautiful, smooth, toffee-colored skin. She was short. She was two or three inches taller than me, but she was short. And she was not my type.

I don't like flat-chested, estrogen-impaired, pointy-

Benin-tittied, can-barely-fill-an-A-cup girls. I don't like undergrown, midget, shrimpy, shrinkie, didn't-drink-any-milk-as-a-kid girls. And if you're going to be a midget, at least weigh something so people can see you exist. I don't like skinny girls. I don't like women who hide their hair. And I don't like straight women. I do not have a dick to give them and they don't have anything to give me. Opal was not my type. But when I saw Opal, tenderness softened me in my heart and between my legs.

She put the phone down and turned to me. "I don't know," she said. "Sometimes, he can be very nice." Louise brought up a pile of dresses and Opal started ringing them up.

"Don't never trust a man," said the customer. She was older and handsome, a gold tooth glinted in her smile. "They don't stay nice."

"Women don't stay nice either. That kind of gender-based dualism only perpetuates sexism," said Louise, folding the clothes primly. "Women must take responsibility for our own sexist stereotypes."

"Fine. Don't never trust anyone," the customer continued. "It's not worth it." Opal nodded sagely, still smiling.

But me, I was looking for someone to trust. That evening, I made my usual, fruitless monthly trip to the Octagon to be in the midst of a hundred and fifty women who couldn't have cared less about me. I wore a tight purple top with spaghetti straps that was barely more than a bra and the black palazzo pants I wore nearly every time I went to a club, it was so slimming. Stashed on the bleachers behind me were my T-shirt, a knit sweater and a coat. I had just bought the T-shirt at the Loft. It read: I'm Butch, and in smaller letters, *yeah right*. I thought it was witty, but the only person who understood it was a black queen who worked in the building where I took a photography class. I think the subtitle was too small for people to read. One white man with long, blond hair rolled down his car window to tell me, as I crossed the street, how great it was that I was a butch. I pulled my leopard coat tightly around me and thanked him.

After gyrating to no avail until the club closed, I agreed to go with Rix, the scrawny West Indian bartender who had a crush on me, to an after-hours place in midtown. It was a second-story room which was a nail parlor during the day. It had a thin beige carpet on the floors and a low ceiling, a row of carpeted bleachers against one wall. DJ Don was at the helm. He was a great DJ (i.e., he played what he was told) and that was the only reason I went, besides not wanting to go home.

As usual in a mixed environment, there were plenty of gay men and we didn't know about the women. After dancing to Joi Cardwell's "Club Lonely," I sat the rest of the time out. I watched Rix dance. Rix was more or less ugly, but she was double-jointed, and I had a great time watching her. I had a great view too because she was the only one dancing. This place wasn't so much a club as a place to go and buy drugs from hip dealers as opposed to dealers on the streets. One of the prime hotshots was this light-skinned balding guy who had his tongue down a different rich bitch's throat every time I saw him. Some men just got it like that, and if the bitches were better looking, I'd wonder why him and not me when I know I have more money and I certainly kiss less sloppy.

A pretty white fag lay down next to me on the bleachers, and, with his head propped, began telling me a long anecdote about Debbie Harry pissing outside the ladies' room at Jackie 60 because she had to wait in line. The punchline was Debbie Harry saying, "Do you know who I am? I'm Debbie Harry." The fag laughed like this was laughable and I wondered if it was so laughable, why he was telling me about it. "Do you have any

Donna Summer anecdotes?" I asked.

"No, I only do Debbie," he said. "I'm a piss hag."

The problem with this kind of place is that you always find out what you don't want to know, and never what you do. There was a black woman in a silver Armani-ish suit sitting with a few drug-dealers and I wanted to know her party line. She had a really short 'fro but dyke chic is in these days so that didn't mean anything. I would have asked Rix her opinion, but Rix was the kind of person who would ask, "So what she got that I ain't got?", and I am not the kind of person who can answer.

I watched the traffic in and out of the bathrooms, wondering what was going on. People were doing drugs openly and the place was illegal anyway, so it seemed odd for the sales to be conducted in secrecy. The trips were too quick to be sex, at least from a woman's perspective. Don's final song was "Get Off," and I got up to dance the last dance. It wasn't easy dancing on a carpeted floor, but I needed to stretch my legs. It was already seven-thirty. I had to be at work at nine.

After escaping Rix' reefer-stinking requests to let her drive me to work, I walked up to Times Square and took the shuttle over and the train down. I would have read the newspaper sitting on a dewy metal chair outside the Metropolitan Library like I sometimes did, but I was hungry. I went into the Greek diner near the 8th Street station for some breakfast, and there was Opal.

She was sitting by herself, eating Belgian waffles with whipped cream. "Hey" she said, sweetly, as I sat down in her booth.

"What are you doing here so early?" I asked.

"This place has the best waffles."

"So good you had to get up early?"

"I had a craving." She smiled bashfully, her teeth showing. She lived nearby, in NYU dorms. She was about to graduate with a degree in History.

I ordered an onion bagel from the inevitably Greek waiter. Opal started telling me about her suitemates who were annoyed with her because she played "Kill the Bitch" at their suite party. They found the song offensive but Opal liked it. "It doesn't bother me," she said. "I mean if you weren't going to like a song because it was misogynist, what would you like?"

That was the kind of girl Opal was. A man's fantasy girlfriend. In line with this, the men that she found attractive were the ordinariest ones around. She was especially enamored of D. Nice. She was probably enamored of Al B. Sure too, though fortunately she didn't share this with me. Not that I had anything to base it on, but I felt that women who liked sheer good looks could be turned, but girls who went for the boy-next-door type were a lost cause.

We made regular girl chat. She asked if I had a boyfriend. I smiled and said I liked someone. I asked her what she thought of the controversy over "Boom, Bye Bye." She shrugged. If I thought I was going to get insight into her ideas about homosexuality, I was very much mistaken. She wolfed down her food.

Women in general mince their food in public, so a woman who wolfs it down has a certain raw sexiness. That was the way Opal was sexy, raw like unrefined sugar. She was nowhere near the raw of porno magazines, the raw of a wound. Most of the time I was rather ashamed by what turned me on, but I liked myself for liking Opal. It was nice to know that just as my palate had a taste for both junk food and rasam saatham, my sexual predilections also ranged from bimbos to Opal.

We walked to the store together. Mona had been there for awhile, so by the time we arrived, it was warm. Opal opened the closet and we hung up our coats. I handed Opal her work clothes; we had to be attired in line with the store's

69

tropical theme, so Opal wore a tight, flowered, pink and magenta dress. Since I was not quite so thin, I wore black pants and a loose giraffe-printed shirt. I peeled off my sweater.

"What does your T-shirt mean?" Opal said, unzipping her dress.

I looked down at my chest. I had forgotten I was even wearing it. I decided to be non-committal. "It says I'm butch, and, you know, obviously, I'm not, so then it says, yeah, right, so it's funny, you know?"

She nodded. "Oh." She was standing in her black sports bra, the open dress flowing over her bare arms. The shadow on her chest revealed the curve of her small breasts. She tilted her head back slightly. "I still don't understand." She didn't move to put on her dress.

How was I supposed to respond? Let me show you, little girl? Come with me, sweetheart, and you'll understand everything? The whole thing was straight out of the first five minutes of a porno movie. Could someone live in the Village and not know what a butch was? Was she for real? Or did she really mean to feed me a line? I shrugged and faced the other way to take off my T-shirt and put on my work clothes.

I stood all day, leaning against the CD rack when I could. The only stool was behind the cashier's desk and Mona's butt was on it. My feet were aching and I felt sleepy. I stumbled around, drinking soda to keep awake and then getting buzzed and irritable from the caffeine. I was in too much of a daze to think coherently, or even to want to. When I asked, all the men I knew, and the dykes, were sure she was testing my waters, but the straight women told me Opal was innocent, that I should leave her alone. Most people are heterosexual, they reminded me, and Opal was seeing some man. I felt too tender to fail. I was through with unrequitedness in high school.

I had things to do, anyway. In exchange for my taking over his job for the month that Simon spent at Tracks with his little friend – a boy who insisted on being called Drakkar, having chosen his nom de gay after a cologne – Simon had agreed to leave his developing equipment in my bathroom. I had some projects in mind – pictures of the Armory, of murals in Washington Heights. I really wanted to photograph people, not things, but women get all coy around cameras. Things don't turn away, at least.

I had this fantasy of taking solarized pictures of women, Man Rayish, but it was of course impossible for me to find models. I wasn't surprised. Women were not about to take their clothes off for me for any reason, personal or professional. "Women are ridiculously self-conscious," I said.

"That's because we are judged primarily by the way we look," Louise replied, wrapping a bowl in tissue and putting it in a brightly flowered gift box. She turned to me. "Are you doing this for a class?"

"No. I took a class but this is for practice. Oh, and to create art. Actually, Simon left his equipment with me and I thought I'd take advantage of it," I said.

It was a late Thursday night and we were trying to get the customers out so we could close. I was wondering whether I should go to the Box. I had once met a woman at a Thursday night party who had come home with me, and I had been going back in the hope that it would happen again, though not with her. She told me I was wicked inna bed, but she also had a lover who later punched me in the eye in the ladies' room at the Box. It wouldn't have been so bad except the woman herself was decidedly not wicked inna bed, and her lover hitting me was just adding injury to insult. The woman had offered to go down on me, but I'd had my period. She'd had her period too, so I just lay on top of her and grinded, which I found quite boring, and she found, as aforementioned, wicked. It would have been pretty funny if we had both been faking it. In any case, she had come home with me, so it gave me some hope.

I was immersed in these calculations when Mona asked me if I would show her how to develop photographs. I agreed. It didn't mean much. Mona and I had made plans a few times to hang out and she had always canceled at the very last second. That was the kind of person she was. She once revealed to us that she would happily be Clarence Thomas if she could have the limos and the respect.

"Drug dealers have limos, and Clarence can't get no respect. Black people don't respect him because he's an Uncle Tom, and white people don't respect him because they know he's under their thumb. I don't know *what* you are on," Louise had replied, and ever since, they disliked each other.

Mona grated on my nerves, too, but I was always looking to go out so I didn't refuse her invitations. I had this picture in my mind of an exciting life in New York City, and going out every night with fashionable people was a fundamental requirement. The one time Mona and I did go to a cafe together, she annoyed me with her dissertation on the illicit pleasures of Anne Rice's S/M novels. Anyone who couldn't see Anne Rice's faghag hokeyness was beyond my redemption. I didn't know why Opal was friends with her.

Opal actually got her job through Mona. They were at NYU together. Opal was involved in black student organizations and Mona frequented coffeehouses and wanted to hang out with fags. One night, when she told me she was in the mood to hang out at a club, I started suggesting various places, from Bacchus to Level 10, and she asked me if they all had sex boys.

"Sex boys?" I asked.

"You know, places that pay cute, half-naked boys to

dance on the tables," she replied. Mona tried to make friends with all the white Fire Island types who came into the store.

Mona and Opal didn't seem to have anything in common. Mona was upstate prep school, summering at the Vineyard, doing X in the East Village before turning Buppie. Opal was the ocean breeze, a candy-striper, someone who knew all about the political situation in Grenada, and not just because she had a subscription to *Carib News*. Mona dated Europeans because black men didn't wine and dine her and brought too much bullshit and baggage into her life, and Opal believed in the black family.

"Are you leaving or are you going to stand there daydreaming?" said Louise.

"I'm trying to figure out what I'm going to do with myself." I went into the back room to change. When I came out, Louise was opening the door for Hailey, her Jamaican boyfriend. Hailey had dreads down to his waist and a thick beard. He was a poet. He did "performances" at the Nuyorican and places like that. His poems rhymed. "Can we let the Man who is farther than/set a plan for us?/Are we doomed/to be broomed/into the dustbin of history/because history is *his* story/and we're too sorry/to pin the din/on the sin/of winning at a time/when rhyme/is the meter of revolution?" Things like that.

They and Mona were going somewhere together. It was the law of gravity of popular people: people went out with Mona even though they disliked her. "Which way are you headed?" Hailey asked. "Maybe I can give you a lift?"

Me, they offered lifts. "No, that's OK. It's close by," I said, and walked out. The Box it was.

I should have gone home, but my apartment was empty and if I stay home too long I get a headache from the dimness of the light. I have two lamps but still the light never seemed to be enough after a while. I was really worried that I was going blind.

The Box was crowded. I went, screwdriver in hand, to the back of the room, and sat on one of the speakers. The music was so loud the vibrations throbbed against my butt and my thighs. In front of me, a menage of three short, shapeless women in denim and "Let's Jam" grinded against each other vociferously. I giggled. A woman standing beside me touched my arm, laughing. She shook her head, still smiling. It's not that she didn't have looks too, but I liked her for knowing why the trio were tacky, the kind of knowledge not always to be found at the Box. My drink was finished. I gestured towards the dance floor. She walked in ahead of me.

She was taller than me, though not tall really, and a warm cinnamony color. She exuded warmth, literally and figuratively. She hadn't been dancing, but her perfume had a richness that usually comes from perspiration. She danced well, with vigor, not that lazy grinding that bad dancers use as a sexy substitute for knowing how to move. Her blouse hung loosely, and I could see her breasts move as she danced. The music slowed down. I moved in closer, partly because someone was going by behind me. I leaned against her shoulder, my body pressed against hers, her tits on mine, and asked her name. She pushed me back, firmly. I smiled, embarrassed, and asked her again. "Sandra," she said.

We kept dancing, song after song. Sandra turned me around, and towards her, and away, with slight pressures of her hand on my hips or shoulder in a manner that I found macho and alluring. I didn't want to be the one to stop.

I tried to decide whether I would ask for her number if she didn't offer it, whether there would be dates, sex. She put her hand on the small of my back, and twirled me around, so it was me who was against the mirror, and Sandra behind me, with her back towards the crowd, when her friend, a pale Latina, came over to her. I watched in the mirror. Sandra turned slightly, gesticulating.

The crowd behind Sandra was dark and shaking, splotches of light settling momentarily on hair and shoulders. Sandra's hands moved more quickly, to her mouth and away. The Latina nodded back to Sandra, her hands rapidly curling and splaying. Our eyes met for a second in the mirror. A deaf girl, I thought and touched my forehead, smoothing my hair back. My hair was thick with sweat.

Girls, girls everywhere, the speaker blared. And I had to get a deaf girl. What was a deaf girl doing at a club anyway? Sandra wound her hips, hands in the air. Her friend the Latina was joined by two other girls, glancing at me and smiling. The music seemed terribly loud in my ears, speakers crackling. It was obvious that they were teasing Sandra about me. I felt horrible. "I'm going to the bathroom," I mouthed to her, and fled.

I couldn't. Period. Not even because there wouldn't be any chats on the telephone or whispering in my ear, but because it was too threatening. Was I such a loser that the only woman I could get was a deaf girl? I couldn't get a normal girl? I felt guilty – it wasn't that I had any prejudices – but I couldn't face anyone knowing. What would Simon think? It was like being in fifth grade, and hanging out with the Korean girl who spoke no English because I had no other friends.

I splashed my face with cold water. The bathroom attendant, a dirty looking woman with an enormous tool belt around her hips, handed me a paper towel. I dabbed my face. The woman leaned on the handle of a plunger. "Tipping would be nice," she said. I looked over at the range of products on the sink: hairspray, Opium, Old Spice, peppermint candies, Kleenex packets. I picked up a candy and put a dollar in her bowl.

Upstairs, I stood close to the stairs to the bathroom and surveyed the crowd. Of the women who hadn't already rejected me on a previous occasion, and who weren't in someone's arms, Sandra was the best of the lot. In the looks, dress, dancing and upward mobility categories, except for the deafness thing. The Latina came towards me, smiling ingratiatingly. Do deaf people have to smile all the time? She grabbed my arm, even though I wasn't going anywhere. She pointed towards where Sandra and I had been dancing. I nodded, and she went down the stairs to the bathroom.

I moved through the crowd, back to Sandra, who had a slim girl in black velvet poom-poom shorts draped over her. The girl was wearing a black halter top that ended in a string in the middle of her back, and spike heels the likes of which I had only seen in phone sex ads in the back of the *Village Voice*. I was walking away – my buzz was wearing off, and a drink seemed awfully inviting – when I felt someone tap me. Sandra beamed at me, her lips puckered in a smile. She tilted her head to one side. "Hi," I said, and went to the bar.

When I came back to the edge of the dance floor, the Latina made a bee-line towards me. She tried to dance with me, shaking her body in the uncontrolled way that white people in '70s TV shows dance, turning back to gesture Sandra towards us. Sandra looked at me, I looked at the colored lights streaking over the wall. Sandra didn't come over. She found the velvet shorts girl to dance with, the girl put her arms around Sandra's neck. I watched them for a while. I asked a woman to dance, and she said no. She was dark and not lovely; I wasn't attracted to her, so it wasn't that bad. I fished the cherry out from the melting ice cubes of my drink, put it in my mouth, and went outside. Crossing the street from the Box to the train station, I saw a girl who looked like Opal, and I felt a heat in my stomach like I had just downed a shot of whisky. I looked again, but it wasn't her.

76

*

It was already evening when I woke up the next day. I looked on my calendar even though I knew what day it was: I had written OPAL in block letters, she was having a party. I felt swollen between my legs. I tried to masturbate, but my mind kept wandering. That's how I can tell when I first like someone, when I try to come, but keep getting distracted. I never fantasized about having sex with Opal. I didn't know what I could want from her. Nothing? This slip of a girl asking me what a butch was.

Maribel had seduced all her (heterosexual) female friends one by one, with a modus operandi she called "being there at the right time," which apparently meant making the most of their moments of unhappiness. "A woman understands what a woman needs," Maribel told them, and she spent her money on huge stuffed animals and thin gold ankle bracelets, spent her time listening to these girls' dreams of modeling or marrying money, making love to them, coaxing them to make love to her. It was as boring as it sounded, so she always had a well-stocked harem of them, beeping her and wondering why she wasn't coming around as much as she used to, kissing the arches of their feet and telling them she knew how to love them. She would check the number in her beeper and laugh.

I've always been terrible at games. I used to be terrible at Mother, May I? and Simon Says, much less anything more complicated. I called Maribel for advice. "Should I go? I decided not to. You know, I've been avoiding her for days. I don't want to make an idiot of myself." Avoiding speaking to her was one thing, but how could I refuse a social invitation from someone like Opal?

"Don't go, you don't know how to handle it," said Maribel. "On the other hand, go. You'll never learn otherwise." She went back to her "wife," a dumpy Dominican girl who had made rice and beans and tostones all through Maribel's numerous affairs.

I got up and got dressed. I wore a white dress shirt and green slacks with a belt, men's shoes with chunky, Led Zeppelin heels. The subway was crowded, and the elderly white man playing the "Habanera" on his violin received lots of change. I even gave him a dollar – despite my general rule against giving money to white people – as if he were a gypsy and it would bring me luck.

I was at Opal's dorm just as she was coming up to the building. "Am I early?"

"No, I'm late. I just got off work. Mona didn't show up so I had a lot of shelving to do." She pulled down the hood of her jacket. "That's Mona." Opal fished in her pocket for her I.D. for the guard, and he signed me in. The sickly fluorescent light that university dorms and hospitals use made my skin look green. I turned away from the hallway mirror.

"So is your boyfriend coming?"

"He's not my boyfriend. Not yet, anyway," said Opal. We got on the elevator. "I invited him a while back, but we haven't talked since then." She shrugged. "You know how it goes."

"No, not really. How does it go?" I leaned against the elevator wall. Just as the door was about to close, another friend of hers came in. Opal introduced us. He was ellipse-headed and lanky, a member of the black NYU social services organization that Opal co-chaired.

Opal's apartment was split-level, and she directed the guy up the stairs to the living room. She took me downstairs. "You know someone likes you because of the attention they give you, you know?" she said, unlocking the door to her bedroom. "And then they just turn away. Sometimes you can't figure out the game people are playing." She turned on her orange lava lamp. "You don't mind, do you?"

I shook my head. A huge poster of Bob Marley stared down at me from over her bed. On the wall next to it was an ebony mask, the kind sold at street fairs by some African guy stationed between a shish kebab stand and a Miracle-Wipe dealer. I went over to the radiator to warm my hands. "I'll only be a second," she said. "I'm just going to change."

I read the spines of the books on her shelf: Angela Davis, Zora Neale Hurston, *The Black Jacobins*. "You burn incense?" I asked. I could smell something spicy and sickening. My only un-Indian traits are a dislike of agarbathi and a dislike of milk. Once when I went canvassing in Jackson Heights with Hari, a group of taxi drivers had invited us into their apartment for some warm milk. Hari gulped it down, but after a few polite sips, I couldn't drink anymore. One of the taxi drivers, a man from U.P. who evidently fancied himself a wit, said, "Well, in Tamil Nad they are not having cows so she is not used to it." Hari had to get me out of there before I decked the guy.

"My roommate does. I don't really like it, but she says it gets rid of bad spirits." Opal took off her jacket and hung it on her chair. "I don't believe in that kind of stuff, but it's hard to say no when she comes in here."

"This is the original American Rasta?" I took my own jacket off and sat down on the edge of her bed. Opal was from Barbados, but she wasn't half so into what her roommate from Mount Vernon, New York, considered "roots and culture."

"I told Stacey, just don't smoke weed in here, and she hasn't, so I figure I can put up with incense." Opal took off her sweatshirt, and stood in a pale, lavender bra. She undid the drawstring of her pants and stepped out of them. She was wearing a pair of lavender poom-poom shorts that covered not more than an inch of her thigh. She slid the door of her closet open and hung up her clothes, then bent down to pull something out of an egg crate, her ass in the

79

air like two ripe melons lying on a folded piece of cloth.

"You know you have a nice ass." The words fell out of my mouth and scattered like marbles. I waited, my skin growing hot, for her response.

"Thanks," she said, smiling, and then her face was covered by the top she was pulling down over her head.

"I have to go to the bathroom." I bolted out, and up the stairs.

Joan, her other roommate, found me, and took me to the kitchen, where everyone else was gathered. She gave me a paper cup full of Antiguan rum, and I took it into the unlit living room, where I sat on the window ledge. The living room was empty except for the stereo system blaring out some DJ Lenny dancehall mix. I lifted the blinds and looked at the lights of the building opposite. I wrote my name on the window mist, then Opal's. Then I erased her name with the side of my fist, the window was cool and squeaky. I went back for another cup of rum.

Opal had come upstairs and she called out my name. "You know how to bogle, right, show me how to bogle." I shook my head. "Come on." Her voice was so soft and feminine, she sounded like a girl saying "Papa, Papa" in a BBC costume drama. I wanted to slap her.

"I'll show you," said Joan.

I went back to the living room ledge. People began to come in. I listened to some handsome double-earringed guy tell his handsome double-earringed friend the latest words from Cali. "They're not saying dope any more. It's hype now. We have to say that now." The friend nodded, leaning into him to catch every word, an expression of utter seriousness on his face. A Cutty Ranks song came on, one double-earring asked a spandex-clad girl to dance and she ignored him. I watched Opal in another corner of the room – I could always spot her from her bare legs – hugging the people coming in. I couldn't tell how much time had passed.

I had been silent so long that I couldn't speak. I only moved when I need to go to the bathroom. I came back and another girl had taken my seat.

I stood in the corridor awkwardly. A huge man who looked like a slab of well-done meat grabbed my shoulder. "I want to dance with you when there's a good song on," he shouted into my ear, and walked by. I went back to the kitchen to get some more booze. I should have just gone home, I thought, but I wasn't ready for the long subway ride yet. I didn't feel high, only invisible. I kind of liked it. I felt like I could walk through walls.

Opal put her hand on my arm, the tips of her nails pressing into me. I stood in the doorway of the kitchen. Someone was trying to make margaritas but he couldn't find the top for the mixer. He opened each cupboard. "Hey," said Opal. "Hey." Some freckle-faced, orange-haired – the only people in the world who have red hair either have it out of the bottle or are brown-haired people who get red-headed when they swim and the chlorine turns their hair red – natural redheads are actually orangeheads and I don't know why they aren't called that. I had the urge to explain this to the guy who was looking for the mixie lid. I felt very sad all of a sudden. I thought of my ma using the mixie to grind pulses for sambar. I was very young, maybe four or five, and she wore a plaid shirt and a long purple maxi skirt. It was the '70s, and she had a beehive hairdo and wore long streaks of kohl. Or was that Asha Parekh? I was drunk after all. I wanted to cry.

"Hey," said Opal. The grip of her hand tightened on my arm, that coarse palm of hers. What did she do to make her hand so rough? Why did she smell like coconut? "Are you having a good time? I saw Mike ask you to dance."

"Mike?" I croaked. I hadn't spoken for hours, my voice sounded inhuman.

"The tall guy? You don't like him?"

I pushed her away. She was so slim I could have snapped her at the waist like Pocky. Strawberry-artificial-flavored Pocky. Bitches. Why was I sweating her like this? "Is that what you like? Huge slabs of meat? Refrigerators? That's what you like? I'm sure they like you too, if they're paedophiles. You have the body of a six-year-old."

"I don't have big curves like you, that's true." She smiled. Her lips were puffed like perfectly puffed puri you were too awed by to prick with your fork. The color of her lips were pink as pink chamcham, naturally so, since Opal did not wear makeup.

"I'm sure all the men in here want you. Is your boyfriend here? He must be really good-looking."

"No," said Opal. "He's okay, he's ordinary." Joan pushed her way into the kitchen to find the mixer lid. Opal stood aside, against the wall. Her face was in shadow, but her chest, until the lip of the top, glowed.

82   "How can you call the man you love ordinary?" I wanted to put my hand on her. I felt like I had a hairy paw. I was turning into a werewolf.

"I don't love him, I'm not even sure he's my boyfriend." She touched my arm lightly. "He's not as attentive as he was even a week ago."

"Maybe he's not sure you like him."

She shook her head, her soft eyes gazing at me. Her hair, which I had only ever seen brushed back close to her head on those rare occasions she was not behatted, was fluffy, a black halo around her face. "I think he knows how I feel, maybe he just doesn't know if he can handle more." Joan called Opal's name. "Excuse me." She went into the kitchen.

"There's no more rum," Joan said to me, as if I had drunk it all. I slunk back to my seat, trying to think. You know someone likes you because of the attention they give you, and then they just turn away, you know? I had avoided her for days. He knows how I feel. I told her she had a nice ass and all she said was thank you. What is a butch. I wished our conversation came with subtitles. Was I finding something in nothing? I felt dizzy and weak.

Louise appeared before me. "Look, you girls are being very bad, you cut day before yesterday, Mona cut today. Two people per day is not enough, OK?" I nodded. Hailey was standing behind her, holding her waist as she swayed. "Why is Buju Banton always singing about facials?" She looked over her shoulder at Hailey, who shrugged. "It's just using beauty products as a way of regulating women." She turned back to me. "Don't you think?"

"No, I think all them bitches should have facials." I stumbled by to the bathroom. A couple were talking in there, a man checking the hair on the top of a beautiful, dark woman's head. I waved them out and locked the door. I sank to my knees. I hadn't drunk that much, had I? I never used to get drunk so quickly. Maybe I was getting the flu. I vomited.

I washed my mouth. It was time to go home. I took a fingertip of toothpaste and brushed my teeth as my great-grandmother had done with Vico Vajradanti toothpowder. I rinsed and spat.

I went down to Opal's bedroom where I had left my jacket. She was lying on a mound of pillows, her thighs slightly parted. She had her arms crossed over her chest. "I didn't realize you were in here."

She looked up. "I needed a break. Are you leaving?"

I nodded, picking up my jacket. It was slightly crumpled. I smoothed the sleeve. "Thanks for inviting me."

"Mona just came."

"Too bad I'm leaving then." I put my jacket on. She got up. I opened the door and she reached up to give me a hug. Her body was so fragile, her small breasts like stingy scoops of mashed potatoes. They would have fit neatly into

83

my palms. I kissed her cheek quickly, cupping her head. She followed me up the stairs.

I found Louise and said goodbye. As I turned to leave, I saw Opal dancing with some huge man. He must have been at least 200 pounds, he was even bigger than Mike. She looked like his child, I half-expected him to pick her up and set her feet on his feet to teach her to walk. I felt another wave of nausea. I went out the door.

On the subway ride home, a black man harangued me for accidentally bumping into him, even though I apologized. "You're just jealous because I have an American passport and you don't!" he shouted. "I can tell you don't by your shoes." I looked down at my feet. They were English leather shoes from Trash & Vaudeville. He spat in my direction. I got off the train at the next stop and got back on a couple of cars down.

When I got back to my apartment, the chair by the window was full of dead leaves.

I went to the Box the next night, hoping my luck would change, that I'd find someone to occupy my mind, but I didn't. Maribel told me I was too desperate to meet someone, too unfriendly, too eager, too stand-offish, dressed too sexy and not revealingly enough, that I intimidated with my intelligence when I spoke and intimidated with my silence when I was quiet, that I shouldn't look for it and that I was missing my opportunities, that I was, in other words, doing everything wrong. I drank, and I danced by myself, and went home with my head spinning. Alcohol made me need less sleep, so I woke up on time more often than when I didn't go out.

When the phone rang at nine o'clock, I woke up immediately, which I would not have done otherwise. It was Raju reminding me that everyone had to be at Hari's by ten. I agreed and fell back in bed, crumpling the strewn sections of the *Sunday Times*. I leaned over the edge of my bed, and drank the rest of the grapefruit soda I had bought the night before for this very purpose. Cola quenched my alcohol-dehydration thirst better, but it also made me edgy. I crawled back under the sheets and masturbated incompetently, orgasm trembling in the distance like a mirage. My head buzzed.

With fifteen minutes left, I leapt out of bed, hurrying through my toilette, slipping on my shoes, and running out the door. I was at Hari's house at exactly ten. He opened the door for me and wandered out. I walked in gingerly. I had never been to his apartment before. I scanned the books on the hallway shelves: biology textbooks, medical journals.

A handsome, olive-complexioned man peered out of a room briefly, and went back inside. I hadn't known Hari had a white roommate. Since he hadn't spoken to me, I didn't want to disturb him. I searched the bookshelves for something to flip through while I waited for Hari to return.

"Don't you have anything to read?" I said, as Hari opened the door. He took out liquid glue and some brushes out of a plastic shopping bag.

"The novels are in here," he said, going inside the room the Italian had looked out of. I followed him, vaguely insulted that Hari had assumed I only read fiction. I did look like a bimbo – I was wearing tight black leggings and a turtleneck sweater that made my boobs look big, a jacket over my arm – but only out of perversity, because I felt that the people in the group thought I was a bimbo. They were older than me, and Marxists. I felt that anyone who had actually read Marx had to be smarter than me, because I had gotten through about four pages of *Capital* before being too bored to concentrate. Adam Smith was a much better writer, I thought. I was a capitalist bimbo. The rest of them worked in the sciences, except one or two of the women, and that too made me feel like a bimbo. I had once dated a bartender who had thought I was a bimbo, but that only amused me, because I was much smarter, and the bartender was too dumb to realize how much smarter I was, and insisted on giving me advice on my intellectual development, such as, "You should really pick up a book once in a while." This was different, and I felt I had to prove to them that it was possible to be smart and look like a 'ho.

Hari had big pieces of bristle board spread over his bed, and he, the silent Italian, and I pasted wooden sticks onto their backs. I turned one over. It read: Down with the Fascist Forces who are trying to Separate the People with Communalist Tactics. "Catchy," I said.

Hari grinned. "We also have VHP Murdabad."

I pasted a few more signs together. The others began to arrive, and another girl took over for me. I found a George Hart book to look at. Hari let me take it with me on the ride over into Jersey. Reading in cars makes me want to vomit, but I loved George Hart. I wrote him letters in my head as we herded out to the cars. It was eleven-thirty, which I had forgotten was what be here by ten really meant. Dear George, I thought to myself, you are a slamming dude. You have brought me closer to my Tamil heritage. You are a down-with-the-program white man. Live long and prosper.

"What's so funny?" I looked up with a start. It was a man I vaguely recognized, someone I had met at a film series curated by a girl who used to like me. Ajay. We were going to all be in the same car. I sat down quickly, pulling my jacket tightly around me. I put my hand over my mouth, and looked out of the window. He sat beside me. "Aren't you Wanda's friend?"

I smiled weakly, over the edge of my finger.

"How is Wanda? I haven't seen her in a long time. You

know that she was supposed to come live with us, but things did not work out." He pointed, no doubt in a vague gesture, but it ended up poking his wife, who was sitting in the front seat, talking to the woman who was driving. The poet who was driving, because that's the way the woman introduced herself, I'm Anna, I'm a poet. "Sundari tried to call her, but Wanda doesn't have an answering machine."

I nodded. Ajay flicked a greasy and droopy lock of hair over his bald spot. In a perfect world, Brylcream would be a controlled substance, administered to Indian men only with a doctor's prescription. "Have you seen her?"

"Not recently," I croaked, and opened the book. I couldn't very well say, yes, Ajay, I saw her last night at the lesbian bar we frequent. Ajay may have guessed anyway: Wanda is completely out. Her lack of discretion and my fucking life. I looked over the edge of the book. Ajay was watching the scenery out the other window. Of course, Ajay and Sundari were Wanda's friends, and they were straight, a couple.

So how did you and Wanda meet?" he asked, turning back to me. He had either been mulling over his repertoire of conversational gambits, or he was baiting me.

"Through friends," I replied, not looking at him. I turned the page. The truth was that Wanda had hit on me at the Box, no doubt thrilled that she had finally found an Indian there. Wanda spent most of her time having unrequited crushes on South Asian women who were either heterosexual or lived far, far away. She was currently in love with "Radz," alias Radhika, who was, according to Wanda, teasing her with flirtatiousness, and probably trying to come out, but was finding it difficult because of her ethnic and class allegiances. Ethnic and class allegiances being Wanda's exact words. Radz was probably utterly unaware of Wanda's crush, if not utterly uncomfortable – as I was, wanting to maintain Wanda's friendship despite my lack of erotic interest. Radz probably didn't mean anything by the polite gestures, off-hand remarks, that Wanda interpreted as flirting.

I was feeling smug, until I thought of Opal. Opal didn't mean anything by it, nothing at all. I kept telling myself that I wasn't getting my hopes up in the way that only meant that my hopes were rising, getting stuck to the ceiling like balloons, string dangling. I thought of Radz and Wanda, and yanked them down.

Anna turned into the motel parking lot. The road to the motel was considered public property, so we were limited to the road for our protest. We pulled the signs out of the trunk and trotted up to the grass-depleted sidewalk to await our instructions from Hari. He had a mike, and list of slogans for us to repeat after him in at least half of India's official languages. No Northeastern languages, I pointed out to him. "Do you know Bodo? You can make one up," he said, laughing.

"If you hadn't perpetuated the marginalization of tribals and Northeasterners, you wouldn't have this problem," I said, wagging my finger at him. "At least you have Tamil." I read it out loud. I could barely understand it.

Once the mike was set up, Hari led the call of the sloganeering and the rest of us responded, jiggling our signs. There were few people to see us. Most of the crowd had apparently promptly assembled for the noon speech by a VHP flunky. "I guess the fundis do make the trains run on time," I joked to Hari's roommate, who was beside me. He laughed. When a car came into the lot we screamed with added impetus, but the suited men and salwar-kameezed women getting out did not even look in our direction. One sullen pre-teen, a girl who could have been me at her age, turned briefly. I waved, nudging Hari's roommate to wave also.

Eventually, Hari, in a bid to prove his equitable attitude

to gender relations, asked me to take over the lead. I glanced at the slogan sheet and shouted out, "Bajrang Bali." Raju grabbed the mike away.

"It's Bajrang Bal, Bajrang Bali is Hanuman," he whispered. He covered the mike so the few "Down, Down"s that were uttered wouldn't be picked up. Those who hadn't heard me properly looked around, confused. Raju took the sheet and read out something lovely in Urdu. Everyone screamed, "Down Down."

"I see you're spreading the DK anti-Hindu message again," said Raju, later on in the afternoon. He was a Bombay-born Tamil, and therefore lost no opportunity in making Tamilian allusions. I ignored him. It had suddenly gotten colder. I undid my hair so it covered my ears, wiggled my toes in my boots to keep warm. "You'll only perpetuate their stereotypes of us as anti-Hindu," he continued. A couple of people sat down on the curb facing the parking lot.

89

The fat white policeman, who had been stroking his mustache like a regular cinema villain, waved his hand. "Get off the parking lot," he yelled. "Stay on the sidewalk."

"We're sitting on the edge," one of us replied. "It's muddy over there."

"Don't you understand English? Get off the parking lot. Stay on the sidewalk." He came towards us, his nightstick swinging at his hip as he waddled. Hari tapped the seated people on the shoulder. They stood up, one boy lifting his foot in the air just over the curb.

"Don't play with me," said the policeman. He yanked the boy by his collar. "I could send all of you people home." A crowd formed around him. I wandered away. A couple of women were at the end of the driveway, sitting in a car. One of them was Sripriya.

I knocked on the car window. "Hey, open up, it's cold." I got into the backseat. Sripriya introduced the other woman, a pale, moon-faced girl named Kausi.

"What's going on over there?" asked Kausi.

"Police brutality," I said, rubbing my hands on my thighs.

"Typical men, having to prove the size of their dicks," said Sripriya. She opened her purse and began to rummage.

I asked Kausi where she was from, and it turned out to be Nungambakam. "Hey, you're Tamil." I grasped the back of the front seat.

Sripriya patted my head. "She's bright, isn't she?"

"Mm, I don't know how to put this, but can you feed me? I'll eat anything. I'll travel. You don't live in Jersey, do you? Please feed me." I sat back, trying to look like a nice guest.

Kausi was a little startled. "I do live in Jersey, but maybe you can come to dinner some day."

"Hey, if you make morsathemthe, I'll come to the ends of the earth. Do you live near the PATH? Or vettha kozhambe, fried okra karmathe." My sinuses cleared at just the thought.

"Oh, you're an Iyengar, is it?" Kausi turned to Sripriya. "They respect food so much they fix 'muthu,' 'nectar' after the name of every food."

"I'll eat anything, though. It's been ages since I ate namba-ur sapade." I told her I hadn't eaten rasam since my mother's death, making pitiable faces. Kausi was examining her gloves intently, as if the knit would spell out whether she could feed me or not.

"I am not a fancy cook or anything," said Kausi. "I hardly cook, only make some rice and sabzi."

"Sabzi?" I lifted up a little to sit on my hands.

"She married a North Indian. Where is Shekar from?" Sripriya, who had finally found her cigarettes and lighter, rolled down the window.

"Does he force you to say 'sabzi'?" I asked. "Ayyo Sripriya, you know how those North Indian men are. Her husband sabzigates her." Sripriya and I giggled. Kausi didn't laugh. "Get it, subjugates, sabzigates?"

"He says poituvarain sometimes," said Sripriya, trying to stop smiling. She put her hand on Kausi's arm. "Right? He says poituvarain, sometimes?"

"I am going to go back," said Kausi and opened the car door. I got up and took her seat.

"Nice going." Sripriya flung her enormous purple felt bag into the back seat where it clunked.

"Hey, it was funny." I giggled again. "Sabzigates."

"So," said Sripriya, taking a puff of her cigarette and blowing out a line of smoke. Smoking is a disgusting habit but Sripriya looked good with a cigarette in hand, like a '40s movie star. With her high cheekbones and wavy hair, she could have been a dark Veronica Lake. "Did you seduce that girl yet?"

"Opal?" I fiddled with the radio knob, but there was only static.

"Another one? I thought you liked someone named Monique."

I sighed. "Monique . . ."

"Yeah, yeah, so who is this Opal?" Sripriya flicked out some ash. I gave her an abridged version of the story. Sripriya always seemed entertained by the stories of my infatuations, and I wanted very much to entertain her. I really wanted to be better friends with her, but I didn't know how to manage it. My life consisted of wanting friends so badly, and making do with people I picked up in clubs (like Maribel, who had liked me) and went to other clubs with.

Sripriya was so smart, studying physics, and had a handsome white boyfriend who adored her. He was study- ing Sanskrit at Columbia, working on Vijjika. They lived together in a plant-filled apartment on Perry Street, which I had been to only once, when I had run into her on

Christopher Street and she had invited me back for a drink. We listened to classical music (Sripriya played the piano too) and drank wine and had a great conversation, until he came home. The spell was broken, and I left soon after. Though I had her number, I could think of no excuse to call her, but sometimes I wandered down Perry, hoping to run into her again.

Sripriya's family was appalled by her living arrangements, but put up with it because she was studying physics, unlike her cousin, who was threatening to major in creative writing. Sripriya's parents were quite wealthy, and her dapper, Saeed Jaffrey-looking father was often mentioned in *India Monitor* ("the only twice-weekly Indian paper in the metro area"), *News India Times, Asia Online* et al., for his funding of a temple in Long Island. Her elder sister, who had graced the cover of *Femina* and was a doctor, had had an arranged marriage, and Sripriya, though she was not in love with the aforementioned blond beau, had moved in with him to forestall similar plans for herself. Sripriya, in other words, had a richer version of the family people usually assumed I had.

"I told them I wasn't marrying John, so they're feeling a bit better. My mother tried to ask in a roundabout way if I had slept with him." Sripriya laughed. "She was hoping against hope. She said, well, maybe we can find some nice Indian divorcé with no issue." Sripriya opened the car door and stubbed out her cigarette with her foot. She was wearing beautiful suede boots. I looked at my own scuffed, fake, man-made something bought used at Manic Panic and felt gauche, though Sripriya could wear something scuffed and used and look chic. She held the door open. "Come on, we should be getting back."

We walked back to the protest. Some people were sitting down on the ground on their placards. No one had gone in or out of the motel in a couple of hours. Sripriya went to check on Kausi. Hari's Italian roommate said to me, "Do you have a cigarette?"

"You shouldn't smoke," I replied. "It causes lung cancer, heart attack, and chronic obstructive lung diseases. Makes your tongue taste terrible." He gave me a funny look. "Makes one's tongue taste terrible."

"Who's going to taste my tongue?"

"I don't know, whoever. You are. I mean..." I pointed Sripriya out. "She has some cigarettes." I went up to Hari, who had stopped sloganeering because the responses had become so desultory. "When are we leaving, yaar? It's cold." My hair was falling in my face, so I pushed it behind my right ear.

"Let's wait until they come out, no? They're coming out soon." He offered me a sip from his coffee flask. The acrid smell of stale, dark coffee scraped my nostrils, then my stomach.

I shook my head. "Of course let's wait. One of your zesty slogans might change their convictions." I put my hands in my jacket pockets. My hair fluttered over my face. "So what's your vellakaaran roommate doing here?" Hari was also a Tamil, but from New Delhi. He looked so much like a burly Jat that I suspected this Tamil connection was somewhat fictitious. Certainly his Tamil slogans were written by some Sri Lankan friend.

"Avan namba ure," said Hari. He sounded like he was choking on a bonda. "And he's not my roommate, he's some classmate of Raju's."

"Your Tamil is pretty lousy, Hari, namba ure is Tamils only." This wasn't necessarily so, but I felt like saying it. In my thin leggings, my butt was freezing. I had been staring at the parking lot of the Sunrise Motel for the whole day.

"Mohan is Tamil," said Hari. He was about to continue when we noticed that the salmon pink curtains in the largest of the ground floor windows were parting. I squinted.

93

Someone was aiming a camera at us. "Those bastards. When we went to D.C. last year, they had known all our names."

"I guess this photo session must be for new members only then," I said, but Hari had gone by me to tell the others. A couple of men lowered their placards to cover their faces, shielding themselves with their convictions no doubt.

The grand finale of the day came. People hurried out of the motel into their cars. We yelled and screamed. Death to Communalism. Down with Sikander Bakht. The People Will Not Be Distracted By These Tactics of Diversion. We chanted Down Down after slogans in languages we did not understand. We stamped our feet in time to keep warm. I felt a surge of patriotic and self-righteous fellow feeling, and I jiggled my placard with vigor at the heavy middle-class people getting back into their stationwagons and four-door sedans, the men on the driver's side, women putting kiddies in the back. Many of the women were dressed in finery, zari-bordered saris or silk kameez in the rich colors of Starburst candy, Kashmiri shawls over their shoulders. The men were generally in suits, unless they were seniors in kurta-pajamas. They looked as if they were going to someone's engagement or a Deepavali party, not a lecture by a member of a fascist organization being demonstrated against by sincere graduate students and untenured professors in vinyl jackets and jeans.

We waited until there were only one or two cars left in the lot. The policeman got back in his squad car. "Where are you going?" the formerly Italian Tamil asked from behind me. I turned.

"I live near Hari. Are you down by NYU?"

The guy shook his head. "I live around here, with my uncle and aunt."

"You know I thought you were Italian." I was staring

right at him, and I still could see nothing Tamil about his face, the cheekbones and aquiline nose, the light eyes. He looked like a white man with a slight tan. His eyes were pale green. Where did those come from? "Are you sure your mother didn't have a little dalliance with some foreigner? You certainly look like a foreigner, though Hari says you're Tamil." I pronounced it the right way.

He denied having any foreign blood, though he claimed no one in his family had green eyes. "Anyway, you don't look Tamil, either. I thought you were Punjabi," he said. "When I saw you pick up the George Hart book I thought, there's another North Indian girl with a South Indian fetish."

"Does that happen?" I asked.

He nodded. "Yes, the IIT North Indian girls have it."

Raju opened the boot of Hari's car for the placards and mike set. "We're all in this car," he said. I looked in the crowd for Sripriya. She already had a group huddled around her car. "I'll drop you off, Mohan."

"I hope you drive fast," I said. "I'm starving."

Raju reached into his jeans pocket and brought out a packet of gum. He thrust it at me as if he had been waiting for just such an opportunity and said, "Bubblegumuthu."

That snitch Kausi had been gossiping about me, and Raju thought he could pass it off as his own witticism. It was pretty pathetic. I would have refused the gum but it was cinnamon-flavored. "Don't you have anything else to say? Amusing anecdotes?" I tied my hair back into a bun.

"Well, a really funny thing happened to me," said Raju, tittering. He raised one finger and made an arc in a typical Tamil way that made me feel a sudden burst of nostalgia right under my ribs. "I was in the Village, and this man made a dirty suggestion."

"Like what?" I leaned over the cool top of the car. The last light faded behind him, leaving him dark.

"It was so disgusting." With much hemming and hawing, he tried to explain. It turned out that Raju had fallen into conversation with some guy coming out of the subway, and the guy had asked Raju to go home with him. Raju tittered again.

"The man has the right to ask," I said. "I mean, he asked politely." I lifted the handle of the backdoor. "Open the door." I found Raju's giggling quite irritating. I supposed that if it had happened to a woman I might have been offended along with her, and tried to make myself not snap back at Raju with "Wasn't his dick big enough for you, size queen?"

Hari and Shetty came, finally, and we all got into the car. "Mohan, are you going to come back to my apartment? You left your backpack in my room." Hari turned around. Raju swerved out of the driveway.

Shetty, who was sitting behind Raju, grabbed Raju's shoulder. "Slow down, Raju, you're speeding."

"Let him speed, make himself useful for once." I was in the middle of the back seat between Mohan and Shetty, and Raju was driving so fast that every time he hit a bump, my head hit the roof, but I didn't want a leisurely drive through the Jersey countryside. The smell of the heated leather was making me want to puke.

"Do you want to have dinner?" Mohan whispered. I shrugged and nodded. "Yeah, Raju, you can drop me off at Hari's."

The ride took a detour to drop Shetty off, but finally we made it to Hari's apartment. Mohan got his backpack and Hari showed us out with a broad smile. I rolled my eyes.

We made a pit stop at my apartment because I had forgotten to bring my lipstick, and my lips were chapped. I had only managed to get through the day by borrowing some from Sripriya. I opened the door gently, not remembering if I had left anything incriminating lying around. Some copy of *Black Tail* opened to a spread of Champagne squeezing her breasts.

"Sit down, I'm going to wash up." I threw my jacket on the couch and went into the bathroom. When I came out, Mohan had put Supercat on the CD player, and was looking at my bookcase.

"Asimov," he said, touching a book on physics I had bought when I was in high school because I thought that I might read it and understand the world. "Popularization of science."

"About as much as I can understand." I smiled.

"Don't be silly, you seem like a smart girl." He crouched to look at the next shelf. "Erotica?" He tried to pull the art book from the stack.

"Don't, okay, the rest will fall." I was miffed by the Asimov crack. "What are you studying?"

"Computer science master's." He put his hands in his pockets. "Will you show me how to dance to this? I've never been dancing because I'm shy to dance."

I knew how that felt, so I stepped back and swung my hips a little, trying to show him the bogle. He gawked at me as if I was Bindu and he was some Indian geek in a cinema hall. I realized he *was* some Indian geek, and just because he looked like he was Italian didn't mean that he wouldn't behave like some Indian geek. I stopped dancing. "Let's go." I grabbed a thin, leopard coat and opened the door. He stood there, looking at me, and then shrugged.

He wanted to go to a take-out falafel place but I kept on walking to the Mexican restaurant. I wanted alcohol. I ordered a Tom Collins as the pretty little waitress gave us our menus. I downed it as he nursed his beer. I ordered another. "Were you born here?" he asked.

"No, Madras." I looked around. It was mostly a college crowd, the college guys bringing their college dates. I envied them their stereotypical experience. I had never even been to a frat party, and though nothing in the idea of standing around swilling beer attracted me, I felt I had missed out by never having been part of the cliché.

"But you grew up here?" He lifted his knife and creased the napkin. I ate some chips and salsa. I used to go there a lot so the waitress knew to put extra chilies in my salsa. Sripriya, that evening in her apartment, had teased me that I was more of an Andhra than she was. Where was my drink? "You must have been brought up here."

"Really, why?" The waitress, so doll-like and petite, curtsied in her flaring rose-appliquéd skirt as she set down my drink and more chips. The hot corn smell made me even more hungry. I ate, Mohan sat in his chair, toying with the cutlery. "You're not eating?"

"I want to have sex with you," he said. I nearly sprayed a stream of salsa, as red as paan juice, in his face. "I mean, you were dancing around half-naked in a very sexy way, and I . . ."

"Half-naked?" I snapped my corn chip in two. The frat couple sitting next to me turned briefly. "How was I half-naked?"

"You took off your—"

"Jacket, I took off my jacket. In my own house. Do you wear a jacket in your house? I was fully clothed from head to toe, I was wearing a sweater for God's sake. I'm wearing the same thing right now." My chair squeaked as I sat back. The waitress had seated us in the middle of the restaurant, and I wished I had my usual table in the corner. Then I would have felt as if my back was against the wall. Damn this geek. "I guess I'm half-naked right now." If I had been a little more drunk, I would have said it to the people eating near us.

"I'm sorry, I'm sorry if I offended you." He made a contrite face. "Really sorry, I take it back. Don't be angry."

I understood how he felt in a way. Here he was in a strange country where, he was led to believe, it was so easy to get sex, and yet none was falling into his lap. I felt the same way when Maribel and I were flipping through Wendy Caster's book on lesbian sex and we read a quote from some woman about how she was just an ordinary, plump girl in the straight world but in the lesbian world she was "cute" and got lots of attention. And I wondered how it was that if standards were lower in the lesbian world, I myself got no attention.

I finished my drink. My mouth tasted sharp and tangy, but I felt slightly blurred. "Okay," I said, benevolently. "I'm sure you didn't mean to offend me, but listen, that kind of line wouldn't work in India, and won't work here. Find yourself a girlfriend. You're a nice-looking guy, with your green eyes, you ought not to have any problems with Indian girls."

I smiled, pleased with my advice. The waitress curtsied again and brought us our dinners, soup and a quesadilla for me, something that sent up hissing smoke for him. The geek was eating beef. I didn't know whether to approve or disapprove.

He asked me about school, my life, boyfriends. I tried to give sensible answers, my tongue moving slowly to enunciate my words. The light in the room was getting softer and warmer. I wished I wasn't wearing a turtleneck. I pulled at its neckline to get some air. I put my hand flat on the table to steady myself, and sent my unused cutlery flying off the edge. Mohan seemed not to have noticed, he was getting up to get a cigarette from someone.

Strangers, smokers, give and take nothing so amiably as cigarettes. Smokers seemed like an international society, something like the Masons, only their evil deeds were more obvious. He came back and set the cigarette next to his fork, waiting for me to finish eating.

"Why don't you buy a pack instead of bumming them off of people?" I folded my napkin deliberately and set it on my plate.

He said sheepishly, "I'm trying to quit." He toyed with his empty beer bottle. "But no girl tastes my tongue; no girl kisses me." He said it in the tone of voice in which people confess that their parents were too poor to buy them Malibu Barbie.

"Then who have you been kissing all your life, men?" I snapped back.

Mohan looked astonished. It was as if I had held a blank, white sheet of paper in my hand, then in one motion, crumpled it up into a ball. He didn't have to say anything. Or rather, he couldn't say anything. His expression had told me, and he couldn't retract it. "It was my high school Hindi teacher," he said, quietly. "He molested me in tenth standard. He used to say the same things you said, that I looked like a foreigner, firangi."

"I'm sorry, I really am." It was my turn to apologize. But I couldn't make the same contrite face he could. I pictured him as a kid, looking a little like the kid in the Amul cheese ads. He struck a match a couple of times but it didn't take. He struck another.

"He would say the same things you said, that I looked like a foreigner." Mohan repeated it like an accusation.

"That's really awful, Mohan." I felt uncomfortable discussing something so personal. Not because it was sexual, sex is not personal anymore, but because it hurt him. The waitress came and I ordered tea. Something to dampen my high, make me more lucid.

Mohan lit his cigarette, finally. "You have an ashtray? Have you an ashtray?" he called out. He made a little circle with his hand, the cigarette in his mouth. The waitress walked by, oblivious. He turned back, refusing to meet my eyes.

"Mohan, was that the only man?" I asked, carefully. It was not. He had had an affair with someone in college. The guy was married now, and refused to speak to Mohan anymore. They had gone down on each other. "Did you like doing it?" I asked, slyly.

"Yes," Mohan said.

I thought about Raju, stupid Raju, saying "disgusting, nasty" and tittering. How difficult it must be for Mohan in New Jersey with his aunt and uncle, and then even his friends act so childishly. I would take Mohan on as my protégé. I would take him to the scene. I would take him to bars. What bars? The only gay men's clubs I had ever gone to were Tracks and Kellers, but neither of those places seemed quite right for Mohan. He wasn't into rough trade, was he? Maybe Simon could suggest some places for Mohan and I to go. It would be great, the two of us on the Village prowl, gossiping in Tamil. And I would prove Simon wrong, I wouldn't try and turn him into a queen. "Listen, there's nothing wrong with being gay," I said. I wanted to hurry the conversation along to the Village prowl part. I did know one other gay Indian – who knew if he even liked Indians – but this was a short Parsi doctor – not that good-looking, but maybe for starters?

"I'm not gay," said Mohan.

"You enjoyed giving a guy head and you're not gay?"

"I only did it because it was an exchange. He did it for me, and I did it for him." He blew out smoke in short bursts. The ash tip of his cigarette was long and dangling, threatening to fall. "I'm not gay."

"To actually enjoy giving, you must have some attraction to the other person's genitals, no? And if you're attracted to a man's genitals, what does that mean? If you don't like the word gay, fine, but…" The waitress brought the tea. It was too hot to drink immediately, I toyed with the tea bag string.

101

"Have you ever slept with a woman?" Mohan asked.

Somehow I was surprised. I hadn't expected the tables to be turned. I thought of the people we knew in common, Raju, Hari, Shetty. I struggled to be a part of the group even though I felt patronized sometimes. Like every time Raju asked me if I was studying English literature. I was a dumb girl, after all. He conveniently liked to forget that we were studying the same thing. Once Hari had spoken in a meeting of "women, our mothers, our sisters," as if women could only be defined through their relationships with other people. I had wanted to throw a shoe in his sanctimonious, progressive face. But still I went back. Being a woman, and the woman I was, was bad enough. Did I have to be a lesbian too? I shook my head. "No."

I tried to rationalize it. I had not gone down on a woman yet, wasn't that what "slept with" meant? So, I hadn't slept with a woman. I took a sip of tea. Mohan took my saucer and flicked his ash in it. Ash melted into the drops of spilt hot water.

"I'm not gay," he said again.

"Bisexual?"

"No."

"You did like going down on him though?" I felt like I was cross-examining him. "You told me just now that you liked it."

"Yeah," Mohan sighed. "I did."

"And how come he didn't want to talk to you after he got married?" The tea had a strong, bitter taste. "Hmm?" Mohan shrugged. "Did you want to again?"

"There's a woman in my canteen I want to have sex with, a Mexican girl. I think of having sex with her all the time." He didn't move, but I felt as if he had leaned back. "I want to have sex with you."

The waitress came over with our check. It was a busy night and we had taken our time. I wondered for a minute if Mohan would cover it, since he wanted to have sex with me. Without looking at the bill, I threw in fifteen.

He paid the rest and I rose, buttoning my coat. I was still a little high, and the wind was sharp outside. We walked towards my house. At least I was walking towards my house. Mohan stopped at the train station. "Thanks for dinner," I said.

"I have a long ride home. I have to take the PATH."

"Wouldn't Hari let you stay there overnight?" I could see my breath.

"I need to go back," said Mohan. He leaned against the entrance wall, one foot on the second stair down to the subway. "You're the only person I've ever told besides my uncle."

Mohan had apparently tried the same suave lines he had tried on me on his uncle's distant cousin, a buxom seventeen-year-old, and his uncle had threatened to thrash him if he didn't give a good explanation for his behavior. "You don't need to prove anything to anyone," I said. I put my hand on his shoulder in what I hoped was a brotherly way. If this was a t.v. show, he'd either kill himself at home or meet a nice computer programmer on the train.

He nodded. "If I had asked you nicely, would you have slept with me?"

I wanted to shove him down the stairs. "If your college buddy had wanted to keep sleeping with you, would you have?"

"Yes," said Mohan, and he went down to the subway.

At home, I stripped quickly to my underclothes and got under the sheets, slipping one hand under the elastic of my underwear. I wondered if Mohan was a portent. We are everywhere, aren't we? I came once, and then again. I decided that the time for dithering was over, I had to do

103

something about Opal. I could win if only I approached the matter in the right way. Maribel had been recommending studly forthrightness for some time.

I'd have asked Simon what he thought – after all, he actually knew Opal – but he was in D.C., and anyway, I felt uncomfortable discussing this kind of thing with him. He took it too salaciously for my happiness. On our one foray to the Clit Club – that dive for bisexual women who want to be gay men and straight couples looking for a third – he had been glued to the lesbian porn videos on the monitors. I had played pool, embarrassed that I had brought him there. No, I had to do this on my own. Do you know what a butch is, she had asked, and I was beginning to. I longed for the next time Opal and I would be working together, for another time she would give me an opening. This time, I'd jump.

On that day, Opal was sitting at the register, massaging her hands. "Hey, do you have a nail file on you?" she said. "I know there's one on Louise's key chain."

"Planning on some fisting?" I turned from the CD's I was dusting to leer at her with just enough exaggeration for it to be a joke. It was my old high school m.o. – jokes whose point I hoped was both clear and unclear. The girl I had joked with joked back with gifts of blue flowers, her thigh-high hose autographed with a felt tip marker, its foot crisp with sweat. She became a legend at school for allegedly sleeping with two men in the woods one night. That's the kind of girl I used to like.

Opal laughed, leaning forward so her thin shoulders jutted up. "I thought only gay men do that."

I was amazed she knew what fisting was – had Dr Frances Cress Welsing discussed it in *The Isis Papers*, because surely Oprah had never mentioned it? "Women can do it too. We have holes." I tried to sound blasé, not shocked that this was coming out of Opal's pink chamcham of a mouth.

"Wouldn't it hurt?" she said, giggling. She lifted her head so even more of her bare throat was exposed.

I dropped the duster and went over to her. I leaned against the counter and took her hand, making it into a fist. "Not with a hand as small as yours," I said. I would never have guessed that one day I'd be feeding Opal femme lines.

"You think so? I should ask Dennis. My cousin Dennis is gay." She opened her hand, palm pale and cut with deep grooves. I flattened out my hand, weighing her. We had never even been alone together socially, except by accident at the diner. That was the first step. I had to invite her to dinner or get her to my apartment on some pretext. She turned her hand over, so we were holding hands. "But he's discreet, you know."

"I won't tell anyone." I didn't dare raise my eyes to look at her. "I mean, about Dennis. I'm very discreet." Butch T-shirt aside, hadn't I been the soul of discretion? No one at Montego Bay knew much about me, except that I was a friend of Simon's, which was no clue in this day and age.

Opal's eyes were half-closed. She had a dreamy, far-away look, the same look she had when she was ringing up the cash register or sweeping the floor, as if there was no connection between what she was thinking and what her hands were doing. "Louise files her nails down. She's trying to get me to stop relaxing my hair too."

Louise came up from the storeroom. "Y'all gossiping about me again?"

I let go of Opal, jamming my hand in my too-small pants pocket.

She leaned over the counter, her breasts coming to the pink rim of her dress, and whispered, "You have really feminine hands, you know. Soft. I noticed that before." She said it quickly, then came on the other side. I backed up so that Louise could dump the new shipment of clothes on the counter. I looked at her over Louise's shoulder. She smiled, her head lowered, and unfolded a shapeless pantsuit.

I was almost glad to take a commercial break from the drama to hang the clothes up. I worked quickly. I tried to decide where I'd invite Opal to, from among the crummy restaurants in my neighborhood. There were about four horrible Indian restaurants which bizarrely called themselves cafés, and several mediocre Chinese places with exactly the same menu. Not to mention Greek diners. Maybe I'd take her to the Mexican restaurant I went to with Mohan.

As we hung up the clothes, Louise began describing the epiphany she had had about women's sexuality on television. "Intelligent, respectable women are not allowed to be sexually voracious. The joke is always that she hasn't gotten laid in years, like Murphy Brown." Opal made demurring noises. I couldn't think of anything to say, my head too full. The phone rang. It was for Opal. She went behind the counter and sat down on the stool so she was facing the wall, and began to whisper. Louise winked at me broadly and said, "He's back."

"Have you seen him?" I asked, but Louise didn't hear me. Had I misread everything yet again? I felt like I had some sort of eye problem which made flat pictures seem three-dimensional. This was silly. I bent down and picked up a hanger.

The racks were already choked with clothes, so Louise was pulling some of the oldest stock out. There were clothes on the racks which hadn't sold since African print first became popular in the '60s. Some of the prints were pretty but the ruffled, baggy style suited no one but the West African women who stitched the clothes, and the only Western-style dresses were in sizes only girls like Opal, Mona and Louise could wear. That is, not me. Louise peeked her head over and asked me to repeat myself.

"Nothing, forget it," I said. "It doesn't matter."

Opal hung up the phone, still holding it in her lap. She sat in the chair, not coming back to help us.

"So your boyfriend's back," I said, coming around the side of the rack. My voice came out a little higher than usual. I tapped the hanger against my palm. At least this had happened before I had hit on her. Well, Mohan was one thing, men have penises and can satisfy each other. How did I know how to make a woman happy? All the hopes I had had only the night before, only a few minutes before, seemed ridiculous. "Well, isn't that nice. Romance is flowering once more."

"Why do you and Mona keep insisting on calling him my boyfriend?" Opal banged the phone on the counter.

Louise said calmly, "Well, Opal, I've done it too. We're just teasing you." She put one hand on the top of the rack, and the other at her hip, looking like she was modeling her white shirt and kente pants in some Afrocentric catalog.

"Neither of them know *anything*..." Opal threw her hands up in the air, and turned away.

I cut in, "I think Mona knows plenty about men. She does just fine. And as far as I know, she does better than you." I don't know how I got into the position of defending Mona.

Louise turned to me. "Mona doesn't know shit about men except how to bilk them for loose change. She thinks she's getting so much out of her little rich boyfriends but she doesn't have a clue how to have any intimacy with a man." She did not use her own relationship with Hailey as an example of the intimacy Mona would never achieve but it was implicit. Hailey did not have loose change that didn't jangle in his pockets, so he was a sensitive black poet instead, always bemoaning the marginalization of Nella Larsen in discussions of the Harlem Renaissance.

"Whatever." It was an argument whose point I had

lost, as I tend to do quickly when I am not the offended one. "Is it that he won't get as close to you as you want him to?"

"Commitment anxiety." Louise drew out the syllables so it sounded like a medical condition.

"Whatever happened to someone saying, I want to take you out to dinner, I want you to be my girlfriend?" Opal was looking at me now, although Louise was presumably the expert. "I don't even like Eric that much." It was the first time I had heard his name.

"Is he big?" I asked. I didn't mean it the way it sounded, and I was grateful that both Louise and Opal knew me well enough to know that I didn't mean it that way. It was one of the rare times that I noticed that I was Indian, and they were black. I had only wanted to know if Eric was the man I had seen Opal dancing with at her party. "Like a slab of beef? A refrigerator?" I laughed, thinking of how drunk I had been and the things I had said.

Opal laughed too, and said my name. "So you like skinny?" she asked, her hand touching her waist, pinching the fuschia cloth of her dress. It sounded gay, the way she said it. Gay people often leave out or third person the gender words, as in "someone who said they liked me" and "you know someone likes you because of the attention they give you." Oh, I was tired of trying to understand what was going on. I felt released from any obligation to behave in a coherent manner.

"Sometimes I like skinny," I said. "But not as skinny as you, Miss No Tits." I threw the dress in my hand at her. Of course Opal had tits, but I savored discussing her breasts. She could go have her Eric, or not. I could say anything.

"I have even less," said Louise. Opal looked as surprised as I felt that Louise was still a part of the conversation. Opal threw the dress back at me. A customer came in, and I finished my work, wanting no more from the day. Opal left at 3 pm and Mona took her place. I felt as relaxed as a thirsty man feeling the condensation from a glass of water dripping onto his lips.

Mona asked me yet again if she could come over on the weekend to learn to use Simon's photo-developing equipment. I agreed. It didn't matter whether I agreed or disagreed, I thought, because she would cancel again. But I was wrong. She called me early on Saturday morning, and was at my house at one. I went to the Box on Friday night. Only two women asked me to dance. The first one came up to me as I stood on the edge of the dance floor, looking at what was on display. She was a fat woman with a dripping jheri curl who had been talking with – monologuing at – me since I first started coming to bars. Feeling both generous and humbled by my continuing singledom, I spoke to her. "Your English has gotten much better," she said. "When I first saw you, you couldn't speak very well." It wasn't a sly dig, she looked at me with utmost jheri-curled sincerity.

The second was a tall woman with skin the color of black grapes. I agreed to dance with her and she swayed with boredom, leaning down periodically to ask me my name, nationality, place of residence, etc.. I asked her if she really wanted to dance. She smiled like she was auditioning for a toothpaste commercial. "No. Can I buy you a drink?" I agreed. We moved to the bar. I leaned against the opposite wall as she fought through the crowds to buy me a screwdriver. When she came back, I said, "So what do you do?"

She put her hands in her trouser pockets. She was a good-looking woman, a perfect face except for the scar on her forehead, but somehow she didn't move me. She didn't have that quality that distinguishes human beings from mannequins – that kalai that Opal had. She said, "What do I do?"

"Yeah," I said. "You know, for a living."

"My job?" I nodded. "Oh, I work for an accounting firm." We stood in silence; she gazed off into the distance. "Am I bothering you? I mean, just because I bought you a drink doesn't mean you have to talk to me."

"No, you aren't bothering me." Boring me, yes, bothering me, no.

"I'm just going to get myself a drink," she said. "I really shouldn't." She giggled. "I've had four already." She went back to the counter. I turned away. The only other possible candidate had turned me down on another occasion – a tall, hard dyke, ugly but smooth, with her latest draped over her shoulder: a blonde this time. When I turned back, I saw Sophia was still at the bar, talking to the woman who had been the focus of attention on the dance floor earlier.

I was about to slip away when she returned. "Have you finished your drink? Do you want another one?" she asked, leaning against the mirror. She squeezed the lemon slice into her Heineken.

"So what did the East African breakdancing queen have to say?"

"East African breakdancing queen, that's so funny." Again she giggled. "The usual boring shit. Oh you're so beautiful, are you a model? I used to say yes, but then they want to know what agency, and what you've done, so I don't. Do you want another drink?" I nodded. She took a swig of the Heineken. "So have you ever just gone home with someone?"

"Yes." I jiggled the ice around in my glass.

"A woman?"

"Yeah." I looked up.

"I feel like doing something like that, something uninhibited."

"Have you ever slept with a woman?"

"Oh yeah, I like it. Don't you?" said Sophia jauntily.

I smiled. "So are you a model?"

"Yes." She finished the Heineken. "So, how are you getting home?"

"The train."

"Why don't you let me drive you home?" I agreed, flattening against the wall to let the crowd pass. I kept hoping someone I knew would see her with me. She went to the counter to get us another round.

After we kicked that back, we got back on the floor for some very desultory dancing where she tried to grind and I slunk away. She was too tall not to know how to handle herself and when she tried to get on top of me, I felt startled, not aroused. She drove me home. When we got to my building, she said, "Well, I'm really glad I met you." She smiled with her perfect teeth.

"You too," I said, and rushed out of the car. Any other time, I'd have dawdled, hoping to be asked my number. Or taken hers.

I got into my cold bed. Even though it seemed like days since I had come, my sheets seemed to stink of its arachified dosa mave smell. I took out a fresh blanket and lay back down.

My sleep turned into an anxious yet gripping dream. Opal and I were at the side of an enormous pool. Opal slipped off her pink dress and dove in. She kept splashing water at me, trying to get me to join her, but I was naked beneath my T-shirt, no swimsuit on underneath, so I sat on the edge of the lawn chair, watching her. Mona called to say she'd be coming over soon. I hung up the phone and dived back into bed, wanting to get back to my dream. I had just fallen asleep when the phone rang again.

It was Sripriya. "Oh, it's you," I said, puzzled.

"What, not happy to hear from me?" Sripriya sucked her teeth. "I thought I'd call and tell you your namesake is going to be on *Eye on Asia* today."

111

"You called to tell me that?" I lay down in bed and pulled up my bra. My breasts were tight, nipples long.

"No, grumpy, I called to tell you that John's gone to California, so I'm having a little buffet party to keep myself from getting lonely, and you're invited."

"I can't cook," I said lamely. I wondered where Sripriya had gotten my number from. I had hers only because I once had to call her on a phone tree about a meeting. Why had she chosen to invite me of all people?

"Bring wine. No, go to the Sinha and get some kara boondhi or something. No, get Ribena and lime cordial so we can have a nostalgia flashback. Maybe I'll make vegetable cutlets. Madras Beach thenga, manga, pattani sundal." Sripriya's favorite uncle had gone to IIT-Madras.

"Chicken tikka speared on toothpicks and sprayed with lemon juice. Dosas from Woodlands. No, no, clay pots full of rabdi. Oh those Bongs. Why is it in New York they only make third-rate motor panir?" My breasts ached.

Sripriya laughed at "motor." "Remember washing them out and then drinking water from them, so cool and sweet? Anyway, love, I've got to run. Bring something and come." She gave me the date, time, and address, making sure I was writing it down as if I'd forget, and left me.

Sripriya wanted to see me. I knew I would be leading a whole different life if I was her friend. I thought of Opal and turned on the television.

Mona called at the time she was supposed to come and said she would be there later on in the afternoon. It's one thing to ignore your own dislikes to accept the interest of chic people, and it's another thing to let them walk all over you, and I was determined to leave my apartment by the time Mona came, but she rang the buzzer while I was still dressing. I pressed the button so she could enter the building, picked up a shirt off the bed, and tried to button it quickly.

Mona was as dark and thin as the girl I had met the night before, only shorter, and she was dressed in an expensive but uninteresting Banana Republic way. I opened the suitcase full of Simon's things, and asked her what kind of film she had brought. It turned out she hadn't brought any film. "What are you going to learn to develop?" I asked her.

"Don't you have anything lying around?"

"I haven't finished my roll."

"What are you waiting for?" Mona dropped her jacket on a chair right beside my coat rack, and lightly touched my dining table as if she was looking for dust.

I was hardly about to tell her that I was waiting to get up early one morning and go down to the Flatiron. "I'm not wasting my film for you, Mona. I guess I can just show you without actually doing it." I did it in five, ten minutes. Mona didn't seem to be listening, and she didn't ask any questions. I sat down on my futon, pulled the sheet over my leg, and wondered why the hell she had bothered to come over.

"That's a nice shirt. Where did you get it?" she said, still sitting at the dining table. People gave me more compliments on this shirt than anything else I wore, maybe because I wore it more often than anything else. It was my favorite shirt, deep blue with purple and green splotches melting into it, like an artist's conception of ocean depths. When I was feeling sexy, I wore it with only a pair of tights and maroon velvet shorts. Lately, I had been wearing it almost every day, even to sleep. Though, because it was long-sleeved, I usually took it off in the middle of the night, feeling constricted. Mona said, "So, can I have something to drink?"

I sighed loudly and pointedly, and rose. I went to the kitchen and opened the fridge door. "Grapefruit juice, grapefruit soda, wine."

"What kind of wine?" Mona called out, as if she was at a fucking restaurant.

"Cheap rotgut I bummed off a wino." I poured one glass and took it out to her. If she didn't want it, I'd drink it.

Mona was bent over in front of the bookshelf. I sort my books by subject matter: general interest nonfiction, how-to, reference on the first shelf, Africa and West Asia on the second, India on the third, then China, Japan and gay. I only had a couple of books of Chinese poetry, a Kawabata novel with bisexual women, so the gay and lesbian books took up most of the shelf. It was way below eye-level, and anyway most of the people I know don't look at bookshelves.

"White," she said, turning around. She took the glass and sipped it. "It's good. I like cheap wine." I went into the kitchen to pour myself one. I felt funny doing this. I hadn't even had lunch, and my stomach had been delicate the last few days. "You have a lot of lesbian books."

I have a lot of African books, I felt like saying, but that doesn't make me a Hottentot. I settled for, "I have a lot of books period, Mona. But not one Anne Rice." Straight people hardly ever think anyone is gay unless they announce it, the possibility seeming so slim. I opened the fridge again and saw the encroaching white fuzz on the strawberries.

Mona was reading something when I got back to the futon. I didn't care what it was, but she looked up at me, waiting for me to ask. "It's lesbian erotic poetry. *The Poetry of Sex* by Tee Corinne."

"It's not by her, she edited it." I twisted to turn the radio on.

Mona, uninvited, began to read out loud. The corny verse sounded somehow less ridiculous as she read it. I began to feel uncomfortable. Surely Simon hadn't said anything? She began to tell me about women reputed to be lesbians at her prep school, at NYU, at parties she went to with her gay men friends. I had never heard the word lesbian so many times in my life, and it's not a word I like at the best of times, though it's not verboten. A familiar song started on the radio, one that I had heard at Opal's party. I still couldn't figure out the words: "keep wanting you so" what?

Opal's name suited her, a smooth pure stone. She didn't have one-off cravings for one-night stands. She didn't smoke weed in after-hours bars. She was not a security guard and she didn't need to be spoken to in small words. She had a decency that I craved. It wasn't even as if I'd seen her rescuing cats from burning buildings – or even from trees – but she was kind to me. She invited me to parties, and kissed my cheek. Her lips were so pink and soft. "So what do you think about Opal and Eric?" I asked Mona.

Mona shrugged, annoyed that I had interrupted her. "He's going to get rid of her. Do you want to order from the Japanese restaurant around the corner?"

We debated what to order for awhile – her refusing to eat Indian because it was too greasy – and settled for Chinese. She told me endless fascinating anecdotes about her roommate, Stephen, a white, Chelsea Gym-going waiter whose only acting gigs were ACTing UP. Mona was in awe of this cliché. I was irritated until I realized I felt the same awe for Sripriya. I tried to explain this to her, but she called Sripriya Syruppiya and I shut up.

After the food came and I poured more wine for Mona only, I asked why she thought Eric would leave Opal. "Opal is too direct. She sleeps with men too soon, and she tells them how much she likes them, and that they should have a deep relationship and be together a really really long time." Mona made wide-eyed, gooey faces, batting her lashes. She looked like a minstrel. I thought of Maribel, who had discovered exactly how to give straight women the love they needed in a way that they could actually receive it. "I've been telling her to get some dignity for months now, and she's finally acting like she has some spine but she'll collapse as soon as Eric whips it to her." She picked at her fish with chopsticks she used expertly. "Although she hasn't been such a sap lately."

"What is being a sap?"

"Telling someone you like them. Not making them come after you. I think Opal is finally getting some sense."

I pushed away my tinfoil container, licking my lips of garlic sauce. The sun was beginning to fade, but I felt like I had already been stewed in the heat and alcohol. The stench of Mona's food was too much. I was going to make a new house rule that people couldn't eat seafood in my apartment. I closed my eyes and saw white streaks against a dark background, nausea rising in my throat.

Mona kept yipping. I leaned against my pillow. "Stephen is going to Trinidad to shoot a commercial and he's excited because he likes black men, but I told him Caribbean people don't go for that."

"What do you mean, Caribbean people don't go for that?" How did her roommate put up with this kind of thing, unless he was one of those gay guys who's into shocking people with his decadent ways. How could she have gone to all those gay parties and still say this? The answer to that was pretty simple – she only went to parties with white men.

"I mean West Indians don't go for homosexuality. They think it's wrong and they don't do it." She waved her chopsticks around as she spoke.

"Mona, almost all the women I've dated have been West Indian." I said it in a fit of pique. Why did I have to personalize everything? Why couldn't I have said, well isn't Audre Lorde West Indian? I was behaving like a lunatic.

"Really?" Mona looked at me as if I were a little more interesting than I had been only minutes earlier. "There's this black guy I know who sleeps with every girl he can, and he started hanging around my suite, around this pretty white girl named Bonnie, very buxom, and from Iowa, and

I asked if he had slept with her and he said, don't worry Mona, I didn't fuck your honey. Everyone thinks I'm very bisexual."

I turned my head towards the futon, but Mona continued on with her true (almost bisexual) confessions. She revisited some of the stories she had told me only an hour earlier, adding herself into it, the lesbian I roomed with in prep school, the woman who hit on me at Stephen's boyfriend's party. I felt uncomfortable every time Mona told me she was perfectly willing to sleep with a woman. I wasn't sure if she was actually expecting me to offer myself – not because she wanted me but because she thought that was what happened.

Mona asked me what clubs I went to and told me about a friend of hers who took a gay studies class at Columbia which had a recommended field trip down to the Box. "That is fucking insulting," I said. "Go stare at the dykes."

"So have you slept with a lot of women?"

"Have you sucked a lot of dick, Mona?" I had my arm on my forehead. I didn't have the guts to ask her to leave. Though I was drowsy, I was too keyed up to rest, and it was threeish, that awkward hour. "Can you keep a secret?"

"What?" Mona put her foot up on the blanket box, her pale pink-painted toenails peeking over next to the plastic packets of soy and duck sauce.

"Forget it." I was just as stupid as Opal was, longing to tell someone who had actually seen Opal, who knew her, ill-advised or not.

"Can I borrow some books from you?" she asked, getting up.

I didn't have the guts to say no, and so said nothing. She made a little pile on top of her jacket. "How many are you taking?"

"Didn't you say you have a lot of books? You won't

miss them. You're not going to be reading *The Marabi Dance* today, are you?" She smiled.

I didn't want her to go, all of a sudden. I was feeling too anxious to be left alone. I tried to keep her with tantalizing clues to my story. "I like someone."

"Yeah, who?" she picked up the leather box on the other bookshelf and opened it. It contained little shells I had collected many years ago, when Madras Beach had shells. She poked her finger in the box and yellow tissue floated out. "Anyone I know?" She looked over at me as if she thought it might be her.

"Forget it." She shrugged. "Opal."

"I knew that." She closed the box.

I sat up. "You knew?"

Mona nodded. "You'd better forget it, though. Opal would never go for it. Whatever West Indians you know, no one in her family would ever be gay."

I almost wanted to tell Mona about Dennis. But what was the point? "You knew," I repeated, almost to myself. Did that mean Opal knew too? Did she know when she changed in front of me? When she turned her hand over so we were holding hands? Of course it was easy for Mona to say it. I wanted her to tell me what she meant by that, to participate in my desire, but instead Mona said we should go to a gay club sometime. I nodded, getting up to open the door to let her go. I felt nervous watching her going down the stairs with six of my books, somehow knowing I'd never get them back.

I closed the door and went to the bathroom to puke. I used to drink as much as I wanted and not get sick. The first time I drank, my friend and I finished two bottles of wine between us and I didn't even feel high. Now, a glass of wine and I was puking. Or maybe it was the bad Chinese food. Who knows what roaches and strands of hair and filth were in the Chinese restaurant's kitchen.

I went back to bed, and tried to think whom I could call to tell about Mona. I tossed and turned for awhile, then fell asleep. When I woke up, I turned on Nick at Night and picked up *The Poetry of Sex*. I had no concentration to read, and I kept picking books up and setting them down until it was finally late enough to go out – time that the club would be reasonably crowded. I felt like the ceiling would collapse on my head if I stayed at home. Or that I would die of an anxiety attack. Every time I closed my eyes, I felt as if someone was smothering my face in dirt. I went out and came back home when the club closed. I fell into a dead sleep until Simon called me.

"Is my stuff safe?" he asked.

"Yeah. Where are you?"

"Just got back. Are you doing anything tonight?"

"No," I said, and hoped Simon would suggest we go out. People would start thinking I was a loser if they always saw me by myself.

119

"Tommy's having a party. I wish I could go but I have to get to sleep so I can work tomorrow."

"I thought you were starting back on Thursday."

"It's alright, I'll go back," said Simon. "Might as well."

Even though I knew that he would have let me work for him if I had explained about Opal, I didn't feel like it. "Did you know Mona is bisexual?"

"Aren't all women?" said Simon. "And all men want men, only they don't know it yet. Even if they don't like having intercourse. That's Drakkar's problem. He just wanted to fool around. So of course we had a fight, and I haven't gotten over him."

"Do you love him?" I asked. "Could you?"

"He named himself Drakkar," Simon reminded me, and there was no more to be said.

★

I ended up going to Montego Bay anyway on Thursday. It was the last time I saw any of them, except for Simon, and even as I stood with them, I knew it would be. Though she was kind to me, I knew Louise would not give me the attention of a friend. I didn't want to be Mona's friend. And Opal? I was too much of a coward to be around her anymore, even though I knew she would never say to me, I need a cock in me and you don't have one. She'd never say, I'm going to tell everyone you know and we will all laugh at you. I'd never say, let's have dinner, let me kiss your mouth.

Louise tried to give me a hug when I came in. "We enjoyed having you in our happy little family," she said, and I avoided her body touching mine. I slipped the CD I had borrowed back beneath the register. It was a sampler we used to get our customers to buy some of the over-priced imports, and I had been feeling guilty for thieving it. "Do come again," said Opal, with an exaggerated accent.

120   "I didn't come the first time, baby. I was just faking." I had no problems being crude now that I was leaving. I felt like a desperado who knew he could never get Miss Mary. No wonder they were so boldly lecherous. No wonder they grabbed her and salivated, tongues lolling out. They knew they would lose, so there was nothing else to lose. I knew I'd never be the hero who left the flashy fishnetted saloon singer for Mary's porridge.

Someone had pulled the stool out from behind the cash register, and Opal was sitting on it, leaning back against the tape bin, her stockinged legs stretched out against the book rack. She beamed at me, or maybe it was just the orange of her dress making her skin glow. "I'm having another party on Saturday. Will you come?"

"You're just trying to lure me to your lair to have your way with me. No, I'm too delicate for fisting."

She smiled and put her hand on mine. I hooked my fingers into hers. We held hands like that as Louise went back to the discussion that they had been having before I entered, on her theory that "The Fresh Prince of Bel Air" presented the typical American validation of amiability over intelligence that Arthur Miller criticized in *Death of a Salesman*.

"It is a television show," said Simon. "A television show." Mona nodded.

I looked down at Opal. "I really can't come," I said. "I am going to my friend Sripriya's." I wanted to see Opal again, but I wanted Sripriya's friendship even more. I couldn't lose this opporturnty to see her. I might never get another chance. I had too few friends, and Sripriya and I might be friends forever, while Opal, I'd barely even see at the party, unless I... did what? Told her that I couldn't masturbate to fruition because of her?

"Is it because you didn't have a good time last time?"

"No." Even though Opal was actually slightly taller than me, her hand was small in mine. And so much rougher. "Not that I had a good time, because I sure didn't. Sripriya asked first, and I said yes, and I even bought stuff for it. Indian food."

I felt self-conscious still holding Opal's hand but determined not to acknowledge it. Mona eyed me with inexplicable contempt. "You still have my books, Mona, don't forget to return them." I let my thumb stroke Opal's palm.

Louise said, "Drop by my apartment sometime. Hailey and I would be glad to see you." Then she left. Customers came in. I felt funny still standing there. Surely Opal's arm, extended up to me, was hurting? I uncurled my fingers, and she withdrew. I said goodbye to Simon, and left too.

Chapter 5
Blaze

How much more one appreciated our great literature
if one loved, thought Belinda, especially if the love
were unrequited!

–Barbara Pym, *Some Tame Gazelle*

Women [will] lose their chastity and wander in the
streets if they see movies.

–T. Chandrasekaran, *Cinemavum Pengalum*
trans. C. S. Lakshmi

I am sick. Outside, the storm howls. I, in what was once my
bed of joy, fester in my soured juices. My skin, never rosy,
has roses now, red roses with pliant, multitudinous lips
oozing dew. Roses on my cheeks, breasts, arms I held out to
Blaise. I try not to think about Blaise, try to rest, try not to
scratch my lesions, but I'm crazy with – rage.

After I found out, the first thing I did was to call him,
more to vent my fury than to inform him. He began by
telling me that he could understand my anger, but finally,

he said, "This is what happens. You are stupid." I hate to believe it, but he's right. Sarah, was it stupid for you, too?

I've been thinking about Sarah so much I gave her a name. I know only two things about Sarah: one of them is that she owns a bookay by Frida Kahlo. I opened this bookay after I picked it up. It was a while later that I saw the buds, a few small nips, tight yet, and roseate, about to bloom into open wounds on my belly, thighs I kept open to Blaise. It's a strange transformation – to have been a flower, chhotisi ek kali, and have been turned, with snips of the phoolwala's shears, into a flower garden.

However, I imagine Sarah's skin is smooth as blank paper, color only on the pink buds of her nipples, clitoris wrapped in darker pink tissue. Or maybe slick and dark as the crust of herb bread at the Italian restaurant some woman tookay Blaise to. He came to me, afterwards. When I saw him through the fisheye, he was leaning against the banister, obviously drunk. I refused to let him in. He begged me to let him sleep in my apartment because he was too drunk to drive home. He sat down on the stairs, his face in his hands. The bulb in the hallway had burnt out and the only light was from the landing below. I opened the door cautiously, and screamed down to his glinting dreads, "You treat my house like it's a fucking hotel. You don't come here for me at all. All you want is a bed to sleep in. Why should I do you any favors?"

"Can you keep it down," my neighbor called out from behind his door. "It's past midnight." With a feeling of inevitability, I told Blaise that he could come in. He lumbered to his feet.

He collapsed on my futon, slurringly telling me he had dropped his knapsack in the tunnel entrance to the basement of the building next door.

The next morning, before he awokaye, when I went out to fetch my morning paper and his coffee, I crawled in and picked up his bag. I brought it back to him, and as I handed it over, as he thanked me in the sing-song way that was his idea of kindliness, the biography of Frida Kahlo fell out.

Of course I knew it was not his, but I didn't stop to wonder then what I wonder now. Whether the owner of the bookay is the Haitian ex-girlfriend who did his laundry, or the model with whom he went to Two Potato and Kellers. Or the white woman whose children he tookay to play in Riverside Park. Andre's girlfriend or Wes's girlfriend whom he told me he had fucked. The dumpling-faced blonde he talked to at Tropicana while I wept. The woman he said he'd once fucked in the 14th Street subway station.

I could ask him. But it would break my last brick of pride, and there's no guarantee that he'd tell the truth. All I can know about Sarah is that she is not me, and the one proof I had had of Blaise's fat-lipped professions of love for me was that I was the only one. Now, all that is soured and ridiculous and I have no place to put my face when my friends are incredulous that I never guessed, had never known. Not even when he had a bookay about Frida Kahlo? No, not for long even then.

Instead, I watched him take the bookay in his hands and read. Then, as he flipped through the pages, I rose and put my hand on his neck. I was so aroused by the sight of him reading about Frida Kahlo, that we turned to half-passionate, if unsatisfying, sex. That's how you helped my love life, Sarah. That's how I became a magdalene with stigmata, my skin dripping with poison, soiling my sheets.

What was it that blurred my vision then? I sometimes think that it was because I was used to having someone to think of when I listened to music. There he was, making my heart ache. And it was a pain familiar from a thousand songs, a pain I could sing however poorly and still touch other people's hearts, a pain that had been prettified for me and made sensible, unlike other pains I felt which had no name nor Lata's voice to give them beauty.

I was forced into a cult as a child. It wasn't something I noticed, though we had special rites that made us different from other people, because in essence all religions are about the same thing: a higher power, losing yourself, dissolving into an atman in this life or the next, whether the atman is a candy-colored heaven with a flowing-haired Christ, or a white courtyard of fountains with houris with jewels in their navels, or simple nothingness. And anyway, the rites of our cult might have sounded different but similar rituals occurred everywhere in the world. Some things happen – procreation, death – and so we prettify them to make them pleasing. And so it happens more often, that is to say, martyrdom.

Even now, I haven't been fully de-indoctrinated. I search for answers. When my friend calls before going to work, I tell her I have a question for her to answer. "Can one live when one's dil is khali of gam? Is ashq okay to drink without khoon-e-jigar? Or are there negative side-effects?" She tells me to lie down and get some rest like she always does.

I lie down, I do try to rest, but I get angry again. I want to go up to heaven, my heaven, and tell them, "Look at your mistake."

My heaven is a wide, black street. A moon hangs like a piece of lemon rind in the sky. A man and woman are walking slowly. I ran to catch up to them. They didn't turn at the sound, even when I was almost right beside them. The woman was dark and full-lipped, damp hair drooping out of her bun. "Can you tell me where I can find Mohammed?" I asked, touching her wet arm.

She stopped, tightening her pallu around her waist, and looked uncertain. The mechanic-faced man beside her said, "Dekho, you can't just barge in on him."

"How can I speak with him, then?" I realized that I lookayed bizarre to them, my ruptured skin, wild, loose hair. "I'm sick. I need his help." They eyed me, as if to see if I was an apparition. The woman rubbed her goose-bumped arm. When she lookayed down at her hand, she saw my blood.

"This way," she said, lowering her head. "Follow us." It started raining again.

We walked until we arrived at a wrought iron gate, its bars decorated with serrated leaves. It creaked open to let the man and the woman through, then clanged shut before I could enter. "Please, uhm…sir?" I called out. There was only the moon in the sky, and behind me the endless road.

I must have said this out loud, because a voice said, "That's not the moon." It dropped down on the ground with a terrifying suddenness. I touched it with my fingertip – it was pitted and soft as an old lemon rind, but smooth as tinfoil on the other side. Now the sky was black and I couldn't see anything but the bars of the gate.

"Gate?" I said.

"You would feel better to see a person? We know you are so homocentric. Everything must be a human being for you." There was a loud sigh. A man in a uniform of khaki shirt, shorts and conical hat, was sitting on one in a row of cement pylons. The gate was gone. "Some more light?" he asked, twirling his thin mustache. I nodded, and light was brushed onto the gate. The road behind me was lined with gas lamps. Behind the cement pylons, the road continued, lined with flower beds.

"I've come to see Mohammed," I said.

"Mohammed, Lakshmi, every day same thing. This is why we are not having Jesus yet. When Jesus comes, every day even more the same thing. How tiring it is for us." He put his hands up. "Although when Jesus comes, we will see

126

even more of the South Indian damsels." He said this in a way that was not even remotely lecherous, and I realized that I had no idea how old he was. He put his hands on his bony knees.

"I'm not looking very damsel-like these days," I said.

"It is the road you are choosing," he replied.

This irritated me, and I felt like screaming at him about the illusion of free will, about insidious pressures, but then he would have known what I had to tell Mohammed, and not let me in. "I can understand that it gets boring after a while. Do you want me to tell you a story?"

"Yes, you tell me a story," he said, and gestured for me to sit on another one of the cement pylons. It was rough and uncomfortable, but another step closer to the other side. I lookayed at the moon near my foot and told him the story of the Ugly Goose.

"There was once a bed of joy that was almost destroyed. Though it was small, it tookay up almost the entire nest of our heroine, the Ugly Goose, and it was where she slept in the warm shade of a Monster.

"Every night, this Monster would go to joust, for it was a knight in the Royal Order of Nightclub Bathrooms. When the knights weren't sitting in a dread-helmeted row at the zozo bar, they pursued their holy goal: in the words of their bard, to "in America...build a Ganja City." But it was, if you believe the Monster, a weak fraternity: the Monster often said the Goose was its only security.

"You are all I have, said the Monster. You are all I have, said our goose. And as they clung to each other, our goose came to believe her Monster was different from the other monsters, somewhere deep beneath its scaly skin. The Ugly Goose believed that the Monster was afraid of revealing this difference, its dark, secret store of love. The Ugly Goose thought the Monster was afraid of loving her because its fellow monsters would make fun of it, and call it an unsuccessful monster indeed. The Goose thought a little plucking would be okay until she won the Monster over from the other side, until love exploded its monster-flesh.

"And anyway, it was only she who had feathers to stuff the pillows with. Could you blame the Monster for not having feathers? That doesn't seem very fair. The Goose believed in patience. When the Monster pissed on the sheets of her bed of joy, she read up on cures for incontinence. When the Monster broke the bed into little bits of wood, she tossed them back at it and thought the fight was over. Our goose washed the sheets in a tub of boiling hot water, Krazy Glued the wood clumsily back together. For the Ugly Goose loved her bed, its broad expanse. She loved the warmth of the Monster's shade.

"But after a certain amount of foulness, the bed was permanently soiled. The Monster too liked bed and its pleasures, the softness of feather pillows, the crisp smell of clean sheets, the sweet sleep. Off it went to find another one, as the Ugly Goose stayed in her nest, trying to fix it. What other choice did she have? She needed to rest at night.

"Still the story is not over, yet. The Goose sits on the floor sometimes, with her elbow on her knees, hand on her cheek, and says, enviously, 'Monster, Monster, who are you being monstrous to now?' "

"This is a terrible story," said the guard, his eyes wet and red. He blew into a large handkerchief, honking. "I am not liking the story one iota." I rose and bent to touch his brown chappals, then touch my closed eyes. His face still half-covered by the handkerchief, he waved me inside.

I went in. Though it was dark, the flowers seemed to exude oxygen. I walked until I reached daylight, and a small story house. A little girl was walking a fat daschund on the front path. I adjusted my silk, peacock blue dupatta over my head and shoulders and walked towards her. "Hello," I said softly, and bent down to pet the dog. I kept my face averted. She was a child, after all.

An upstairs shutter opened. A man with a face like a brown egg called out, "Chhoti, open the front door for our visitor." His familiar, mellifluous voice diffused in the air like the smell of sandalwood. The girl beckoned me to follow. We went into the house and up a sunless flight of stairs.

The egg-faced man sat on a wooden swing towards the back of the room. He rocked back and forth, holding his shawl closed. A white ceiling fan swished air. I tookay off my slippers and set them neatly in one corner.

I pulled my dupatta away as soon as the girl went down the stairs. The sunlight stung my skin, fetid vapors rising from my body.

"You can close the shutters if you wish," he said.

"No, Mohammedji," I said. "You can see more clearly with the light." I slung the dupatta over my shoulder, my cankered arms, throat, face exposed.

"Will you have some tea, my child?" He came to the edge of the swing, and poured from a pot into stainless steel tumblers.

"I'd like a screwdriver." I crossed my arms.

He shook his head. "I'm a teetotaler," he said, holding out a bowl of banana pakoda. "It is a better way to live."

"Don't you tell me about the way to live." My voice was shrill as a bird's.

I walked through the room, the tile floor cool against my feet. At the windows, I hooked the shutters closed. "I used to listen to what you had to say about how to live," I said, more softly. "I wasn't the best of pupils, Mohammedji, but I listened. Every weekend, we went to the hall and heard you. My parents bought cassettes. I used to pin a dupatta to my hair with a hairpin and dance to you in my

129

room. I gathered hibiscus from the garden and scattered them on the floor. Baharon phool barsao, mera meheboob aaya hai." I pressed my cheek against the shutter as I sang. "I practiced scattering flowers for the day this skill would come in handy. I might as well have been sewing my funeral garland."

I twirled around, my dupatta in my hands, my kameez billowing out. The gold bangles on my wrists slid up and down, chafing against the lesions as I danced. "Tujhe Ganga main samjhunga, tujhe Jamuna main samjhunga." I stopped, suddenly light-headed. "Your voice taught me so, Mohammedji. My head was dizzy with longing, following you sliding up and down the notes. How could I want anything else but that emotion in my life? How could my heart not fill with desire for that thing only? A love that I could surrender to, could dissolve into. A love that would make the sound not just beautiful, but more meaningful, more mine. So it would be the playback for my own heart, if you'll forgive the conceit." I sank down to the floor, in the middle of the room, where the shutter left slits of light. I sat as married women do, in the half-lotus, with my chin against one knee, and fiddled with the bells of the ring on my second toe. "Why couldn't you ever sing about the noble struggle to be a civil engineer or something?"

"You know my father did not want me to sing these songs," Mohammed said softly, then leaned back, his finger to his lip. He tookay a sip of milky tea. "He was a very religious man, singing only of God and the Prophet. My brother convinced him to let me go to the city and sing for films."

"Why did you stray? Why did you worship false gods?"

Mohammed shookay his head. "Love is not a false god, is it?"

"This love is. That's why Khomeini banned musical instruments, Hindi films, all of this refuse. Don't get me wrong, it's beautiful refuse. But truth is this." I stretched out my arm, its roses rotting and oozing. "Aankhon mein sharaab hai," I sang, tunelessly. "Why were you, a teetotaler, extolling sharaab?"

He put his tumbler of tea down, and folded his hands in his lap.

"I have a hangover, okay?" I said, bitterly. "I spent so much time on this that I could have spent on fruitful things. Things, not people. People are cruel. Except sometimes for imaginary people."

"I sang many songs about God," he replied.

He sighed, rewrapping his shawl. "It was many years ago. The young feminists had just begun writing on the cult of romance as a patriarchal invention. I did not read them, as I did not know of them. It is only recently that I began." His voice was wan. "But it is not just you who come here. Some days, the garden is full of young men who heard my voice in the mouths of heroes. They come here and cry, and unlike you they will never go back." He held out the bowl of pakoda again. "Eat. What else can I offer you now?"

"Zindabad, zindabad, mohabbat zindabad," I sang, softly, because I couldn't help taunting him. Pearls of pus formed on my throat, and I touched them with my fingertip. "Although we were willing enough dupes, weren't we. What happened? Our prince became king, found another, and lived happily ever after. While the girl died or at best, was banished. We saw the end, we knew, but we believed only the middle." I looked up, and laughed. "Maybe we didn't know we were the girl."

Mohammed shook his head, not amused. "You knew, you always knew. Whether I made it easier to bear or more inviting, I don't know. It's a question for my conscience." He swung more rapidly. Outside, the girl called the little dog's name. "Why didn't I sing that no prince was worth it? That monarchy was a terrible idea, anyway? That Bahaar probably would have made an excellent ruler. That song about civil engineering." He closed his eyes. A fat tear rolled down his cheek.

"They were beautiful songs," I said. "I listened to them for years instead of crying myself to my sleep. They told me what happiness would be like, that someone would look in my eyes and see sharaab." I tilted my head, smiling. "They were my dreams."

He wiped his tears away with his thumb. "There are those who come here to tell me this."

I rose, gathering my dupatta around my shoulders and wrapping it so my head was covered. "Thank you for listening to me."

He smiled, and it cut the fog of unhappiness that had settled around us. "You listened to me," he said, graciously, and he rose to show me out.

I walked into the garden, and said goodbye to the girl and her dog, then wandered out of the light back into the darkness. There were others to blame, for romanticizing gangsters, for making dasis sound valiant, but that would have to wait for another day, another place. The gate swung open noiselessly. I walked on and on.

No wonder I feel so exhausted. And yet, I can't sleep. I rise to sponge my sore back, my breasts, with warm water. The tub is too dirty for a soak, and I'm too tired to clean it. I fill the sink with warm water and pour in a drop of cherry-scented bubble-bath. I have to somehow muffle the stench of my skin.

I unbutton my shirt. It's Blaise's shirt, he forgot to take it with him the last time he came to my house. I love its melting colors, the deep blue like the ocean, green algae and purple foam. I'm still trying to decide whether I should get rid of it for its bad juju or ignore its provenance.

I squeeze a few drops of water on my lesions, those pink and wet openings into my body, then dab lightly with a sponge. I must clean myself so I can heal these marks all over my body that reveal even to strangers what I have done – been a pussy, had a pussy. The second time is farce, and my skin itches with the white inverse of anticipation. What should I call this pus? Knowledge?

I am not much of a drinker, only tookay little sips of the bottles of wine, cognac, Cointreau, I kept in the house. Blaise drank most of it, as he ate most of the meat, and used all the little tissue-wrapped soaps I bought in Spain. I could forgive it for the higher joys. The joy that squeezed me until I went blind to everything but joy, as plush and crimson as the upholstery in five star hotels. I even bought a coat that color, and it flared out if I twirled. I felt glamorous every time I wore it. A red fur, a brutal and handsome lover, youth. It was a movie unfolding, and I was the star. Lights, camera, action!

The smoke machine blurred my vision with silver, glittery fog. I touched the banister to steady myself. A woman in star-shaped pasties danced in a cage dangling from the ceiling. She clutched the bars and meowed at us, staring at her. Lance, beside me, whispered, "The first time I came here, I thought, this is what a real nightclub is."

We went down the stairs, me being careful not to hookay my heels into the grating. I followed Lance into a room where they were playing a rap song I liked because it mentioned my train. When the train's name came, we, and everyone else, jumped up and down, my breasts rising out of my bra. Jumping up again, I caught a glimpse of Blaise over someone's shoulder. I pushed through the crush of bodies to him, and slid my arms around his slim waist. "Who are you here with?" he asked, over the noise of the music. I reached up on tiptoe to reply into his ear, my lips brushing him.

He gave me a sharp push into the crowd and walked away, glowering. I skittered, in my heels, and the girl I had

133

fallen into jabbed me back with her fake nails. Lance came to get me before the girl picked a fight with me. "Where did you go?" he asked.

"Blaise is here," I replied. He shookay his head.

I spent the night trying to speak to Blaise, but he evaded me, and once, grabbed my wrist and returned me to Lance, like a rejected sack of potatoes. Or jewels. For he was furious, jealous, my green-eyed god, that I was with another man, and I was gorgeous, my hair flowing to my waist, huge eyes glittering like the night sky, pink lips, soft, tightly-nippled breasts, round hips that led to firm, shapely legs. I was a woman after all. His anger was delicious as a spicy gazpacho.

I danced by my stellar self, shimmying my hips, arms outstretched, until Lance asked me if I was ready to go home. I agreed, and we went into the coat room to get our coats. I slipped into my red fur, pulling the plush collar to my cheeks. Blaise was at the exit but I said nothing to him, stepping carefully as if a red carpet had been unfurled in front of me, and all eyes were watching my progress.

Then, he grabbed my arm and yanked me against the wall so hard that the first button's elastic band broke. In front of everyone, his friends, Lance, he yelled, "What the fuck is going on?"

The wind scratched at my bare throat and chest, between my fingers holding the coat's collar together. "What the fuck do you think you're doing?" I yelled back. But I was delighted, no matter what I said, and though my new coat was ripped, because Blaise was so open about claiming me, vulnerable about wanting me. The cold was on my skin, but the blaze of his desire was within me.

I used to remember that night with such giggly happiness, but now I can only wonder if the girl with the long black hair I saw him talking to near the bar was Sarah. Blaise, I used to hoard the thought of that autumn night when I was dancing with my back to you and the man in front of me grabbed my hand, when you reached around me and said, "She is mine." I used to. Now I can only think of the fact that as we were pushing past the velvet curtains to the dance floor, we passed a blonde with a knife-cut mouth, and you said, "Hey Linda. Hey Lili, so what's up?" I gave a name to each of your qualities, and you gave your one name for me to another woman. For me, any man's name was you. But for you, Blaise, I think any girl could be Lili.

I think of the phone calls he made from my house. I think of the time when he laughingly made plans for the night, and when he saw my eyes on him, he said, smiling, "Why are you so jealous?" His jealousy was like a cocktail he made for me, a "women's drink" with fruit and little umbrellas that got me drunk and tasted sweet. And I was addicted – I'd bring home phone numbers on slips of paper each night I went out, so he would make me another in the morning. Even the one time he hit me, I could forgive him because he did it out of jealousy.

135

I thought you were jealous because I was beautiful, Blaise, but now I know that you were jealous because you were afraid I was doing to you what you were doing to me. And what you have done shapes not only the present and the future, but the past, because the past isn't fixed, it's a movie we watch through the lens of the present. I used to rationalize my surrender by thinking I had something Blaise didn't have and couldn't take away from me: the memories of my intoxication. But though my soul will survive this ordeal, it has almost destroyed the cherry-flavored memories of the way he sipped his jasmine tea and the coiling way he danced until three or four or seven, because they *can* take that away from me. It's so easy.

At least if you're Blaise, who is so adept at taking and giving – a maang for you and for you and you and you and you. The yellow, discolored skin on my neck is charmed with red medallions. The lesion on my forehead oozing blood is my sindoor – mera, tera and Sarah's. If I had a potted tulsi in my angan – if I had a front yard – I'd break it. Enough of all this religion. It's what makes you take Cortez for Quetzacoatl. I'm taking up stamp collection instead.

I pat myself dry with a towel, then slip on underwear and a fresh Hanes T-shirt. I would wear a bra but the underwire chafes my skin. I reknot my hair and lie back in bed, in the faintly rancid sheets. I am so weary of this bleeding. But I can't lie. I try to resist my education, but I still find my succor in romantic videos with couples entwined on beaches, in moaning jazz songs where women bewail inevitable, ineluctable love, Um Kvithvm droning that people hate her, you hate her. I have had a surfeit of it, and I'm sick, but I still eat it up. It feeds me. And in my weakened state, I'm sometimes even less capable of resisting, now that it seems even more true, all those songs I heard, the books I'd read, the words I'd mouthed now given emotion to their meaning.

That's what I liked about Blaise, his gift for the cinematic. Even now when we speak, he asks if I will lie once again on his chest, on his heart. Did you lie sucking his nipple, Sarah? Did he make you spaghetti and call himself Daddy? Did he drink wine out of your navel? Did you lookay down at him after the first time you had sex and think he was ugly? Did he ever return the money he surely borrowed?

I'm accosted by images I have no match to burn. I can see them together, though her shape, color keeps changing, but always the same sting in my mouth. I can laugh in his face when he asks me to take him to the doctor, but at night, I shift in the sheets and go crazy that I can't feel his chest against me, soaking up my anger and anxiety.

136

I try to make up convincing excuses to call him, but pride stops my mouth up from letting the real questions escape my lips: why I was turned back from a goddess into a rotting pumpkin, why Sarah was better than me.

In our last conversation, I said, "You have to tell the women you slept with."

"There was only one that I was with besides you, and I'm not talking to her, because she is a carrier."

"*You* are a carrier, Blaise. You have to tell her. This is serious."

"I'm not going to talk to her. I knew there was something wrong with her. Her pussy smelled funny. I saw some strange stuff coming out of her hole."

I didn't ask him why he fucked her, then. Because she was beautiful? Because she gave him money? Because she was knowledgeable about twentieth-century fucking Mexican art?

Lookay at me, then lookay at Sarah. Lookay at her slim, firm body. Her creamy skin, her cunt the deep red of port wine jello. I wonder if she ever got Blaise to eat her pussy – that's what they say in love advice columns, anyway, that girls who give poison, receive pleasure.

Or else, they say that for ladies, O.P.P. means something different. The night I finally slept with him, after our summer of separation, I had asked him to tell me the truth, I had asked him if he had been with someone else after me. "No," he'd said laughing, and after weeks of refusing him, I said yes. I tried to go to the bathroom to get something, but he said, "No," again, and pulled me back to the bed, and climbed on top of me. This he doesn't mention, only that I had said, yes, as I had before the first time we had, when he said, "I'm not forcing you – you make the choice. No or yes?" I had giggled and felt free, in my lacy white nightgown. No one had ever given me such freedom. "okay," I said, and liked him all the more for it. Words, to

137

me, made all the difference. So, I believed him when he had said there had been no one else.

Now, rage drools out of the mouths on my skin, each crying out. The noise pollutes the air around me. How nice it would be, and convenient, if warriors rose from this blood, if I was Raktabij, but instead they only cry out like babies. I put cold cream on and try to soothe them.

Darkness drains out of the sky. It's the hour when the clubs are closed, the coffeeshop coffee is drunk and the toasted bagels or ham sandwiches are eaten, the street-cleaners come into the streets, and the garbage trucks, the hour Blaise calls, or will call me back if I page him. My fingers itch. Blood, salty as tears, flows from my weeping wounds. I want his skin to dry myself on. The phone sits stubbornly on the night stand.

I think of going into the kitchen to heat up some kurma and rice. Of course, Sarah eats nothing but steamed vegetables, though she makes fried plantain and jerk chicken. Sarah, it would do me so much good to know you. Whether you were stupid for him too, or whether you fucked him and dumped him and don't think about him. I wonder what and who you are – you're the only one who gave him what he deserved, but when is karma simple or easy? Someone tell me, is he crying raththak kanneer yet? I have done everything but scream, "Aththaan." I wait for him to call.

Or is he with you now, Sarah? Are you pressing your slim, boyish hips to his, your pink-tipped breasts caressing his face, your hair falling like a rain of gold to the bed? Are you a model, Sarah, or the artist Blaise told me about when he saw my drawings, or an ingenue? Are you a black girl, light as Vanessa Williams, with Malcom X glasses and bell-bottoms and a thing for brothers with dreads. Or pertly Japanese, the one who bought him the leather jacket with tassels. Though I try to forget, I have sharp shooting visions.

This is my exercise in madness: see Sarah and Blaise reading from the biography of Frida Kahlo, see Sarah and Blaise fucking, see Sarah and Blaise. Isn't syphilis supposed to cause insanity and blindness? I'm crazy but I can still see. His golden skin, his broad, scarred chest. I can still, with my inward, diseased eye, see: Sarah and Blaise and me.

Jesus on the wall, standing in his snazzy all-white outfit down to snazzy white shoes, is frowning at me. "So help me," I scream out. "Help me if you don't like to see me behave this way."

I slip him into the machine, and he says to me: "Zamaane ke baazaar mein woh shai hai, ki jiski kisiko zaroorat nahin hai." I kneel before the stereo, re-wind to this section again and again until my fingertips are sore.

139

Chapter 6

Excitement

> The pattern will remain, unless you break
> It with a sudden jerk; but use your head.
> Not all returned as heroes who had fled
> In wanting both to have and eat the cake.
> Not all who fail are counted with the fake.

–Nissim Ezekiel, *Case Study*

N woke up at about three in the afternoon. She ate around
seven, and by ten, was at loose ends. She sighed. The t.v.
had been stolen the week before. She had been reading for
the last few hours. Who was there to call at ten on a Saturday
night? And to say what? How dull and listless she felt. It
was late summer, and hot, uneventful days stretched into
hot, empty nights.

She paged Paul, whose girlfriend she putatively was.
They hadn't seen each other in weeks, but he had called in
the morning. Speaking to him was like a game of chance.
Would he be busy and barely attentive? Tell her she should
learn to buy him presents if she expected to have him,
and learn to cook, sew, fuck? Tell her to stop going out
every night, taking home other men's numbers? Tell her

140

he was faithful to her, and couldn't they be kind to one another? But Paul did not call her back.

She rose, showered, stared at herself in the mirror. Her big breasts, belly, hips were consigned to a girdle and an orange leotard. She pulled on tight, acid-washed denim jeans studded with metal squares at the cuff and a dark blue jersey with a hood. The jersey was comforting as a security blanket and hid the body she was used to thinking of as fecund and womanly. It made her look ever so slightly hard, which both scared and excited her.

She took the train down to the Box. At one time, she would have been full of the exhilarating feeling of holding a secret which might leak out at any minute, but she had made the trip down so often that summer that its thrill had waned. No one had ever seen her entering the Box, but she still didn't feel completely safe because the sushi bar Paul went to was not far from the Christopher Street station. As she reached the street level, she casually looked over her shoulder for his familiar profile. She crossed Seventh Avenue.

The crowd had overflown onto the streets. Under the August moon, there were: sweltering dark women in too tight denim shirts and jeans, reed-thin prima donnas almost toppling under waves and waves of cascading hair, b-girls and more b-girls in baseball caps wearing large fake gold earrings, light-skinned hard women with their small hips swaying to the beat of passing car stereos, petite, noisy girls in push-up bras and peek-a-boo blouses, punky types in leather jackets and boots, butches with close-cropped hair in sweat suits carrying beepers, femmes in black velvet catsuits deeply cut to expose mounds of cleavage, women posing against the wall and hoping someone would pay attention, drinking soda across the street, smoking reefer in doorways, sitting on cars. There were so many people she recognized and did not know.

It was Latin night, and Barbara would have been easy to spot over the heads of the Latinas. She was Dominican, but black, and tall. Barbara, N thought, would be someone to dance the night away with, but she would no doubt want to hold hands the entire time. This irritated N because she knew it would go no further unless she seduced Barbara, and she didn't like to have to be the one to take the initiative.

She squeezed her way through the crowd at the bar, and to the edge of the dance floor. No Barbara. The music turned from playing hiphop to reggae. The dance floor expanded as women clung to each other. N positioned herself in front of the mirror and slowly began to wind. When she first met Paul, she didn't dance particularly well, but she had learned so much. She arched her back, thrusting her hips in the air. She made waves with her hips lower and lower on the ground, then higher and higher. Even without looking, she could feel the stares on her body as she danced. She closed her eyes.

When she opened them, Selma was behind her. "You enjoyin' yourself?" Selma said, her warm island accent smothering her words. N smiled. "How long ago you got here?"

"Half an hour," N said, drawing Selma onto her thigh. The one benefit of dancing with someone shorter was that N could move her thigh along the girl's inner thighs without raising her foot off the ground. That was about it.

Try as she might, N couldn't be stimulated by Selma. It wasn't just that Selma was short, but she was over two decade older than N and though she was still pretty, she did not look young. Light-skinned women, as the saying goes, can't hide their age. Selma was a housekeeper, and after first telling N this, she said sadly, "You don't like that? What class of people you like?" N could have excused everything if Selma had had a certain elan, but the weight of her vulnerability was too much for N to bear. N was

142

used to being the vulnerable one, and was afraid of the greediness this unexpected turn of events inspired. As much as she wanted to be, for once, the one in power, she was afraid of abusing it, and so Selma confused her. N preferred complaining that she did not have what it takes to draw people to her as she was drawn to Paul, draw them with a desire that opened their hearts and legs and wallets.

She didn't know why she was with Paul. Whenever he did something to anger her, she thought of her own cheating and lying. He had liked her with more consistency than anyone else, and most of the time that seemed enough. He didn't really know her, and N didn't mind, because it gave her the protection of distance. She even felt superior to him because she had a secret.

She moved her hands down Selma's back to her hips. The music changed. They danced, drank, danced some more, sweat running down their temples. The small dance floor was crowded and someone was smoking a joint. The sickeningly sweet odor mixed with the musk of women's bodies and perfumes and cigarettes. N took off her jersey and tied it around her waist. She had dark, wet half-moons under her breasts. Her hair was matted with perspiration. She tied it into a messy knot, then reached for her drink. N sucked slowly on a maraschino cherry and offered it to Selma. "You're bad," Selma said, admiringly. "You a bad girl."

The tingling that began over N's cheekbones moved through her body and sank between her legs. The bar was getting more and more crowded. Cigarette fumes choked the air. The speakers were crackling with sound, and N could feel the vibrations against her thighs.

Eventually, the merengue started. There was a mass exchange of populations as the Latinas came on the dance floor and the others left. N stood against the mirror. Barbara had tried to teach her the right moves but she hadn't gotten

143

them down yet. "Come on," Selma said, but gave up when a squat, crop-headed woman asked her to dance. N watched them for awhile, then went outside, squeezing past an older woman in a pink, frilly prom dress.

N put her jersey back on. It was 3 am. She realized suddenly that she was a little drunk. She closed her eyes. The morning paper was out. She could take the long train ride back uptown and begin her Sunday rituals of crossword puzzle and cream cheese on a raisin bagel, but she didn't want the night to end yet.

While having found Selma spared her the vagaries of standing around waiting to be asked to dance, or trying to get up the courage to ask someone, and the attendant rejections of being ignored by the women she made eyes at or refused by those she asked, it also denied the possibilities, and excitements. There is no excitement without risk, she thought. She positioned herself on the front step of an apartment building.

No one so much as looked her way. A woman she had once gone out with, a crazy woman from Texas, had told her that with her light skin, long hair, big breasts and femininity, she would have the (black lesbian) world at her feet. It wasn't even at her side.

She got up, slapping the dust off her jeans, and walked around. She thought about visiting Paul at the bar. If only Barbara was there. Or any of the Moniques. Or if that tall one over there would return her gaze. Was it that men were more lecherous or more courageous in their desires?

Usually, being among women made her feel free. She could come to the Box alone without necessarily being seen as desperate or sluttish, which was not the case if she went alone to a straight bar. She did not have to suck her gut in and mince unless she wanted to. Boldness may be rewarded, as it never was with a man. She could grind and wind all over a girl without it making any sexual promises. Yet with this freedom was a loneliness. With women, N thought, there was no knowing what would work, so all that was left was to be yourself. And go home alone. She went back inside to Selma.

N put her arm around Selma's waist. "You still single?" Selma asked. "Why you ain't with nobody?"

"If women want me at all, it's only to cheat on their lovers," N said. "None of them are single."

"I can't find no good woman neither," Selma replied, slowly. "You goin' home now?"

"Are you?"

"Where else can I go?"

N fingered Selma's lapel. No, she didn't want the night to end. Not without a climax. "There's an after-hours place in Alphabet City."

"Straight club?"

"Mixed," N replied, and even though it was not a lie, she felt anxious.

145

"We go for coffee, first, okay?" Selma said, dubious.

So they sat in a Greek diner drinking lousy coffee. N flipped through a copy of *QW* and sulked. Selma said nothing. "So, you are taking me?" N said finally, as the Pakistani waiter brought them their bill.

"Aap kaise hain?" the waiter asked N.

"I'm fine," she replied, coolly. He retreated to huddle with the other waiters. Suddenly, she felt very protective of Selma. "We don't have to go. It's okay. It's fine."

"Let's go." Selma leaned towards her. "It's not straight?"

"Mixed." N wondered why Selma kept asking.

They took a taxi from Seventh Avenue to Avenue B, which N chivalrously paid. When they got there, Chris's bright red jeep was parked outside the open door of the club. The snide, fat bouncer in the doorway and the crowd of dreads milling against the graffittied walls were the only signs to the place. N's stomach tightened. If Chris was there, there was a good chance that Paul would be there too. Chris was Paul's best friend. On purpose not thinking, N paid and hurried through the long, dark corridor. She bounded down the narrow stairs of the club to the basement, Selma following behind her. She didn't want to run into Paul. She didn't want him to discover what he already suspected, or confirm what he thought he knew. But still she was excited by the thrill of nearing her secret to sunlight, bringing closer together her inner and outer world.

"I said I'd take you, you know," Selma said, and offered her the money. N declined.

The place was not yet full. She sat cross-legged on a battered metal box. It was only the third time she had been there. How she had disliked the place when Paul had brought her there on their first date. The smoke had nauseated her, the low ceiling had made her feel claustrophobic, she couldn't take the extended re-mixes of dark, repetitive house and sonorous rap, and she had been practically the only woman of color. "There are too many white people here," she'd said. Paul had laughed. He had been wearing a golden yellow turtleneck that flattered his complexion. In the subway station, for the first and last time, he had put his tongue in her ear.

N turned her head. The memory and the alcohol she'd had and her too-tight jeans made her ache between her legs. It had been so long. Paul and she no longer had sex because he made it pointless – he always insinuated that it was something *he* did for *her*. She had been more or less faithful for the last few months, except for one groping on the Christopher Street pier. She had cheated on him with a man once long ago, and that had been so disgusting that it had depressed her. She thought of Paul as her man but still, these days they were both ready for it to be over and unwilling to stay away.

She felt a hand on her neck. "What's up?" Chris looked out from beneath thick, phallic dreadlocks. N shrugged. He sauntered away. His movements had such feline grace. N couldn't decide if what she felt was more lust or disgust. Part of her attraction was his unavailability – he was Paul's friend, he apparently only liked them from white to Japanese – but the other part was his sexual confidence. Once, when she was drunk, N had taken some gum from his mouth with her mouth and thereafter N felt a complicity between them. It was their secret from Paul. Which he probably doesn't even remember, N thought, her eyes following him. He turned. Their eyes met. His tongue darted out in a deft lick.

"Who's that? Your boyfriend?" Selma asked.

"If he was my boyfriend, why would I bring you here?"

"He used to be your boyfriend?" Selma tried to make eye-contact. "You remember you saying you was with some dread who stole your money?"

"That's not him."

Selma didn't seem to believe her. "This is a straight club," she said plaintively.

N pointed out the slim blond man in a tutu with blue letters painted on his chest, other white men in see-through shirts and nipple rings, transvestites in Tina Turner wigs, shirtless men with Chelsea Gym chests, two women who had been at the Box. She gestured at Chris. "He's a fag. He wears all those baggy clothes so you can't tell his maxipads." Selma spotted a leather dyke couple she had seen parade at the Pride March, and relaxed.

Besides the homosexuals, there were: Haitians with dreadlocks or shapeless hats covering incipient dreadlocks all of whom more or less knew Paul; white girls with hair down to their waists who worked at *Interview* or Tommy Boy or were photographers; awkward rich Japanese; boozy, stumbling white men; a thin, dark-skinned girl who was

147

obviously a dancer. N remembered how these people had intimidated her with their hipness, how boring she felt among these chic New York types, club kids whose life she imagined to be one long, tingly high.

There were more people on the cement dance floor, and for some reason, this made the basement seem bigger than it did when it was empty. The music was deep house and a beautiful transvestite began to vogue, sauntering along the length of the club, then standing on a metal bench to pose against the pillar in the middle of the room. A happy Haitian rubbed his crotch on the ass of a bland, long-haired girl whose blank face was a sign of the drugs she had taken. At least she was mobile. Once, N had seen a girl collapse at Chris's feet in tears. She had wondered what the girl had wanted, whether it was drugs or him that made her incoherent with need. An older man who was at least sixty was dancing with a Filipino who turned around at regular intervals to spray himself with perfume. A drunken woman who had once caressed N's palm with her long nails was on all fours, and a b-boy was pretending to hump her. The clean-cut all-American fag sitting next to Selma cut coke on a dollar bill. As dark and ugly as it was, the club attracted N because it seemed anything was possible. Paul had told her he had once seen a man give another head in the back of the room near the D.J. booth.

The pipes along the ceiling began to drip. The last time she came, a man had explained that it was the condensation of the sweat body heat had evaporated. N moved to the side. An ugly dread winked at her and smiled pointedly. N told Selma they were going upstairs.

They squeezed up the creaky stairs – people were pouring in, now – into the other room. It was a larger room with red walls covered with blue ideograms, and red and blue furniture. Chinks in the paneling revealed slashes of daylight. Some jazz had been playing as they entered but now it was heavy metal. N looked down at the sawdust floor. "You wan go?" Selma said. They were near the exit.

N didn't respond. She felt cheated. To intersect her two worlds hadn't been as exciting as it seemed. Nothing was happening. "We'll dance first, no sense in wasting money," she said at last, but didn't move. Chris went by, disappearing behind a partition. She didn't watch too closely. She knew what he was but didn't want to see. She felt a derision for him that she didn't feel for Paul. Paul was sucked into selling drugs through lack of initiative, but it was Chris's lifestyle. There was something feral about Chris that wasn't in Paul at all, N thought.

By the time Selma and she returned downstairs, the D.J. was playing reggae. N loved dancing down to reggae, imagining a lover between her thighs, feeling eyes on her lascivious hips. She began to resent Selma's presence. She couldn't dance with Selma because she knew how fast gossip traveled. The risk in coming there was not only the drama of running into Paul but being under the eyes of his friends. She didn't want to hear Paul's taunts, hear him asking if he could watch: it was her secret. She couldn't dance with a man, not with Selma beside her – she would never behave that way, too many women did. It was Paul she told on the stairs of her building that he couldn't spend the night after all because she had a friend staying, when Marita wanted to sleep beside her. It was Paul who waited outside her building for three hours in the morning cold and filled her answering machine with asking where she was after she had told him to come over, because she would rather be thrilled at sleeping on Alyssa's couch. It was Marita she took to dinner and whom she was ready to be utterly faithful to. She gave each woman the truth, canceled plans with him to be with them, talked to them whenever they called, even if he was waiting beside her. She took off work for Marita, and kissed her breasts like it was prayer.

With Paul, she lay there and acquiesced.

Paul had once seen a picture of Marita sitting on N's lap, and warned her to be careful of taking pictures like that because others might misconstrue them as lesbians. Paul, who at least called her his own, for whom she had been the only woman unlike the women for whom she was a diversion before they returned to their lovers, Marita to Diane, Jeannie to Tanya, Barbara to Maria, Jamie to whomever, Alyssa to everyone. Paul, who called her to see how she was, how work was going.

Paul, who had hit her until her nose and lips were bloody and swollen.

She looked at Selma. She felt tired and guilty. She had been thinking only of herself since she came into the club. Selma gazed at her with her large, watery eyes. N ran her finger down Selma's cheek. Selma smiled. N led her to the back of the room. She would take Selma in to the recess in the wall under the stairs, run her hands along Selma's body.

150

As she reached the alcove, she realized that somebody else was already there. She saw Chris dimly. He was sitting in a plastic chair facing the wall, his head thrown back, one foot aginst the wall. Someone else's hands gripped his thighs. Curious, N craned her neck. The figure crouching in front of Chris was almost completely obscured. Chris shifted, and the person turned his face up slightly, dreads sliding down his bearded face, and then was blocked by Chris's thigh.

"Let's go," she said to Selma sharply. "Let's leave."

"Why?" Selma demanded after her, but by then, they were already up the stairs. N strode out into the startling sunlight. Selma screwed up her eyes. The street was filthy and strewn with garbage. They walked by the junkyard lot piled with rusty car parts and tires. It was hot, but N put her jersey on. She suddenly felt very sober, and very bored.

Chapter 7

There's No Place Like Home

> They fuck you up, your mum and dad.
> They may not mean to, but they do.
> They fill you with the faults they had
> And add some extra, just for you.

> –Philip Larkin, *This Be The Verse*

You do it when you're pregnant. You don't know whether the hormonal imbalances of pregnancy are making you act crazy or whether the possibility of a child draws you to the possibility of a mother. You're careful to call it "the possibility of a child." You're still not sure what you will do. The man – and if people ask what man, you point to your stomach – the man isn't much help. He isn't much of anything, but the two of you would have a pretty, frizzy-haired child, and this appeals to you. This kind of attitude is definitely inherited from your mother, which is another reason she's on your mind.

You haven't done it since you were fourteen. It hasn't occurred to you except as idle fancy. You haven't wanted to any more seriously than you've wanted to be a blonde. Recently, it's become somewhat easier to do – you were invited to – your father told you that his sister told him that your stepfather had called her to ask you to call your mother. You laughed. What would be the point? Why drag mess back into your life? Your mother is mess. It's an equation. Then your life gets messy on its own. You're pregnant. You've been lying in bed for almost a week, in the same filthy shirt and underwear. Your home pregnancy test is still on the dining table, on a urine-smeared newspaper. Plastic bags of half-eaten delivered food, unread mail, half-read magazines, dirty clothes litter the floor. You vomit every time you eat and you have diarrhea. The smell of most anything makes you sick. Trained by your mother that religion is a weak man's crutch, and death is followed by worms, you shake with fear and you're afraid of drowning in the shower. Your vagina leaks white paste. Your sheets are foul. Your hair is greasy and matted. You're tired from being alone. The man doesn't call you. You wish he were next to you. You hate him. You're tired from not being sure who will stand by you if something goes wrong. You're tired of not having anyone to notify in case of emergency. You couldn't be any further away from home.

You turn the t.v. off. You sit up in bed and retie your ponytail. You pull the phone to you. Its back is streaked with dried bolognese sauce. You grope the pile of newspapers and mail on the floor for the right piece of paper. You feel reckless. You call your mother.

You left your mother at fourteen. The memory smells of earth after rain. The first new night, lying on a mattress on the floor because the bed hadn't been set up yet, one foot resting against a cardboard box of books, you thought about his kiss, that hours later still made you feel like a balloon filled taut with radiance. You pulled off your shirt and churidar, and lay in a skimpy black leotard, running your hands over your lips, your neck, and those yet uncharted places, your breasts, your stomach, that moist, fragrant thing between your legs. You counted the details over and over again, his lips, the sun, his tongue. You pulled the yellow sheet over your bare legs and listened to the rain falling past your open window.

You gently fell asleep as if you were floating on water. Then awoke, thinking of yourself as a lotus, that flower which symbolizes self-creation, beauty that rises from muck. You descended the staircase with slow elegance to get some lunch, and when your mother didn't respond to your greeting, you barely noticed, still smiling. Your mother cut sandwiches, her neck bent, eyes focused. Your brother said, "Good morning, Akka."

"Hey." You flopped down on a chair in front of the telephone, rubbing your arm. Your mother took the sandwiches and two glasses of juice out into the backyard. Your brother pattered out after her. You picked up the phone.

You would have called Robyn, but she lived in another area code and you weren't allowed to make long distance calls. You called Nicole instead, and buttering slices of brown bread and sprinkling them with fennel, you told Nicole every detail of what had happened, what James had said, what it had felt like, what his house looked like, down to the waffles his younger brother was eating.

Before your mother came inside, you scurried up to your room and closed the door, not wanting to let her disturb your happiness. You sat on the mattress and drew your schoolbag to you, unzipped it, spilling its contents to the floor. The novel you'd borrowed from the school library fell on your toes, Grace's present clattering further away. You picked it up and unwrapped it, picking at the Scotch tape with your fingernails. She'd told you to wait until your birthday, and you had.

You played the cassette, and leaned back against the

wall, taking the novel into your hands. The music was jazzy and languorous. You thought about love, passion, the fruits of the world you would one day eat: tart, green apples, white cherries, pomegranates, blood oranges from Morocco, bland Haitian mangoes. You stared at the purple-flowered, green-leafed wallpaper until it turned into green-eyed, violet-lipped faces, then drew your notebook to you and doodled pictures of James looking at you, eyes heavy-lidded, lips parted. Would he remember your birthday, would he call? You reached up to your brother's Smurf tape player and rewound to Paul Weller singing "Paris Match" again. You lay flat on your back, the sheet tangled around your legs, your bare arms prickled with goosebumps.

That summer, you listened to "Paris Match" and read novels. There was no money for anything else. The money you'd earned babysitting lay in your mother's bank account. How could you get it? Your mother didn't even reply when you asked permission to go to the library. You found her behavior strange, but you went out and got directions from the neighbors. When you got there, the library was closed. You went to the McDonald's next door and spent your last three dollars. You sat in the grass behind the library, gently sucking apple out of the rectangular pie, and thinking of James, his straw-colored hair smelling like Ivory soap, his eyes too blue for metaphor.

Feeling expansive, you decided to go home and try. Only the screen door was closed; through the netting you could see everyone posed in the living room. You entered. "Hi" you said. "Hi."

Your stepfather's eyes briefly met yours. "Hi Akka!" The ebullience in your brother's voice was so out of place that even he noticed and fell silent.

Someone skateboarded past, wheels screeching. Your mother didn't turn.

They were playing a geography game. Your mother

continued, "There's another airport in London, isn't there? Heathrow and something else." You sat lightly on the arm of the couch, right behind her. The door to the backyard was open. Light began to fade, the sun was setting.

"I don't know," your stepfather said guiltily.

"Gatwick." Your voice was edgy. This was so boring. His lips, his tongue, that sweetness.

"Gatwick," your stepfather repeated.

"Yes, Gatwick. That's what it's called," said your mother. You rose.

You mounted the stairs to your room. As night fell, you began to listen impatiently for the sound of their footsteps going to the floor above. The master bedroom, above your head, was where your mother slept. Your stepfather slept on a blanket in the room across the hall from her because he snored. Your brother slept with your mother. His bedroom was across the hall from yours, it was empty. Your room held the broken shelving unit stacked with paints, brushes and turpentine, the frame of your bunkbed, a cardboard box of financial documents, a large piece of canvas, a pail. Your stepfather had stored them in your room as you lay sleeping.

155

You turned sideways on the bed so you faced the wallpaper instead of the mess, and finished reading *La Chamade*, played "Paris Match" and felt hungry. You did feel confined but knew you weren't wasting your time. You thought of yourself as a caterpillar creating the cocoon in which to wait, in which to turn into something suited to the next stage. You avoided the others as much as possible, an uneasy peace was better than any disturbance. You leaned against the window sill and listened to the rain, listened to Sade, thinking of the day when you'd be wild as Friday night, when, if he looked good, you would hope he could dance, when you, and life, will have changed.

All summer, at night, it rained. You waited as long as it

took for everyone to have gone to bed, then descended the staircase from your bedroom to the kitchen. You got food quickly, by the light of the microwave. You wrapped peanut butter or butter-fennel sandwiches in paper towels, gathered laddus and apples. You got a tumbler full of tapwater from the bathroom, then lounged in bed for your meal, thumbing through the art book you'd stolen from the school library, rereading the few books you had. Your mother didn't believe in buying anything but reference books, so there was little to choose from. When you were a child, your mother brought you books from the library, abridged Dickens and George Eliot, Ian Fleming, Mickey Spillane.

One day, after you had already re-read almost everything you had, when you heard the slam of the front door, and when you looked out of the window and saw that all of them were leaving, you slipped upstairs to the bookshelf in your mother's bedroom. It was forbidden to you, you guessed because of the sex manual on how to satisfy women. You'd already read it in the library and discovered nothing you didn't know. You went to the shelf and read the titles quickly. There was no telling when they'd get back, there wasn't much time to choose. You skipped the thrillers, the baby care book, the dictionary. You eased out a copy of *Hollywood Wives*, and hurried back to your room.

Your mother was an intellectual. She had proclaimed this many times, along with her contempt for other men's wives, who read Mills & Boon or Harlequins, depending on the continent. When you saw the well-thumbed pages of *Hollywood Wives*, you felt disappointed. Your mother wouldn't buy *you* anything but reference works, but she owned this book? You skimmed it quickly and lay in bed with nothing to do. You wanted to keep yourself occupied, not thinking about James, who had made Robyn tell you he would not call. You picked through your box of books again. The only thing you hadn't reread was a copy *Madame*

Bovary that you bought with a bookstore voucher you received as a school prize. You were reading it for the second time after five years, and for the first time, it made sense.

You had tried to tell Robyn, the weekend before James kissed you, that he gazed at you intently when he thought you weren't looking, but Robyn had said, "Jamie?" and laughed.

That was the weekend your parents moved house. You stayed over at Robyn's. Late at night, you huddled together, eating palmfuls of chocolate chips pilfered from her father's baked goods business, whispering your plotted and replotted fantasies, yours about Antonio, hers about Jeff Sloan. This is what you talked about. There's proof, since you taped your conversation for posterity, Robyn's Walkman on the pillow between you. The man accidentally listened to the tape and said, "Men, men, men. That's all you ever had on your mind." You didn't reply, didn't try to explain that what you talked about was the skin containing 157 what you couldn't say to Robyn, that showed no marks because your mother was neat that way – spreading, splashing pain, blood rushing to your nostrils, but no bleeding. You didn't explain, you hushed then and didn't explain and he took you in his arms and you could pretend he was completely yours.

At the end of that weekend, Robyn's mother drove you to school, and after school, you gathered in the mall with Robyn and her friends, James, Antonio, Todd. Your mother had given you the address to where they had moved, but you didn't know where it was. It was James who said he would help, that his mother would chauffeur you to your new home. Afterwards, it all seemed weird, which is why Robyn burst into laughter when James told her and he became embarrassed and wouldn't speak to you again, but this was the way it happened. Somewhere between going to his house to meet his mother and arriving at your house, he declared his love for you. Of course it was funny – blond, shy James and dark, bold, noisy you. But your heart was awash in gratitude and you gazed into his eyes, yes, Flaubert, those eyes more limpid and more beautiful than the mountain pools in which the sky is reflected, and told him not to be jealous over Antonio and you kissed and you still remember the warmth of the sun and the radiance in your body as his tongue entered your mouth. Never mind that his mother was driving, and no doubt could see all that was going on. No wonder Robyn laughed!

But still it seemed romantic. Like Françoise Sagan and Emma Bovary, growing up to be a woman, glamorous, exciting and free. That summer you were afraid of nothing. You leaned against the window pane at night, and with thickening confidence, tried to think rationally about what to do. The fall was coming, it was time to make your move. You needed shampoo and Kleenex and toothpaste to set your mind free from scheming for the moment they went out, when you could filch some toothpaste from your mother's bathroom in small amounts congealed onto your empty tube's dispenser cap, unroll some toilet paper to use as a sanitary napkin, or do without. Once, you controlled your distaste, and as your mother was walking across the landing, you opened your door and asked her for sanitary napkins. She walked down the stairs, oblivious, and you wondered if you had actually spoken or only thought of speaking, and retreated. But washing your hair with a hoarded cake of soap was fine when you were biding your time, but you had to enter your real life. You hadn't even stepped out of the house except for that one time to the library because you were afraid of making the situation worse. It was time for change. James' flicker of love had convinced you that you deserved better.

The next time you were in the house alone, you called Nicole, and she said she'd help, but when the time came, her mother said they were going out to dinner which they so rarely did and therefore couldn't you get someone else. Her father told you to make an effort and maybe things would go back to the way they were. You couldn't explain that you deserved better. You packed your schoolbag and your brother's old diaper bag full of clothes, put what change you had into your pants pocket, and went to the McDonald's near the library, trying to think of whom to call. You sat there for hours, your hand over your mouth, watching people eat. You finally called an old teacher. She called the police. They carted you home.

The police told you you were a fool, an idiot. You were assigned a social worker, a former Moonie who told you you were self-engrossed, a narcissist. You found the school, and got up with the dawn, watched from the window to see when the teenager who lived opposite left his house so you'd know when it was time. Once, after coming home, you found the house empty and locked, so you went around to the back door and jimmied it open. Just as you entered, your mother came in through the front door. She sprang at you, her fists raised, and you with your lousy aim, missed the first strike you ever laid. But it was not so bad a moment, you coming out of your cocoon forever.

You lived in the house of an old white woman with large dogs and shit-clogged toilets. You cleaned the shit stains around their toilets and the shit the dogs left and your life was endless shit: such an improvement. Then, your father's sister called. She thought you were your mother – the phone nearly slipped from your hand. She had gotten your number from your penpal when they'd met at a party. You went dizzy with money when it began to come your way, buying suitcasefuls of Kleenex, toothpaste and shampoo, storing them in the basements of friends, just in case.

You read your mother's phone number scrawled on a

sodden Bengal Cafe take-out menu. The years of silence has been like perfecting the insulation of a window pane. At one time, when you were beginning to trust an uncle's beautiful bride, you leaned over the kitchen counter and told her about your mother. "I know," Vijaya replied, chopping up tomatoes. "You still love her." She plopped them into the sambar. You looked at her in surprise, the banality unexpected. No one who puts your life in the position of scheming for toothpaste can be met with love. Wasn't that obvious? Curiosity or corrosive anger, yes, but not love, not your rich, creamy, buttery, raisined, saffroned, vermicellied love. But still, you are looking for somewhere to serve this paysam, someone who will hold out the tumblers.

"You want your boyfriend to be your Mommy and Daddy, and I'm not up to that," the man said, when you told him you're pregnant. "You're a child to be having a child and I am not up to taking care of a wife and a child." He wants to give your baby, if it is a boy, to his grandmother. "If it's a girl," he said, laughing on your answering machine, "just flush it down the toilet."

But you've no idea how to take care of a baby on your own. You're afraid of what lies molten under the surface of your skin, afraid it will surge out of you like spikes and hurt her. When you found out you were pregnant, you cupped your belly, saying, "My baby girl." Your mother's grandchild. Your round-cheeked baby girl. "Do you think she would like me?" you asked your friends. I'd be a good mother, you said to yourself as the area in the square flushed pink. She is the baby girl you have always known you will have, the daughter of the mother you have always wanted to be, but you don't know if now is the time. You don't know what to do. You call your mother.

Not that you are thinking about her as a person: "mother" is not a word that brings her to mind. It makes

you think of Michelle's mother who helped her get an
abortion and took her temperature the day after, or Joyce's
mother raising Joyce's niece. You think of that Christmas
Day in Astoria, lying in a soiled, petal-strewn bed after
losing your virginity, wishing you hadn't wanted it so badly
and been so unsure you would get it, wishing you had a
mother to tell you not to throw yourself away on an alcoholic
waiter from sheer ignorance that better individuals existed
to love you.

Your mother brings to mind not the woman she is but
the food she made: porichche kute, garlic rasam, fried black
chilies with thayir saatham, pushnika morkozhambe, lemon
rasam, tomato goche, mor rasam, podalanga sambar,
avacka, covacka, pavacka, things whose tastes you crave.
Deliveries from restaurants and Campbell's cream of celery
soup and spaghetti à la Harold can't assuage these heady
desires. You vomited the rigatoni bolognese, your head
clouded with memories of sauces of bitter vegetables, sour   161
vegetables, sharp vegetables. This is what you are thinking
of. You are not thinking of the hot tomato soup slipping and
scalding your back so the flesh sizzled and bubbled and
you screamed, running up and down the room, screaming
and your mother looked at you blankly and told you not to
fuss. This is not what you are thinking of. Your mother is not
who you are thinking of.

You tell people your mother's dead. You told the man
the truth so he could understand you, but he replied that all
parents discipline their children, crossed his scarred arms
over his face and went to sleep. After you received the
message to call your mother, the man told you he would
like to meet her and shake her hand, and you hated him,
purely and intensely, before your need overtook that
emotion. He first saw his mother when he was seven,
pointed out to him on the street.

It's not that you don't think you need mothering, but

she has no relevance to that need. You are not calling because you expect it from her. You are calling because the growth in your uterus makes you turn and look back.

You call because all you know is the weakness you feel. It's an impulse fulfilled before it's considered, like being drunk and vomiting, and similarly brief. You get under the cheap, green polyfill comforter stained with food and your come. The light in the phone is a faint yellow glow.

You barely get to speak. She commends your healthy self-esteem when you tell her you are in college, explains that she is not alive to be the librarian to your past, inquires of your goals for your relationship with her, informs you that she is not interested in recriminations, guilt trips, blame-allotting, dredging up the past, because good and bad are relative, admits she is into New Age philosophy and says she's not interested in your judgments, screams that she wants a civil, sharing relationship, responds, when you point out that she's screaming, that niceness isn't her strong point. "Look, Neelam, are you interested in having a giving relationship or not?" she yells.

"No," you say, and hang up the phone. You lie back in the bed, stunned.

You realize that you'll never talk to her again. There's no use in feeling helpless, but you do. How could you inflict this on a child? As much as you like the idea of valiantly singing *Tu mere saath rahega munne* as you cup your swollen belly, you know that you have to wait to have your baby girl. You repeat it to yourself: I'm all alone. Even clicking your heels won't help. There's no place like home. Then, feeling empty, you push the comforter aside, and stand up. You pull the phone to your ribs, and call Irene. "I'm going," you say when she answers the phone. "When can you come with me?"

Chapter 8

Becoming a Man

> Nam agar puchhe to koi
> batlana peenewala
>
> —Harvishrai Bachchan, *Madhushala*

Pussy.

Chick.

"Look at the words you use," says Stephanie Banks, walking into the room. She is not looking at you. She has paused at a slip of yellow transparent paper in the folder in her hand. A piece of letterhead drifts out. She frowns, handing the receipt to you to file. "You might as well be a man."

As well?

You think of her words and smile. You decide to wear the

dark green jacket to the $300 suit you bought at a going-out-of-business sale at some men's store in the Village and the clerk thought you were crazy maybe because you were fish, maybe because the trousers were loose around the waist and so tight around your hips. This is why you wear only the jacket. And a square-necked green dress that clings to your bust and falls straight, but not far. This is your costume to show off breasts, big legs, your hair in a tight bun. You put on heels with long and pointy toes.

The better to fuck you with, my dear.

You walk with Parveen over the humps and valleys of Broadway to the liquor store. The sun is setting, and though Parveen bores you in general, the boredom she inflicts is poignant around sunset. It's getting late. You rub your bare wrist. Parveen tells you again about her mother, her missing father who used to call her kali kuththe, black bitch, when he hit her, all the men who pick her up in subway stations. Dr Qureishi who took her to the Sufi mosque in Jersey with his wife and children. She says: his wife behaved so strangely. Do you think Dr Qureishi is hitting on me? Your mind drifts, thinking about your missing watch. Parveen is one of those people whom you tolerate because you think you have been where they are. You weave past Dominican stores spilling onto the street, boxes of loose soap and toothpaste and colored plastic things with inscrutable uses. The soap is clearly marked: not to be sold separately. A coffee-bean colored man sits on the edge of the sidewalk, indolently waving a rattan fan, his eyes white flashes, watching for thieves. Two Zapata-mustached Banglas on a beaten-up powder blue car say: hola chicas. Muchas bonitas. Parveen says: kamineh, and she bursts into giggles.

It's getting darker. The wine shop is not too far away now. Past the racks of striped T-shirts. A white bucket of cut, shriveling roses. Battered records – Donna Summer, Andy Gibb, the Sherelles – spread on a dirty white bedsheet. The Sri Lankan Tamil in the liquor store has a long, bulging scar like the back of a crocodile over his left eye. Parveen says: woh Tamil hai, kya? Aap ke log? You are searching for a Gallo. So it's cheap. You will take the price tag off before you get to Melanie.

Melanie is pretty. Melanie speaks in the simple, exclamation-marked declarative sentences of women's magazines: My great new pedicure set makes my nails sparkle! Mo Better is a really cool restaurant with good food and professional black people! Sometimes her conversation induces the tranquil boredom of a waiting room, sometimes it is disconcerting. The only idea she has ever proffered to you is that because the first man on Earth was black, black people have the possibility of bearing children of other races. Her cousin, a dark-skinned woman with a dark husband, had a light-skinned, blue-eyed, sharp-nosed child, she informs you. She doesn't have any relatives who have had an East Asian child for no apparent reason, but she is sure it is possible.

When you first met Melanie, she asked you how you like to be fucked, and told how good she was at fucking, and asked the size of your bra. Told you she wants to taste you, smell you. Months later, she explains to you that she talked that way to test if you are a niggerlover. You say: I guess I am a niggerlover. It's the nappy pubic hair, it's irresistible. She says: don't think you can use that word with me.

One night, as you straddle her hips, rubbing your pussy against her pussy in what is at best a butt and hip exercise, somehow excited that you are bored and she is not, she says: oh, honey, that feels so good, how come you move your hips like a black girl? You could tell her it is because your parents are really black or give her Patience's theory that Dravidians are Africans sent to colonize South Asia or you could say this is how an Indian girl moves her hips but instead you snigger.

She says: can't you even pretend to like it?

Riding the cool train after bidding Parveen goodbye, you think of things Melanie says in bed. You sit back in your seat, read the ads for abortions at Lincoln Women's Center, Malboros, ads in Creole about AIDS, return to the religion of your ancestors for Passover, and Melanie saying: work this pussy, you know how to do it, oh, you're incredible, suck my pussy, God, your tongue is amazing.

You walk from the subway station to her apartment. It's in Hell's Kitchen, but in a nice building, doormen, brass, revolving door. Expensive, but there are ambulances constantly wailing by to the hospital up the road. You watch them, late at night, while she is sleeping, untroubled, or seemingly untroubled, and the streetlamp seeps light through the rustling venetian blinds. The air conditioner is always on, never mind that it is barely spring. That's Melanie. Detroit reptile. 'Bama bitch. Cold, cold as an American. You press a blind down with your finger, watch the light, the ambulances, the homeless men, the tip of the doorman's cap, the light, strange as if you were underwater, but not buoyant, never buoyant. You think: maybe her pussy juice is a depressant, and you laugh. Melanie says: what is the matter? What's wrong with you? Get in bed. You know I have to get up early in the morning.

Sometime she feels guilty and so she tries to roughly grab your tits, but you stop her, because she doesn't know how and besides you don't need the charity. She says: don't tell me in the morning that I am selfish and insensitive because I just tried, and she goes to sleep. You used to cry and masturbate quietly, huddled on the edge of the bed. You felt sorry for yourself, waves of orgasmic humiliation flashing in your belly. You climaxed slowly, exhaling. Quietly, too, because Melanie is easily disturbed. Soon, it stops being worth the trouble; instead you watch the ambulances late at night while she is sleeping,

167

Sometimes you recite poetry:

her carefully distinct sex whose sharp lips comb/

/I've got the fever for the flavor.

When you arrive at the front desk of her building, the Italian concierge rings up but there is no answer. You stand with your legs crossed so he can not see the sewn-up hole on your left shoe. He says: does she know you are coming? Maybe she's in the shower. You can go up. He has seen you before. Mornings when she herds you out of bed with her, she dressed in expensive suits and heavy gold jewellery, you in whatever you were wearing the night before, your knapsack over your shoulder. Mornings you are always bitter. You fight over how lousy she is in bed. She is unapologetic. As you pause at the traffic light, she squints at you through eyes encircled with black eyeliner so they look even beadier, and says you reject her minimal effort and she is not inclined to do more. Honestly, you prefer complaining about her incompetence to suffering it, so you do repulse her advances. The light changes. You walk. Her hair, straightened and pressed every morning with a curling iron into artfully messy waves, glitters from a coat of hairspray. Her plump, pretty lips glisten. A uniformed delivery man whistles at her. Then a man in a car, his window rolled down. Businessmen look at her over *The Wall Street Journal*. Melanie is the kind of woman other people think is pretty. She's pretty but really, you think, that pretty? You don't feel capable of scorning her because there seems to be something you do not see. You had to introduce Melanie to Irene simply to get Irene's opinion. Irene said: she's the kind of woman that other people think is pretty.

168

Her pussy at least is beautiful. Salty, nappy-haired, neat. Really, she lied and said it was the way it was naturally but later admitted she trimmed it down along the lips and over the mound to give it that extra cute and available five o'clock shadow of pussy fur and the one tuft of hair like a Brahmin's ponytail over the tiny bead of her clit. It is the first pussy you have eaten. After the first time, Melanie says: that was good. I haven't had it since my ex-girlfriend did it four months ago. She rises off the bed to turn the television on. Did I tell you about redecorating my office? Somewhere in the middle of something about Elvis, you scream.

You have never asked. Well, once you asked what would happen if you ever asked. She said: I don't feel that way about you. You get a burning sensation behind your navel, a line being drawn in gastric juices, halving your body, deadening your nether regions. They are dead. You wait to grow something else.

You used to have fantasies about fucking her. Opening her thighs and plunging in your black cock with your foreskin pulled back and fucking her until you are about to come and shoving your dripping cock into her mouth. This is until you realized that she is not gay, though she said she was when you first met. She now says she is bisexual. She lies in bed, her breasts, the size and shape of cone drinking cups in doctors' offices, peek over the blanket like dogs' snouts. She tells you she enjoys you. Enjoys you cleaning her pussy with your tongue? you ask. She demurs, says it's great that it's only fucking around, there's no involvement, she can't get pregnant, low risk of disease, and multiple orgasms. You put your fingers between your lips and think of your last lover while she tells you she fantasizes about sleeping with men. You do not fantasize about Melanie again.

169

You stand outside her door, the gray carpeted corridor endlessly lined with closed white doors, fluorescent lighting glimmering on the brass knockers. You knock. Once. Twice. You can hear the television set. Screeching tires, fast pounding music, thumping bass, drum machine. You knock again. No answer. Damn. What are you going to do with the bottle of wine?

Melanie asked you over, and before she could say the usual things, you agree. These are the usual things: it will be different tonight, don't you want to see my peasy fur, you can hone your skills for future lovers, I'll satisfy you this time, you get me so hot that you could take advantage of it.

You agree because you don't want to stay home alone. Home alone, you will begin thinking about the world and your place in it. Better to be with Melanie, who leaves you with a strange intellectual numbness. There is no need to think with Melanie, no need to summon up conversation. "Are you just going to sit there like a bump on a log, not saying anything?" she hisses to you over dinner one evening. You are at Jezebel's, and you run your fork through your artfully arranged dinner, scraping the china. The meat on the ribs is juicy and succulent but the sauce uninspiring. The greens are tender and soft. Your wine is white and dry, a nice sharp contrast. You take a sip. Your mind is a clean slate. You don't feel the pressure to be amusing, to be the center of conversation, that you feel with other people – no matter what you say, Melanie will blankly respond "that's good, honey" – and this frees you to experience your dinner more keenly. With Melanie, you note every aromatic and savory detail, the way the white tassels hang from the ceiling, the discordant note struck by the mudcloth vest on one of the busboys, the soft thud of your spoon falling to the ground, the nasal voice of the blonde girl on the swing. Melanie hisses: I am never taking you out again. Do you think you are behaving normally? Don't you know how to have a conversation? You reply: I don't recall you beginning a conversation. She gives a disgusted look and turns away. The maitre d' smiles at her. She smiles back. You dab your lips with the napkin, leave a red mouth on the white cloth.

170

Lipstick stains are so hard to get off. Restaurateurs must hate you. You take another sip of wine. It begins to go to your head, it fills your nipples. Melanie pushes her plate away and lights a cigarette. She lifts her glass of wine. Her wine – you tasted it – is sweet and fruity. It is her third glass. She calls for the check. You hand her a twenty dollar bill. She says it's okay, she'll get it. You put the bill into the pocket of her suede jacket. It's enough that she is willing to pay. You don't want her to. She isn't nice enough to accept presents from, or bad enough that you don't give a fuck what she thinks about you. When you leave the restaurant, she asks if you can stop by the bodega on the corner. You say okay. You don't think about what she is about to buy, but if someone asked you you would guess dessert, or toothpaste, or cigarettes. She buys a 40-ounce of beer. You have never even seen anyone drink a 40-ounce before. You have heard about it, seen it in rap videos, but never seen anyone drink it, after dinner, on the way home. Her apartment is sparsely furnished, dimly lit and stylish in the way that something is stylish if it is color-coordinated. In the short hallway to the bedroom, there is a framed picture of a Ralph Lauren Safari ad. Melanie strips down to her underwear. You sit on her leather couch. Politely, she sits on the other end of the couch before she rolls her joint. The t.v. is on. Arsenio Hall. The blast from the air conditioner makes your bare legs prickle with goosebumps. You cross your legs, lean your head back. Your mind is a clean slate.

171

You take the elevator down.

You say to the Italian doorman: she must have stepped out. Can I leave the wine with you? I'll be back soon. He agrees. You walk out, head towards the lights of Times Square.

It's nine o'clock. Too early to go to the club, but you don't feel like going all the way back home. With ridiculous pleasure, you realize Patience lives nearby. Oh how glamorous, and sly.

The difference between Melanie and Patience is this: Melanie says: why do Indian women have red dots on their foreheads? You say: that's where we menstruate. Patience calls you: Urmila, Rani, Jayashree, the names of all the Indian girls she has known.

From a pay phone outside a pizza parlor. You get Patience's number from Information since you don't yet remember it. Her son answers the phone. He gets her. She says with genuine pleasure, "Hello."

"Hey, baby, what's up? Can you come out and play?"

"Where are you?"

"In your neighborhood. Have a drink with me."

"I can't, you know I can't, I can't leave my son alone. Just because last night, I came to your house. . ." Her voice trails off into a sigh. "Girlie, you know you teasing me."

"Look, I'm calling from a pay phone. Just bring your butt outside and we'll have a drink." The b-boy using the phone booth beside you briefly turns. His friend peeks at you over his shoulder, eyes bulging and watery. You say, "Woman, bring that soufflé butt of yours outside."

"I just had a shower you know, my hair is a mess. If I'm going to come out, I have to do my hair and what about my son? You're being impossible. I don't know what's gotten into you . . . You horny or something?" Patience pauses. "I wish you could come here, you know, but you can't. I know you going to disrespect me if you see how I'm living and it's only because I am so busy these days and I haven't cleaned . . ."

Calmly you reply, "I told you I'm at a fucking pay phone. I don't have time to discuss your housekeeping. Are we going to have a drink or not? I'll meet you in front of Tower Records. Tower Records in twenty minutes."

"No, I have to do my hair—"

"How come black women schedule their lives around their hair? Now, if you were doing something important, I'm not going to say you should break your plans for me or nothing, but you got the time. Bring your butt out. I want to rub up against it." You lower your voice, not in decibel level but in pitch. "You remember that? The first time you came to my house and I kept slipping off you because your butt's so big?"

"Huh?" she giggles. "It's not that big."

"Please. You know it is. Why you flirting." You smooth back your hair. You say, "Twenty minutes. Tower Records. Bye." You hang up the phone. You call Melanie to see if she answers her phone. She doesn't. She must have gone out, but she's not the type to leave the t.v. on by accident and the doorman would have noticed. She has probably passed out drunk again. You'll find out what happened soon enough. Luckily, you have been smart enough not to leave anything at Melanie's apartment or lend her any money so you don't really have to see her ever again.

173

Behind the plastic curtain, buckets of flowers stacked on metal tiers: resilient carnations, tired iris, colors of roses with baby's breath. The stumpy Mayan guard stationed outside the grocery store eyes you warily. You walk on. In any case, Patience told you the night she met you that she hates romance. "You hate it," you said, tipping back in your chair, "because you're afraid you won't get it." She protests with a flash of her accent, that's not true. It's not true at all.

Your mother says: why can't you be content seeing flowers grow? You just have to pluck them, even though they'll wilt so much sooner. You're selfish and greedy, just like your father.

"User," your mother says. "You just take, take, take. You suck the blood out of my life." You run your fork in circles in the lumpy upma she has made. You hate upma. She throws the lid of the stainless steel pot at your head. It barely misses, landing on the table. You watch the condensation trickle onto your yellow plastic placemat. "Bloodsucker," she screams.

174

There are no flowers growing here, or butterflies. Not even in parks, you think last Sunday as Melanie sits beside you on the bench, cradling the *New York Times*. You watch passers-by. A woman with soft thighs and tight jeans that reveal her lips, leading her daughter by the hand. The daughter is the color of honey. She has round eyes, a small flattish nose and a wide mouth. Her hair a short frizzy cloud. You wave. She smiles. She has a broken front tooth. She turns her head. You turn to Melanie. Melanie reads the newspaper: first the Metro section, the entire Macy's catalog, a quick look at the stock prices, the t.v. guide. You watch. She says in a Southern-fried accent, Damn, I missed *Basic Instinct* yesterday. That was a good movie.
You didn't find it heterosexist? You don't know why you opened your mouth. You regret it immediately.
No, it was hot she says. She closes the t.v. guide. There's

this part where Michael Douglas fucks Sharon Stone from behind. She whistles.

You turn your head away, memory imploding. Is that what you want someone to do to you? you ask, your voice held even.

She says, No, that's what I want to do to a girl. *That's* why we don't get along. We both want to do the same thing.

You say nothing. The bench is beginning to hurt your butt. Melanie fumbles in her bag, eyeing a Latin boy in a lavender jogging suit and large white sneakers. He is leaning against the railing, smoking a cigarette. You say, Melanie, you didn't miss the movie. They don't print yesterday's schedule in today's t.v. guide. The movie is next Saturday.

Gee thanks, honey, she drawls, picking out her box of Virginia Slims. It's so nice to be with a smart woman. She hails the Latin boy and asks for a light. As he is leaving, she watches his retreating back and says, Doesn't he have a nice body? You shrug. She is smiling. You think of Patience. You watch the sunlight dappling the dirty Hudson. You watch old couples and lean joggers and little children on tricycles and big dogs leading their owners. As you leave, Melanie says: didn't we have a nice time together? You smile enigmatically. She puts her hand on your back. You say: take your fucking hand off my back.

When she touches you below the neck, it is an offensive reminder of the regions that other people still have. Once when she says she misses you, you ask flirtatiously: which parts exactly? She says: your mouth. You ask: what else? She says: your tongue.

Shut the other things away. Lock the lock. What kind of lock shall it be? Plastic? Silicone? As the boxes in a store on

Christopher Street read: flesh, mulatto or black? You say to Irene: I guess black people don't have any flesh. She laughs, leaning against a rack of leather-jacket-and-pants sets with cut-out ass cheeks. You have only just told her about this part of your life, and you are trying not to be too outrageous, but then you examine the price on the box, and you cry out, "Sixty-five dollars and you don't even get a harness?" The whole store convulses in laughter.

Melanie will not let you do this to her. She once asks if you would like her to do it to you so you can feel something. She will suck your breasts because what harm can that really do and plastic is safe, right? She likes to grind. When one night she calls you and tells you she wants to go down on you, you curtly refuse, and the next day when she calls and says, Did we talk last night? I apologize for whatever I said. Honey, I was so drunk, I threw up all over the bathroom, you are unsurprised.

You have long hair but you do not otherwise resemble the women Melanie likes: light, bony, utterly feminine. Melanie's ex-girlfriend is gorgeous, a perfect body, she could pass for white but has a little something to her face that gives her away. You are doing the *New York Times* daily crossword puzzle and you are only half-listening until Melanie pauses after the word "has." As usual, your mind races to finish her sentence. What is Melanie going to say? "A touch of the tarbrush"? Melanie says: a little something to her face that gives her away.

You laugh, walking the dim night streets.

Melanie's ex-girlfriend is gorgeous. Like Melanie's gynecologist. Like the waiter at B. Smith's. Like the director of a radio station in Ohio she once had dinner with. She calls you up afterwards to tell you all about it. "I know she's straight, straight women are so soft, but it's business so I can't . . . She's just so beautiful . . . Are you bored?" says Melanie. "Do you want me to let you go?"

Once in bed, with her on top of you, her poky hips digging into the rippling flesh of your thighs, you cup her face and say: tell me I'm pretty. She says: don't tell me what to do.

You stop letting her lie on top of you, one more thing the two of you will not do. This leaves: you on top, you going down on her.

177

Melanie tells you all about hot sex with her gorgeous ex-girlfriend, the fruit, the whipped cream, the rope. Melanie says: and she would scream, "Melanie, Melanie!" and I wouldn't untie her, just sit there eating ice-cream. Melanie's voice is nasal and harsh, and her imitation of her ex-girlfriend's voice sounds less erotic than shrieky.

I tried to touch you when I came to your house the first time, you didn't let me, says Melanie. I thought you were sexually abused or something, so I leave you alone.

You cross the street. A gaggle of olive-skinned boys in corduroy and yarmulkes huddle near a newspaper vending machine. A restaurant's glass wall reveals flickering candles and heads bent in discussion. There is a line of white people in front of Lincoln Cinemas, tweed coats and earnest voices. Men with thinning hair, awkwardly alone.

A young couple, matching backwards Yankees baseball caps and worn denim overalls, both with gold earrings, hers heavy bamboo, his small and round, their fingertips barely touching as they walk.

Sometimes you feel like the come you haven't come forms a clog of unguent in your pussy, like mucus in your nasal passages preventing you from breathing properly. What to do? Masturbation is like blowing your nose, at best a temporary remedy. A wise sage in a cave at the top of the Himalayas makes his yearly proclamation. He says: stop wanting to breathe.

178

You will block your passageways. You will be watertight. You will, in public places, grab your crotch. You already don't, in public places, sit down when you take a leak. You read *Soldier of Fortune*. You want to buy a gun.

Let me, you tell Trent, explain to you why Melanie will let men fuck her but not women. It's the Bessie Smith School of Bisexuality. Men bone you, and you envy them the power of boning, but you couldn't respect a man you could bone enough to deal with him, so you bone women. Other famous graduates of this school are Vita Sackville-West, Billie Holliday, Tamara de Lempicka, Marlene Dietrich. Which is why femmes are the true lesbians. Vita went on to fuck Roy whatever from the BBC, you know, after she led Violet around like a dog on a leash.

Trent, who has been eating a cannoli with concentration, says: you said the same thing about Mona.

Exactly. All gay women want a butch and all butches want power not pussy. Trent lays down his fork. He asks in all earnest faggot seriousness: what does it matter if it's for the power or the pussy as long as you are coming?

Oh Trent, please. I never come. What does that have to do with anything?

You stand against the wall of Tower Records, in the orange neon shade of the lettering, across the sidewalk from an old dread playing "All of Me" on the xylophone. Patience is late. You look up from the book you are reading, *The Unbelonging.* It's only a white couple walking by. You decide you will leave soon. You could go down to the Village for a coffee, before heading to the club. You return to the book. Finally you see her. She has her hair pulled back in a ponytail. She is wearing a white T-shirt, a white shirt, spinach-colored trousers and a dark jacket. You say: you're late. This is what I had to wait here all this extra time for?

179

You pull her T-shirt with a hooked finger, peek at her breasts. They are plump as New York City pigeons. She blushes, moves away. You let go. The T-shirt snaps back.

You say: I missed you. She says: I don't want to hear your lies.

Patience and her son sit uncomfortably in the restaurant.

She says: you didn't say we were going to a restaurant. You reply that you could hardly take her son to a bar. The son wants to eat. She says: you have to pay for him, you know. I don't have no money. You hail the waiter and order minestrone. The son orders pizza. The waiter says: you have such beautiful eyes. When the food comes, Patience eats from her son's plate. They both complain it doesn't taste as good as Ray's. You sip your wine. White and dry. Patience, at first, won't talk, because she can't believe you called her out like this, but you point out that it's silly to have come to meet you and then sit silent, and you start telling her about how much you like Joan Riley's novel. Patience tells you about Samuel Selvon.

Patience has Chinese eyes, skin the color of therati pal, uneven teeth. The flavor of raw potato. A lilting Trini accent. Trent has told you but now you learn on your own that the Trini is the most musical of all island accents. Patience has short nails and rough hands.

A woman once advised you never to sleep with guitarists because their callused fingers make them rough lovers, pulling harder because all that guitar-picking has made their fingers less sensitive. You said: I want a conga player.

Patience would let you fuck her. Do anything. "Now, you don't mean you'd let me do just anything?" you whisper in her ear the first time you go out. She is leaning against a pillar in the subway station. "Yes," she says. "Anything."

You know two kinds of sexual feeling. One is sharp and

sour and located on the surface of your vulva. The other is heavy and radiates out throughout your body with its focus at the root of your clitoris. The first kind leaves you cold afterwards, the second doesn't. The first kind is your immediate physical reaction to naked girls. The second is more complicated, submissive, something to do with your emotions, though let's not aggrandize and call it love. The first kind gets you off quickly. The second gets you off longer. Melanie doesn't do either; Patience, after saying, "anything," is firmly and unfortunately in category number one.

Suck my dick?

You don't have much of an imagination. Patience, leaning against the pillar on the subway platform the first time you go out, agrees. You turn your face away. You have hit the jackpot. You turn away because you are not good at hiding your emotions. You press your back against her, smoothing your dress down. A herd of Queens-bound, peasant-faced, Brylcream-haired North Indians stares at you. You grin. Patience is looking her best. You wish she was wearing lipstick.

Patience doesn't wear a bra, either, because she used to be flat-chested. Her breasts bulge against her T-shirt and press the edge of the table. You toy with the candle-in-a-glass, its ridges hot against your fingertips. Her son gnaws on a crust of pizza. "I want to go home," he says, his eyes almost sealed with sleep. She looks at you helplessly. You call for the check. Under the table, you lift up the edge of her trouser leg, rub against her calf. She is smiling. She tells you to stop.

Tell me your name, the waiter says, as he hands you the bill.
Vyjayanthimala Bali, you answer.
He asks you to repeat yourself. You laugh.

In Tower Video, where you have stopped for her son to play
a video game, you lead Patience to the adult movie section.
There is no one else there. You pull various lurid video
cases, ask her if this turns her on. *Beverly Hills Cock. White
Men Can't Hump. Two of a Kind. When Larry Ate Sally.*
Patience says no, you know what turns me on. And you do.
Dark-skinned boys because they remind her of girls. Why
not girls then? Because she'd feel guilty for fucking a little
girl. She also likes the idea of female-to-male transsexuals.
Women with dicks. You point out that a F2M has no more
sensation in her dick than a woman with a strap-on, but she
says the F2M's dick will feel real to her. You tell her she just
hasn't encountered a sophisticated dildo. Your voice is
casual, older, urbane. Wink, wink. Nudge, nudge. Inside,
you are horrified.
We all, you tell Trent, want to use or be useful. Now, how
are you going to be useful to a woman?
Trent plays along. The cannoli long finished, he sips his
café mocha. You go down on her? he asks, timidly.
Yes, but a man could do that. Now, I know there's this myth
that women do it better because they are women, but
Patience says only men have made her come by sucking
her, okay? The thing is, I bet men probably are better at
giving head to a woman, because they can't just assume
their partner will like what they like. Anyway, eating pussy
is skill, not essence. How is your body, your woman's body
useful to another woman? What can your lover do with
what you've got to give? Fisting? She sticks her hand up
you and gets pruney fingers and this is supposed to make
her happy? Your cunt can never be a gift, it's just this greedy

fucking hole, and if that's all it is, I don't want it. You lean
forward. Sex is where one person is a stud and the other
person is beautiful. How can you give a woman permission
to violate you? To do what? Without a dick, there is no
violation. Sex is dirty. Dicks are dirty. No dick, no sex.
Do you really believe this stuff, Trent asks.
"No." You sip your café au lait.

Patience has slept with, not necessarily in this order: a
Trinidadian man she loved before and after he raped her, a
dowdy Latina, a fifteen-year-old boy while she was the
lover of the dowdy Latina, a woman who dialed her number
by accident, this woman's boyfriend, this woman and her
boyfriend, a man she picked up on the streets twenty
minutes earlier because she was really horny, an Indian
with a big dick (Patience says: he must have had some
black blood because nobody heard of no Indian with a big
dick), an African with a small dick (Patience says: black
men have big dicks but Africans have small dicks), a Haitian
man who loved to eat pussy but did it badly and who is also
the father of her son, the man who was her husband when
she became pregnant with her son, a butchy white woman
she loved because of her own internalized racism, a
Jamaican drug dealer who was quite butch, etc. "You are
the first femme," she tells you. You are standing against the
wall, reading the back of *Beach Blanket Bimbo*. At least, you
are looking at the words. "The rest were soft butch.
But you act harder than all them, you know. I don't know
why you acting like this. I am not used to this. It's too
much." She pulls the tape box from your hand and puts it
back on the shelf. You roll your eyes, set your face in
indifference. "You look so sexy, got such big titties, you
won't let me touch anything. I want to suck your cunt so
bad."

You say, "Shut the fuck up."

"See you can't even stand me talking about it." She turns, her sandals slapping. "It's late."

"Baby," you say.

"Are you going to let me touch you?"

"At your house?"

"I can't." She is worrying something in her right jacket pocket, the material shifts and rolls.

"You can come to my house but I can't go to yours?" you say. Let her say no and that will be the end of it. You want to go down to the Box anyway.

"My house is a mess. Let's go to your house. My son can sleep on the floor." Patience looks into your eyes. You shake your head. "I could suck your cunt so good."

You feel a wave of nausea. So what, you want to say, but you don't. You walk past her and towards the exit. Her son is engrossed in the video game. Let's go, she says to him.

Maybe Cervantes is wrong. Maybe hunger isn't the best sauce. Maybe it turns your mouth acrid, makes everything taste like dirt ever afterwards.

At the end of your first date with her, Patience lies naked on your bed. You finger her, watching her face. She lifts her hand, tugs at your sweater. You say, stop, come on, stop. Let me concentrate. When it is over, she tugs again. You say: I can't, really I just can't, I'm . . . Be nice, to me. Hammy as ever, you lean against her as you say this, your chin pressed into her shoulder. You are almost whispering, watching the trickle of light from the building behind the window, telling her about Melanie. Patience says: I'll suck your cunt. You say: it's not about that. Patience gets up, her breasts swaying, the great arc of her rump passing in front of you. She says, grabbing her clothes: I never heard of this shit before. I loved Sonia and she wouldn't suck my cunt, I used to beg her to put her fingers inside me and she wouldn't, but I ain't heard of no woman like you who will suck cunt and not let nobody do it to her. You won't even take your clothes off, it's too fucking weird. You're just too fucking weird.

Melanie says: you went down on me so quickly, I have to wonder about you. I was sure you were lying when you said you never did it before. Patience says: you suck my cunt the first time we go out, and you fucking want me to wait because you won't take your clothes off? I don't know what to think about you.

185

Patience stops walking so her son can take a leak behind a garbage can. When he's done, you walk the two blocks left until you reach her home. The building is a red brick '60s monstrosity whose elevators smell of urine. "The crack-heads come in here to take a leak," says Patience.

"Even the crackheads urinate indoors," you say. She tells you that you have internalized the rules of the White Man's civilization, but you ignore her. She opens the door of her apartment, you stumble in. The light from the living room's one naked bulb barely reaches into its nooks and crannies, much less into the hallway. The space is crammed full: television, plastic tables, Soloflex machine, computer, dressmaker's dummy, sewing machine, rolled futon, bicycles, the floor covered with wires and cords, the ceiling low. The kinds of books sold in flea markets like the one on 125th Street, where Patience sells the clothes she makes: histories of the Caribbean and Africa, Paule

Marshall, Memmi, orange Heinemanns, Sartre (whom Patience quotes approvingly on the plight of black Americans), Fanon of course. The only decoration on the wall is two wooden stands for spools of thread and a brass-framed poster of a brown-skinned baby with rolls and rolls of toilet paper. The poster was a gift.

Patience rolls the thin futon mattress out on the floor. You sit down and unlace your shoes. She takes her son into the bedroom. You stretch out on the mattress, lean on the pillow, arms behind your head. The pillow bulges out of the pillowcase and is rough and grainy against your elbow. The blanket is yellow and brown in some kind of psychedelic floral pattern. It smells like a wet bath mat, but only if you put your nose to it. Patience comes and lies next to you. Her son pitches pennies down the narrow corridor. They plonk and roll behind the mattress, behind the Soloflex machine, near the wheel of the chair in front of the computer.

Jabril, go to sleep, says Patience.

I'm sleeping, he calls out.

Stop throwing pennies, says Patience.

I'm not, he yells back.

You say, I guess it's just raining money. Too bad it's not dollar bills.

She snuggles against you, her warm body filling your curves. He's just jealous, she says. You say: I notice. She says: when I called you honey on the phone, he got so angry. Nobody is supposed to be honey but him. She says it like an offering. You are not moved. You are faintly repulsed. You lift her pyjama top until it is a white veil over her face, touch her plump breasts.

Does that are twin.

This line always bothered you, as if the poet felt the reader would otherwise assume one doe was bigger than the other.

Her belly like a heap of wheat. You are full of poetry.

What are you thinking, says Patience. You say: you got some nice breasts. She says: I hate it when you say that, it's not true, I just put on some weight. I never need to wear a bra. You say: I guess you don't wear one so you can make David's dick hard. David is an unwashed, rotting-toothed, light-eyed pseudo-Rasta who sells psychedelic T-shirts with pictures of King, X, Mandela, Garvey, and the fifth saint, Bob Marley, up on 125th Street, next to Patience. He is after Patience. He wants to show her what a dick can do. Patience says, "If I want a man, I can get a better man than David. I know a lot of nice men, a lot." She pauses, looks down. Your face is blank.

On 125th Street, beside Patience, beside the woman selling plastic jelly shoes and beside the mudcloth vests and caps and cheap sunglasses and the rest of the latest in Made in Korea, and before the corner of Lenox where the West Africans sell rolls of kente and cowrie-studded leather belts and masks and the Rastas sell incense and oils and listen to Chaka Demus, are two young black women selling T-shirts: Bacdafuckup, Throw Your Gunz in the Air, Mike Tyson: I'll Be Back, Ain't nothing but a G thang baby, Black by Popular Demand. You say: I can't believe those two girls are selling the Mike Tyson T-shirt. Patience says: I don't have no faith in Desiree Washington. She just got mad that Mike Tyson wouldn't fuck her so she said he raped her. You say: just because you enjoyed being raped doesn't mean that every other woman does.

You used to have fantasies about fucking her. Opening her thighs and plunging in your black cock with your foreskin pulled back and fucking her until you are about to come and shoving your dripping cock into her mouth.

"I'm not no lesbian. I like women, I'm not looking for no man, but I'm not a lesbian. If I met a nice man, a sensitive man, maybe, I'm not looking for it, but maybe." Patience is sitting in the shade of a large plastic umbrella emblazoned with a hot dog. She is sitting on a fire hydrant across from the fence on which the clothes she made are hung. She wears a straw hat, and with her East Asian eyes, she resembles a Vietnamese peasant. It is hot, your face is oily and sweaty. You are sitting in the shade of the umbrella, on the wooden folding chair. On your lap is Chloë, the child of another street vendor. Chloë is five years old, tanned to your complexion, large eyes shaped like mango pits, her long limbs waving as you bounce your knee to the beat of a faintly heard "Murder She Wrote." Chloë wears a multi-stained pink cotton T that keeps hiking up to expose her soft, small belly. "I want to see my mommy," she says. You scoop her up in your arms, her little butt resting on your forearm, her arms around your shoulders, and carry her across the street, weaving between the cars. The light is green, but traffic is congested. You bump a fender with your knee, tilt, "wheee!" says Chloë, confident this is just a thrill, not a danger. On the sidewalk, you twirl in a circle, her legs fly out in an arc, Daffy Duck shoe laces dangling, pointing to the Earth, she giggles, giggles. You say: do you want to come home with me? She nods, her chin going down to her chest and back up, then says: I can't go home with you. I need my mommy.

Trent says: Brazil?
That's what Stephanie Banks said. There aren't many gay men in Brazil because Brazilian women know how to appreciate their men.
Please. Trent says it in a put upon "diva" way.
Yeah well, Patience says Indians are clannish, tricky.
Patience just said that to hurt you because she felt hurt. Trent spoons up whipped cream off his café mocha. You should work with her, she likes you. You almost tell him she called him a faggot, a pantyman, but you don't.

189

Patience, the first time you went out, leans over the small table at Cafe Orlin and says: when I'm horny, I'd let any man suck my cunt. She tells you about the sissy German who came to her house, and she opened her legs so he could lick her, and then sent him home. She says: with women, it's different, but I'd let any man suck my cunt.

And a man would let anyone suck his dick. What is wrong with you? What is wrong with you?

You would let anyone suck your dick, too.

After a short silence, Patience sits up a little. You have your arm around her hips, your cheek against her breasts, cupping her butt as firm and tender as a ripe cantaloupe, her pyjama pants rough with pilling, your palm bisected by the elastic of her underwear. Patience tells you about her father. He abandoned her as a child, married a white woman in England, found Patience again, treated his "white" grandchildren better than Patience's son. She says: imperialism has shaped my whole life. Do you think he behaved the way he did because he was a bad man? Everything he did, it was imperialism. You almost say: when he tried to have sex with you? You catch yourself in time. She says: I hope there is a God. If there is no God who is punishing black people, then I have to believe that the white man is superior. Sometimes, I try to understand why God would give the white man everything. I think about these things, you know. Without God, you have to believe in Darwin—

What does Darwin have to do with the white man being superior?

190   —let me finish. Her voice is sharp and raspy. You settle into the pillow. The light from outside glistens on your knuckles, her forehead, her elbow. She talks. Her voice coarsens with anger. She gives you a brief history of European expansion, a convoluted and inaccurate description of Darwinism, a treatise on the sorrows of the black people. Her voice reminds you of the dull roar of the t.v. after the programming hours are over. Ksssh, kssssh. You put her dark nipples into your mouth. She lets out a small cry.

You suck, kindling a slow heat in your abdomen. Like a gas fire when you first turn it on, you feel a snap, crack, in your belly. You open her thighs. She shifts to allow you access, her breasts sliding out of your mouth, trailing saliva down your chin. You shove your hand past the twisted elastic of her pyjama pants, through the long, hairy thickets of her bush. Patience's Chinese blood gives her barely any eyebrows and long pubic hair.

She is wet.

You peel off her pants. You slide two fingers inside her vagina. Patience's plug is quite short, you press your fingertips against its hole. You try to slide a finger into the hole. Patience yelps.

She says: you rough, you know.

Patience and Melanie describe good sex with a woman as being sweet, gentle, soft.

After you send Patience to the bathroom to wash it, you eat her pussy. She is not noisy, so you keep raising your head to see the expression on her face. You have too much performance anxiety to be able to zoom into meditative tranquillity, that unselfconscious, almost Tantric state where you lose awareness of everything but the tip of your tongue and the tip of a clitoris, and tip to tip undying is, that time when you understand the Buddhist concept of union with Nothingness and why clitoris is "languette," little tongue, in French. At a certain point, Patience gets sore, so you have to stop. It makes you uneasy that you have now gone down on her twice and she still hasn't come. She grins at you. You suck pussy so greedy, she says, stretching, eyes hooded. You pick up her breast with your mouth the way a cat picks up a kitten. You run your hand down the side of her warm, naked body, over her ribs, down her waist, up her hip to the hump of her butt, your first two fingers ashy with her dried-up juice. You lazily lick over her clavicles, finishing touches for an aftertaste of salt. You reach down and press between your legs.

191

You have all your clothes on.

She lifts up the edge of your dress. "I give you everything you want, and you won't even take your dress off," she says.

Does she? Is sucking her pussy what you want? You confess: I feel like saying I do give her everything *she* wants. What audacity for her to think sucking her pussy is what *I* want. Trent crosses his arms over his chest. So you're charitable? Ornery. You toy with your fork, scraping the plate. It's nice, but it's not enough. For Patience, it's the price she's willing to pay to have me. This is why Melanie doesn't respect me. Because I don't demand my market price. If it's a price, why should anyone pay it? If it's that defiling, I don't want it. I've closed up shop. I've thrown away the key.

192

Your hand is on your thigh, holding the dress down. You can feel the mesh of your tights underneath the rayon. You say: don't start. I've explained to you why I can't. The small window is open, spilling a fan of light on the ceiling. She keeps talking. I want you so bad, she says. Let me suck your cunt.

Barbara doesn't do it. Marita knows it's wrong but she only did it three times in three years for Diane. Jeannie is glad you don't want it. Tracy assures you that the two women she was with did it for her, not vice-versa. Dance hall superstars don't like informers and bowcats. Erica Jong, to her dismay, agrees with the guys that it isn't appetizing, all that hair in your teeth. In movies, the sensitive lover does it, the other one takes the heroine from behind.

Sensitivity. Fuck sensitivity. Well, sensitivity is great in its place, in board rooms and car parks and school yards and when your arms are full of parcels, but in bed, you want greed.

Patience says: I can't put my fingers in? Don't you like me at all? You sigh. You peel off your tights. You have a queasy feeling. She penetrates you. Going inside, it feels good, but once inside, you can feel the hilt of her hand slamming against your opening and instead of that sharp shooting pleasure, you feel disgusted and repulsed, maybe because she is not pressing against the roof of your vagina or maybe it's because she's not doing it fast enough, or maybe you are too swampy and overheated to feel anything, or maybe because you didn't want to do it in the first place, your body convulses in rejection. It makes you think of having sex with a man in a hotel in Paris; his dick moving inside you made you feel like you were shitting through your vagina. Stop, you scream, stop, stop. She keeps going, and you keep raising your voice, wriggling away, until she finally does stop and you say: I'm sorry.

193

You pick up your tights. You have been lying on them. You wonder if there is a run. She says your name, low and slowly.

You catch your breath.

She is screaming.

I explained why, you say. Your voice is weary. You think about going to the club. What time is it? Almost midnight. Good. The train or a cab? Cab.

You pull your shoes to you.

Fine, leave, go home, she says.

Who says I'm going home? You slip your feet into your heels, the familiar dents and curves welcoming. Your feet hurt, but that's too bad. Femme drag to get the girls; butch sex to keep them coming back for more. You're every woman. It's all in you. You stand. The dress is somewhat crumpled, but who's going to notice in the darkness of the club? You look around the room for the jacket. Finally, you see it hooked on the handlebars of her son's bicycle. You put it on.

You're going out? How do you expect me to accept this? Just get up in the middle of the night and go to a club? What's wrong with you? Patience's hair has come loose from her ponytail. Greasy tufts stick out. She looks tired and haggard. In the fluorescent light, she looks her age: nearly two decades older than you. I'm begging you, don't go out to the club, I can't take it, she says. Don't go.

You go out into the empty, lit hallway.

She says: if you're not going home, don't bother calling me.

You do like Patience. You do like her. Why is she always raising her voice?

When you were younger, you had a fantasy that went something like this: Gorgeous woman hits on you and tells you she is incredible in bed. You ask her to prove herself with your friend (male). You watch. She excels. Over and over again, you have this fantasy. Beautiful woman wants you, fucks a man. Because of course how could she fuck you? What would she do?

You take the elevator down.

Don't go. Don't go, she said. You go.

A man's gotta do what a man's gotta do.

Maitenant fort en mon ombre/mon seul compagnon fidèle.

Between your legs you feel as smooth and solid as a Barbie doll. You feel strong.

195

Stop wanting to breathe, said the sage. You have stopped wanting. This is the power of the ascetic. You snicker.

Don't go. Melanie said this once, standing in her nightgown in the corridor. Don't go.

I called you. You weren't there. Where were you?

You laugh. Outside Patience's building, the air is crisp, the night clear. You stand on the edge of the street, just next to the sidewalk, your feet light and tapping, hips swaying. I called you, you hear in your mind the voice of the stoned-sounding white girl and the back beat. Maybe you will request the song from the DJ.

A fat Sikh screeches his cab to a halt. "Christopher and Seventh, Sardarji," you say, clambering in. He smiles too, offers you halwa.

Under the umbrella, you have switched places. She's on the chair, you on the fire hydrant. Patience sews a button on a pair of baggy pants and says: do you know what a Dravidian is?

"Main to Madrasi hoon," you tell the cabdriver. Madrasi, he sighs, and tells you that you look just like Vyjayantimala. You smile and tell him you've heard that before. You undo the bun of your hair in preparation for the club, and talk about going home. He plays Kishore Kumar. The green, pine tree-shaped air freshener swings from the mirror. You sing along under your breath: main hoon Don, Don, Don, Don.

There are some people outside the Box but not many. You unwrap a piece of gum. It oozes sweet and strong in your mouth, but not in a flood, your jaw too overworked to chew hard. You pull the heavy door of the Box.

Mandir ho ya madhushala.

The air-conditioning hits you as soon as you walk in. You

pay, you stamp yourself on the back of your hand as the cashier counts out your change. You walk down the corridor, and sit at the bar, order a screwdriver, flirt unrequitedly with the dark, concave-cheeked bartender with dreads. At the other end of the bar sits a woman who was once in your bed. She has cut her hair short and dyed it the color of the butter flavoring they use on popcorn. She sees you and smiles. You finish your drink and order another one.

The talent show is on. You don't move. The bar area gets quieter as people crowd around the dance floor to watch tonight's singing contest. Could be worse.

Arm-wrestling. Wet T-shirt. Embarrassing dance contests. Strip contests. Drag queens lip-synching, Angie Xtravaganza to "Pride (A Deeper Love)," some big white queen dressed as Scarlett O'Hara to "The Greatest Love of All," dykes sliding folded bills between the silicone-fat breasts of drag queens. A stripper with boomerangs of fat on her sides unsnapping the halter of her black vinyl leotard, then unsnapping the crotch, lying on her back, her pussy exposed until a b-girl drops over her and humps her. Says Lady Sade, "My house is a home, but don't y'all come at once or you'll have to stand in line." A pale stripper with the nicest small titties you have ever seen. Not much there but effectively shaped, not conical as most small breast are, but round. A West Indian girl with a boyfriend, who the night she stripped, said to you as you came in, "I've got something special for you." One hard, hard woman toasting over the beat of "Trailer Lode." There weren't that many people in the house that night, and you felt too shy to start clapping alone. She was so fine.

You are almost done with the second drink. You think: when the fuck is this damn singing contest going to end. You tap the woman sitting next to you. Straightened hair. Eyes like eggs. Black and white striped sleeveless T-shirt. Horizontal stripes, so maybe her tits aren't really that big. "When is this thing going to end?" She says she doesn't know.

You go down to the crowded dance floor. It is dark, the strobe light swirling too fast and too faintly.

You are dancing with the egg-eyed woman.

198   You've got to show me love. You sing along to the words to your reflection in the mirror. The egg-eyed woman is a Jamaican cop. Her name is Dolores. You tell her your name is Pakeezah. Dolores says: what would you do if there were no more mirrors? Her smile is as mild as Opal's. She buys you another screwdriver. Your whole body is pulsing with alcohol.

The most beautiful girl in the world. Pearls, I would buy her pearls, you think. You say: Hey, you are really beautiful. You are the most beautiful girl in the world. Whatsyour-name? The girl says: Lorraine. Dolores is a few feet behind you, dancing with someone else. You say: I know I'm way too femme to be of any use to you, but you really are beautiful.

I'm very intelligent, and I can type, you tell Lorraine. I can't cook very well. Do you like poetry?

Give me the he-man's solid bliss.

Did you just tell Lorraine how well you suck pussy? Or just think about it?

A pretty girl who naked is.

I'm interested in pinhole photography, you say.

Mel kisses you wetly on the cheek. What is his trip? Is it a name thing? Melanie too kisses wetly, and you wipe her kisses away with theater, grimacing, scrubbing your face.

She's not my type, you tell Dolores. Do you think she's pretty? You are pointing to Lorraine. Do you find her attractive? Is she your type? Dolores says no. She's beautiful, you say. We're both femmes so it doesn't mean anything. What's your type? Dolores says: you, you're beautiful. She cups your face in her hand. You draw away, go to the bathroom. Take a hot leak, careful not to sit on the seat. You have to concentrate carefully on pulling up your tights. Banging on the toilet door, hurry up, hurry up. You stagger out. A wet kiss on the cheek. Oh, hello. Yeah, how is everything. You say to Dolores, as you pick up your barely touched fourth screwdriver: I'm getting high, I shouldn't finish this. You set the screwdriver down on the ledge against the mirror and it spills, splashes. "Will you take care of me?" She is Jamaican. Not an American. She can be trusted. After all Jamaican patties are more or less samosas. You try to explain this to her. "You know samosa?" You say this more slowly so she can understand. The sleeve of your jacket is wet.

In the pizza store. "I need to eat. If I eat, I'll be okay," you say. You pull out a wad of bills from your pocket, dollar bills falling to the floor.

A taxi. White male cabbie. Balding. The only female cabbies you have ever seen in the City are West African, Ghana, Côte d'Ivoire. Not like Paris. Women drivers everywhere. And they smelled so good. "Paris? Have you been to Paris?"

"I'm going to throw up."

The spotted pavement swims before your eyes. A wad of pink gum. Black gunk. A piece of cellophane. Nothing happens. Dolores shoves you back into the cab.

Home. The wrong key. She says: I'll try every key until I get the right key. Gimme that, you say, then politely: I'm sorry, but the house is a bit of a mess. You stumble into the bathroom, the tile edged against your knees. Vomit. You forgot to lift up the toilet seat.

Covers.

In the morning, you open your eyes. A woman in a leather jacket is reading the titles of the books on your shelves. Who the fuck is she? She turns. Egg eyes. Striped top. You are about to lift up the comforter to go to the bathroom, but you realize you are naked. I'm naked, you say. She says: Yeah, you ripped off your clothes, telling me you hadn't had sex in six months, squeezing my breasts. She pulls a book out. Don't worry I didn't take advantage of you.

But, you tell Trent, there's the rub. How could a woman take advantage of another woman? In the state I was in, she could hardly make me eat her pussy or trust me to fist her or anything else. This is the difference between men and women: a man can get his orgasm without the willing co-operation of his partner and a woman can't. You shrug. I can't be a man by imitating a man's sexual independence. I have to go the opposite route.

Jan Brown wrote: It's the lie we tell that says butches don't hunger for someone who would know what we needed instead of believing what we told them we wanted. And who would take us down . . . Butch is who we are, but also who we had to become . . . We cannot face . . . the contempt in our partners' eyes when we have allowed them to convince us that they really do want to touch us, to take us, that they really do want to reach . . . into the cunt we both wish did not exist.

You poke at the froth in your mug with a straw. How am I supposed to sleep with a woman in my own body? Melanie is afraid of getting pregnant and Patience is after the next best thing to a little boy.

Trent looks at the bill. Don't you think you are being a little reductive?

You push your mug aside. I don't know.

He says: I wish I knew what to say. What do other lesbians say?

You laugh. In unison, they sing the praises of the stone butch. You pick up the last morsel of your fruit supreme with your fork. You say: as usual, men have the better deal. Gay men get house music and lipstick and gay women get theorizing about dicks.

The Texan wanted to have one. Patience too. Melanie sort of. Florence King in *Confessions of a Failed Southern Lady* misses the thrust of it. Eileen Myles in *Chelsea Girls* misses the thrust of it. Meredith Maran in *Outlook* reveals she wishes sometimes that she had a penis, and sometimes she wishes her lover did.

Dolores says: as soon as I saw all your books, I felt better about taking you home. I guess it's my job, you know. I felt responsible.

You sit up.

She has two books under her arm: a lousy lesbian mystery, a book about a gay FBI officer.

She says goodbye and leaves. You get up and close the door. You find a rag, scoop up the pizza-smelling vomit off the toilet seat and the floor of the bathroom, restructuring the night's events into a more suitable form. I felt like Sam Spade, waking up with a strange woman in my room. As soon as she turned and I saw her tits, I placed her. Yeah, I brought a strange woman home with me last night. I honestly can't tell you what else happened. I was drunk out of my mind. She had eyes like my high school calculus teacher. I'm doing some crazy things, aren't I?

Lukewarm shower. Go out for soda; you need the sugar, the water, and the caffeine. Then, you get back into bed. You call Trent. You ask him to meet you at Caffe Rafaella for fancy coffee and dessert that evening. You lie back and stare at the ceiling, reach into your skimpy Victoria's Secret underwear, fingers on your spongy, firm head, gently kneading. It becomes erect. You pull on it. Your whole body feels painted in that chocolate syrup you pour over ice cream that in a moment hardens into a shell. You are protected, safe, rigid. This is the apex of Hindu philosophy: you will not desire what you cannot have. You will be what you never wanted to be so you can be who you are.

203

You are: the hollow man, the (stuffed)
Man.

Coda: The Know Better Blues

Jab rath ham jaise mathwali
Phir subah kaalam kya hoga, phir subah kaalam
kya hoga?

–Shakeel Badayuni, "Yeh Dil Ki Lagi"

Kinnie left yesterday. Her candied yams are still in the fridge, and I don't know what to do with them. I can't eat them alone. I mean, she made barbequed chicken too, but it's finished.

Since she's been gone, I've been thinking about the things that have happened in the last two years, not just to me, but to so many of the girls I know. Things like Blaise.

Kinnie's Blaise is named Kevin, and he doesn't deal drugs. He's unemployed, though, and Kinnie used to spend her money on buying him clothes and shoes. They gave her a couple of hundred for furniture, and she slept on a pile of old carpets. He beat her nearly every day. Well, he needed to, since she always broke down and admitted that she had been sleeping with whatever man he'd suspected her of being with – and whatever women. She capitulated to all his fantasies.

Last summer, somewhere between Marita and Jeannie,

Kinnie called me to tell me she was leaving Kevin, that she needed my help. To keep her occupied so she wouldn't miss him. We went to bad action movies, to clubs, talked on the phone. I told her she could call me any time she wanted to. I was so happy to save her, to have someone to go out with, to have someone who would save me. Blaise was no match for her, with her head for calculus, with her good sense, my high school friend. Then, she was gone. Her phone was disconnected. For a while, I worried that she had been in an accident, that she was lying in a ditch somewhere, but Irene said I was being naive. She had gone back to Kevin.

As I went back to Blaise. I loved Blaise. It was a great story, my love for Blaise, his betrayals of me, my betrayals of him. The leaves fell last fall and I fell back into his arms. And then everything changed. I filled up with death. No, I mean the death of the person I was. And in a way, I blame it all on Kinnie. And Magali. And all the girls I was friends with. Not the girls I hung out with, or the boys, those fly-by-night people I met in clubs and went to clubs with and talked to about clubs, people who bored me so much I could only stand being with them in places with loud music, but the girls I knew from high school, when we talked about other things. Kinnie wanted to be a doctor. Magali wanted to do international law – which I knew was silly, because she was itching to leave school. Now, she has. She's living with a baby in Redhook, and the man who made her pregnant is married to someone else, while a third woman has a child of his who is two months older than Magali's daughter. The stories get so complicated after a while.

Kinnie came back to me this summer. We lay on the floor, playing Scrabble and drinking Coke at three, four in the morning.

"Kevin knew you were a lesbian," Kinnie said. "He just knows things, it's amazing."

"Kevin knew *you* were a lesbian," I replied. "And he

made you admit you were sleeping with that droopy-breasted, fifty-year old white woman in your suite."

"Forty. She was in her forties," Kinnie said, making ice-cream circles on an old *Village Voice* with the bottom of the Breyers container. "He made me say I was sleeping with all my roommates."

And that was the way it was. I wanted to ask her why she went back to him last year, why my friendship wasn't enough, why she listened to him when he told her not to call me when she didn't listen to me when I told her not to call him. I wanted to tell her that I would have given up all those people I slept with to be with her, except she'd think I was making a pass at her. And I really wasn't. This was the biggest secret I had – that I wanted to be Kinnie's friend. I wanted all of us to save each other from the lives we were leading. The drifting, the fucking, the lies we were telling each other. I want to talk to Kinnie about Helen Leavitt, or the obscure blaxploitation movies she loved or even whether the Freemasons were plotting to take over the earth as Malcolm X had said and Kinnie believed. But Kinnie and Magali, who could wait on street comers for hours to see these men, rarely ever saw me. I only saw Sripriya once or twice. Irene, you're so far away. Mostly, I drift through the day, the nights reserved for strangers. Even when I was pregnant, I went out almost every night, too scared to be alone.

Simon and I went to Nell's last night. It was my choice. We saw people we hadn't seen in ages. "If you hang around long enough," Simon said, "you see everyone over and over again."

"There are people I haven't seen in a long time. Remember Shelter Monique, the tall girl?"

"The one who said she was a detective like on *21 Jump Street*?" Simon shook his head.

"Yeah. And the other Monique? Cicely always said

she looked like she could fuck hard. Not that it matters anymore. I think when they stuck that needle in they anaesthetized everything permanently, Simon." And as always when I said something serious, he asked if I was drunk.

I would have checked him on it, but we had had that conversation so many times before. I looked around the room, but there wasn't much to see. No one to fill the space with new experience, so that I wouldn't look at the walls and think, there, I first kissed Marita's breast, and there I once flirted with a man who looked exactly like Blaise, only taller. There, Lance put my hand on his dick.

"Were you talking about Blaise at the time?" Simon asked.

"Shut up."

"Aha!"

"It was funny, the way it happened. I had just paged Blaise and he had called and been obnoxious, as usual, and I was so depressed."

"So you touched Lance's dick?"

"He put my hand on it."

"Then?"

"We went home and fucked."

"How was it?" Simon finished his beer. His ex-lover looked a bit like Lance, and Simon liked to be kept abreast of Lance's doings.

"I don't know. I wasn't paying attention. I was busy crying. I made him do it from behind so he wouldn't see my tears."

"Spare me the details." Simon pressed his beer bottle against his cheek. "Was it big?"

"I thought you wanted me to spare you the details?"

"That's not a detail."

I shook my head. Some reggae came on, a slow song called "Tempted to Touch," and I danced. A man asked me

to dance and I said well, actually, I was already dancing.
Simon sulked. He always gets annoyed when men in straight
clubs assume he's not my boyfriend. "Lord," I said, when
the guy finally went away. "He once asked me to dance
three times in one night."

"Me too." I turned to look at Simon's face. "Tracks."

"Really? The woman-killer."

"Don't start."

"I have nothing against gay men, okay? Bisexual men,
however, make me think of AIDS. I don't know why. Gay
men don't make me think AIDS."

"Because we keep it to ourselves."

"That's not it." I stopped dancing. "I'm sorry."

"I was only joking anyway, I've never seen him before.
I'll try and forgive your ignorance."

"This is coming from a man who said 'there are those
hard, man-hating lesbians, and there are other lesbians,
who sleep with men.' Men are fundamentally the same, gay,
straight, whatever."

"That's what Drakkar said. Every time I want to do it,
he said, 'Men. That's all they think about.'"

I wondered for a minute if Simon had completely
misunderstood my point, or was simply uninterested in it,
then decided not to ask. I pointed one of the zozo guys out.
"Him, him in the white, I saw on the street corner right
outside my building. I thought it was home delivery for a
minute."

"And it was a blondie."

"Getting breakfast."

"When you got it, you got it."

"But Simon, why? One night at Opera, I saw this tall,
ugly guy with braids done in a big loop on top of his head.
He was bony and scrawny, his skin was on his bones like an
animal skin over a stick hut. He wore this ill-fitting jacket
that ended an inch and a half in front of his wrists, he was

not cute. And the man had two, not one, but two, count them, two, girls draped, and I mean draped, over him. Not bad-looking girls, well-dressed, upper class girls. Two. Draped. One on each arm. They were fawning all over him, their hands on his chest, their hair tumbling, tumbling over his shoulders. Blonde girls, of course. Model-types. What does that man have? What does this guy in the white have?"

"Attitude."

"I have attitude."

"Not 'take me, take me' attitude."

"Even when I'm tough, I don't get it."

"You get it."

"I don't get what I want."

"What you want is more complicated. This guy just wants breakfast. Speaking of breakfast . . ." Simon leered at me. "Are you going to get some?"

"Patience?" I shrugged. "She told me not to settle for her."

"You told her you were settling for her?"

"No." I began to dance again. Simon went to the bathroom to piss out his beer. While he was gone, a friend of Blaise's came to flirt with me in his own, inept way. They know I'm single now, and they figure Blaise has scored. I replied to his questions with icy brevity, and he slunk away.

Simon came back and danced with me. He put his arms on my shoulders. He was too short for this to be in the least bit appealing, even if I did like being touched on the dance floor, which I don't. I shrugged them off. Blaise had just appeared in the doorway.

My toes began to tingle, as if I was thawing. I think it's because there is no way in hell my pussy could want him, my toes were tingling. "God, Simon, you know Haitian babies are hard to kill?"

"Girl, don't start."

"She would be born around now."

"They told you it was a girl?"

I wanted to strangle him even though I was the one who had started the conversation. "Fuck you. It didn't have a gender. It was six weeks, okay? A third the size of my finger. I didn't kill a baby." Simon asked again if I was drunk, and I didn't reply. Blaise leaned against a table, avoiding my eyes. He shifted his heavily-dreaded head from side to side to the music. He had shaved his beard, and his face looked fat and cruel.

Simon took my hand and, with his eyes half-closed, began to do the merengue. It was finally a song he was not complaining about, so I hesitated to interrupt.

The song finished, and he pointed out a girl we knew from the Limelight, she was a box dancer there. She was a small, dark girl, and she was wearing a fluorescent pink bra and shorts under a vinyl see-through dress. She clung to the arm of a stocky guy with hair like a jheri-curled poodle. When she saw us, she waved with her free hand.

"Delia is wearing nothing tonight, boy," Simon said, and whistled.

"Can I tell you, Lance was pushing me with that girl even though she is totally not my type? I think he just wanted to fuel his fantasies. He called me the other day, and he was like, 'How come you never get serious about a female. You should get serious over a female.' I was like Lance, you get serious over a female, okay? He has a different bitch every week."

"Typical. Trying desperately to prove his heterosexuality." Simon and I often amused ourselves by finding gay clues in Lance's behavior. Heterosexual promiscuity was trying desperately to hide being gay; gay promiscuity was happiness.

"Opal saw me with him at Island Lounge one night and thought he was a queen." I shook my head. "Did I tell you he called the police to get his girlfriend out of his house so that she wouldn't see him cry?"

"Really?" Simon assimilated this new piece of information. "Well, yeah, he's kind of wimpy." We went to the bar
and got another round.

I stirred my drink. "So is he still there?"

"Who?" said Simon. The music turned to lukewarm
house and he danced a few steps, grudgingly.

"Fine." The drink tasted horrible, too much soda, too
little syrup. "He called me just last week. From his girlfriend's bed. No joke. She was trying to hang up the phone.
He asked me if I talked to my mother recently." We moved
back to the dance floor, and I put my elbow against the
loudspeaker. "He's such a fuck."

"You should have asked him if he got a job recently so
he could pay you your money back."

"He's got the life, man – sex, dealing drugs, getting
paid for getting laid and women who love him." Blaise was
grinding with someone. She was white, and wide-hipped,   211
and short. I tried to figure out if she was heavier than me.
Blaise had always teased me about being short, but she was
short too.

"And no job security. Wait till he gets old."

"He'll be cruising the nursing homes. He'll be boning
little old ladies and they'll be buying him Ben Gay and
bifocals. What have I got?" A house full of dust. I had not
opened the books I had ordered from India, Raghubir Singh,
Raghu Rai. It was easier to go out, look for the flattery of
someone's leer. "Remember the times we've had, Simon?
Singing the Billie Holiday songbook on the train at four in
the morning."

"That time at Metropolis when you kept saying we
were all going to be dust one day."

"Or that night at Tropicana when I was pregnant."

"It was the same night, Neelam," said Simon. "Right
after I came back from D.C."

"Remember Don, the Disgusting DJ at Opera? He was so ugly."

"I never saw anyone snort coke in such an obvious manner. That man put his paper plate right on the plastic crates full of records, took out his straw and snorted." Simon and I wandered into the other room, and sat down on one of the couches.

"He had a mondo dick." Simon's eyes became huge. "No, I didn't sleep with him." I haven't slept with any man but Blaise since I met him, except for once with Lance. I'd call him by other men's names to annoy him, but he was the only one. It's hard to believe I had been meaning to break up with him from the beginning, that I had just never met anyone else to jump ship to. Kinnie hadn't been there to take me to bad action movies or go to clubs.

"How come you know his dick size without sleeping with him?"

"Have you slept with every guy who has put your hand on his dick?" Simon nodded. "Well, you've slept with every guy you've ever kissed."

"Kissing is intimate, you know."

"I went down on Patience before I kissed her."

"It's a fucked-up world."

"I never did it again."

"No wonder she doesn't want you to settle for her."

"That's not why. It's because I don't think Whoopi Goldberg and Ted Danson make a cute couple. Patience decided it was because Whoopi is so dark and he's so white and that I had been colonized by the Man, and I told her that being colonized is being obsessed with the Man and she said Indians have never stuck by black people and they didn't even join the Black Power movement in Trinidad and they don't care about black people's problems and I said it's not like black people care about Indian people's problems, and that was the end of the conversation." I sucked my teeth.

212 ·

"She's from Trinidad?" Simon put his feet up on the coffee table, and I put my head on his shoulder. "So was Drakkar."

"Well, she's a nympho."

"So, let her eat your pussy and have a good time." I tried not to think this was some homo cliché: Trent had said exactly the same thing. Although Trent had been a little less crude.

"What about love?"

"What's love got to do with it?" Simon straightened up. "I slept with him." He pointed out a slim Hispanic guy wearing a baseball cap, going backwards into the men's room.

"Him? When?"

"A couple of weeks ago. He drove me home from Two Potato." Simon rose, and dug the coat check ticket out of his jeans pocket. He had checked his backpack.

"You didn't tell me."

"Telling you now. Let's go. I haven't called him since." It was almost closing time anyway. I followed Simon to the coat check and up the stairs. He slowed down once we were outside. "So what's the head count?" he asked.

"Eleven. I'm wearing next to nothing, so I should have had some more guys asking me to dance, but on the other hand, I was with you. Once at Level 10, while I was pregnant, I had twenty-six. I kept saying no because I thought it was cheap to dance with another man while I was pregnant, so I was like a mystery woman." We crossed the street, running ahead of the taxis. "You know, two different women at the Box have asked me whether I was pregnant, after my abortion. Do you think I'm having a phantom pregnancy? It's the Devil's child after all, it couldn't be that easy to kill. I should've called him that instead of Claude, I should have called him the fucking Devil."

"Hush," said Simon. "Hush." He opened the coffee-shop door.

We went inside and sat down. "I didn't get much exercise," I said, finally and sipped my Coke with lemon.

"You'll be out tomorrow," Simon replied.

"Probably." We sat there for awhile, Simon flirting with one of the guys who worked there who was trying to give him a meat-colored, thick twisted cruller. I toyed with my drink, trying to decide whether I should check my messages.

Blaise came in. At first, I thought he was alone, but then the wide-hipped white woman followed, looking bland and ovine. I wondered if I had looked like that, so unattractive that it was obvious why Blaise was with her, so stupidly unconscious of what was going on. God, what was her excuse?

"Oh, I forgot," said Simon, and called for water for both of us. "Cheers. Happy Birthday." We touched paper cups, gently.

"I know better than to ask, but do you believe?" I said as we left.

"What," said Simon, turning around. "Still love is possible?" I nodded. Simon skipped down the stairs to the subway. "I try not to, Neelam. Maybe you should try not to, too."